D1216766

1st Ave.

Dead in the Water

Dead in the Water

BROCK YATES

FARRAR, STRAUS AND GIROUX
New York

First printing, 1975

Printed in the United States of America

Published simultaneously in Canada by
McGraw-Hill Ryerson Ltd., Toronto

DESIGNED BY GUSTAVE NILES

Library of Congress Cataloging in Publication Data

Yates, Brock W.
    Dead in the water.

    I. Title.
PZ4.Y3342De   [PS3575.A76]   813'.5'4   75-11657

To my favorite unsinkables:
Claire and Wreet

Dead in the Water

Prologue

SUMMER TRAFFIC. Hugh Twitchell sagged in the seat of his Pontiac Laurentian and eyed the sluggish passage of the Canadian National freight. He was mired in a line of cars—sedans and campers bearing tourists from every corner of the continent, en route to Niagara Falls, nine miles away.

A faded purple station wagon with Kentucky license plates was stopped ahead of him. Its bumper sticker announced: "We've been to CHIMP CITY, Elyria, Ohio." A tiny boy, perhaps seven, stared at him through the smeared rear window and reflectively tongued a sucker. The thought of ingesting a sucker at 7:20 a.m. prompted a slight convulsion in Twitchell's stomach.

He never ate much in the morning, especially on days when he had to fly. Too much filled his mind to permit diversionary thoughts of hunger. Today was the beginning of a four-day assignment with a film crew from the Canadian Government Travel Bureau, and he wanted to be at his best. He looked at his watch. Six minutes late. The town of Thorold, where a small hangar housed the Bell Jet Ranger II and the three-place Bell

CJ-5 of Twitchell's Vertical Flying Service, was a few miles distant. He estimated that he could make up part of the time on the open road just beyond the grade crossing. This particular job, at $425 an hour, involved filming from the Jet Ranger over the great Welland Ship Canal. It was better than most. He usually had to fly around the Falls and the gorge of the Niagara River, where the nasty updrafts and the hydro lines and the monster observation towers that studded the shore made low-level work dangerous. But maneuvering over the Welland, which sliced like a clean incision across the flat Ontario plain, was a simple task for a man who had spent sixteen years flying military and civilian helicopters.

He examined himself in the Pontiac's mirror. His eyes were hidden behind a pair of gold-rimmed sunglasses and he tentatively fingered his right temple, where his wife had spotted a gray hair two days earlier. He did not like his nose. It was too upturned, too pert to fit his self-image of a rugged man of purpose. He pressed his index finger against the tip, pointing it downward, and tried to see his modified profile in the small area of the rear-view mirror. A horn sounded. Behind him, the driver of a Ford pickup, which was tilting under the burden of an aluminum camper body, was announcing that the train had passed and traffic was moving. Shocked out of his brief dalliance with narcissism, he started the Pontiac and bustled off toward Thorold, leaving the overweight pickup far behind.

As he turned down the crushed-stone road, he heard an engine rumbling behind the corrugated-steel hangar and watched his little CJ-5 Bell lift clear of the roof. The other pilot, Les Riggin, was taking off with a Hamilton real estate man and an American client to examine an industrial site somewhere along the prosperous Golden Crescent that hooked around the western end of Lake Ontario, from St. Catharines to Toronto. A white-and-red panel truck bearing the logo "Rubicam Productions" and a 450SL Mercedes-Benz were in the parking lot. He sighted his five passengers standing in the shade of the hangar. The unit director was most visible: a tall, soft-faced man uniformed in perfectly faded Levi's and a denim shirt with shoulder loops. Other members of the crew were rummaging through a collection of metal shipping crates. One, a wiry man with stringy hair and bad posture, was fiddling with a 35mm Arriflex fitted with a 12–120mm zoom lens. Hugh Twitchell had reservations about cameramen. Since he had invested in the special Tyler Mount that made his Jet Ranger a vibrationless platform for aerial photography, he had found that the men who operate movie cameras for a living were fearless—even semi-crazed—and they seemed prepared to sacrifice themselves, the aircraft, and the pilot for one superlative shot. Once they began sighting through the eyepiece of an Arri or an Eclair NTR, they suspended concern for survival. Fortunately, this assignment also included the unit director. Twitchell had found directors, as a group, to possess lower thresholds of bravery. With the guy in the clean Levi's and the blue shirt on board as a tempering influence, he knew the entire operation would be easier and safer.

He guided the Pontiac to a stop beside the Mercedes and shut off the engine. A brittle-voiced radio announcer on a Hamilton station was beginning his seven-thirty newscast. Twitchell paid little heed as the voice announced that the 1976 Olympics would open in Montreal under heavy security, with no indications that the terrorism which scarred the 1972 Munich games would be repeated. He snapped the radio off and got out of the car, heading toward the film crew.

The CJ-5 was above him, hovering a few hundred feet above the field, when he heard the pitch of the rotors change. Looking up, he saw the craft alter its attitude until the low morning sun produced a fireball of reflection off the plastic canopy. It was descending, coming back to land.

"Excuse me, gentlemen," Twitchell said absently as he

scurried past the crew toward the point where the helicopter would touch down. "My other chopper. Better check on that first."

Riggin, a reedy man in his late twenties, jumped out of the Bell and scuttled from beneath its rotors, which were flopping at idle. The turbulence chewed at his fuzzy hair and sent mad ruffles across his short-sleeved white shirt. He was a straight, uncomplicated bachelor who admitted that he could conceive of no happier moments—not even with a woman—than when he was at the controls of a helicopter. Twitchell trusted him completely.

"What's the matter?" Twitchell yelled over the engine.

"Nothing. I was wondering about you," said Riggin with a trace of shortened breath.

"Me?"

"Yeah, I saw you drive in, which kind of fooled me. I thought you'd already left."

"How could I have left? The film crew's still here," said Twitchell with slight exasperation.

"I know, but the Jet Ranger's gone."

"What? Gone? Where?" Twitchell spun toward the hangar. The bay which held the Jet Ranger—an aircraft he had plunged into deep debt to purchase—was vacant. He broke into a hard sprint toward the hangar, with Riggin pumping along in pursuit.

He stopped, panting, in the open space where the Jet Ranger should have been. "Jesus Christ," he said softly.

"I didn't think anything of it when I got here, Hugh. I just figured you'd taken it somewhere. You know . . ."

"I know," answered Twitchell. They stood in silence, then Twitchell paced to a corner of the hangar. "Who in God's name would steal a helicopter? Especially a Jet Ranger?"

"Remember that outfit in Buffalo who lost one four or five years ago? They found it down in Tennessee or somewhere."

"Yeah, but that was just a little one, like the CJ-5. That wasn't any Jet Ranger. Jesus, I can't believe this is happening to me." Twitchell paced the floor some more.

"Hey, look at this," said Riggin, lifting a packet of matches off the dirt floor. He held it up to his face, then propped his sunglasses on his forehead while he read the type. "Café la Poudrière, 12937 Boulevard St. Laurent, Montreal." He looked at Twitchell. "Could be the Frenchies have taken it?"

Twitchell walked across the hangar and took the book of matches. He studied it, then returned it to his pilot's out-stretched hand. He snorted brusquely and said, "Not bloody likely. You can keep it for the police if you want, but I'll guarantee you it wasn't them. They're like the Newfies. There aren't a dozen Frenchies in the whole of Quebec with enough brains to fly a Jet Ranger, and I doubt any of them would have the ambition to come all the way down here to steal one. No, Les, the police'll find it—probably in the States. That's where all the thieves are."

1

IT WAS TIME to raise a little hell. Pancho Farnsworth drained another can of Genesee Cream Ale and flung it into the wake. Belching, he sat down at the wheel of the *Red Dog* and reaimed it into the middle of the St. Lawrence. He was running too fast, he knew that. Around him, outboards puttered through the chop. Some were flat-bottomed scows filled with fishermen; others, fleet fiberglass runabouts with tumorlike motors hung on the transoms, whipped water skiers in wild arcs. Among them bloated yachts pressed ahead with self-righteous dignity. The *Red Dog*, a twenty-eight-foot Bertram, ripped through this jumble at nearly forty knots, striking for the open water that lay to the east beyond the bulging outline of Deer Island. Behind it, little Alexandria Bay was cranking up for another Friday night, perspiring until the coolness of the great river would purify the humid July day.

Roy Enderle shouldered his way out of the main cabin with a brace of freshly opened Genesees in his monster right hand. His stubby fingers nearly concealed the cans, as a normal person's grasp might overwhelm a pair of flashlight batteries. At six feet six and two hundred fifty-six pounds, he made even Pancho Farnsworth—who was twenty pounds lighter and three inches shorter—seem almost like a regular-sized human being. "Hey!" shouted Enderle as the two Genesees tumbled through the air, trailing foam like aborted, flamed-out rockets. Farnsworth turned in time to snatch them out of the air before they thudded against his head. With a raucous laugh, Enderle leapt onto the flying bridge and sat down beside Farnsworth. He had two more ales in his hand and another cluster stuffed in the waist of his Levi's like grenades. "At least we've got enough of this shit until we get to Jessup's," he said, cracking a can.

Ahead, an eighteen-thousand-ton bulk freighter slogged downstream, picking its way through the buoys of the main Seaway channel like a fat lady in a theater aisle. It was broad-beamed and rusty, with a gawky superstructure perched on her stern. A tattered Liberian ensign, its colors murky from oil smoke, flapped from the fantail. A couple lolling against the rail waved as the Bertram sped past. The man was young and swarthy, with long hair and a thin mustache; the girl was fair-skinned with bold, Slavic cheekbones. Small boats bobbed in the wake of the ship, their crews tending stout lines that probed for muskellunge, the strongest, most ferocious fresh-water game fish on earth. Around them, odd-shaped islands dappled the water, some large enough to support stone-and-brick mansions; others, granite pimples where a few scrub trees and bushes elbowed each other for the available space. The *Red Dog* overtook a stately fifty-six-foot Matthews Voyageur, glowing porcelain white in the softening afternoon sunlight. A plump brunette was lying on the foredeck, face down, with the strap of her bikini halter unhooked. Farnsworth gave the *Red Dog*'s horn a blast, but she did not move.

"Goddamn, I'm horny," said Enderle.

"Tonight's the night," said Farnsworth.

"Betcher ass," Enderle answered. "There'll be some action at

Jessup's tonight." They bounded along in silence, slugging ale and savoring the approach of darkness. Then Enderle said idly, "The Browns will kick the shit out of Oakland tonight."

"Maybe, but we never win exhibition games. Never have. Hell, when we won the NFL Championship in 1964, we lost six straight in preseason. We could have beaten Kansas City last week but we just never got it together. It's weird."

"It might have been better if Slater hadn't played like a damn rag doll," Enderle said angrily.

"That son of a bitch. I could have plugged the middle better on one leg. I don't have to tell you, Enderle, I was rattled when I heard they traded for Slater. I figured, O.K., Pancho baby, your ass is headed for New Orleans or Houston, but after that act he put on against the Chiefs, I'm looking a lot stronger. A lot stronger."

"You think we can get the game on the radio up here?" asked Enderle.

"No way. Landsman said he tried last week to hear the Chiefs game. Couldn't get shit."

"Poor ol' Zach, the jock sniffer," mused Enderle.

"Ol' Zach's all right. Hell, he's given us the run of his marina. That ain't bad."

"That's what I mean. If we weren't a pair of pro-football studs, he'd have thrown us out long ago. Zach's a sniffer, so we stay."

"Half the goddamn world are sniffers. Otherwise they wouldn't pay good money to see dudes like you and me kick each other in the head."

"They may have coughed up their last buck to see you and me play," Enderle said bitterly.

"We'll play. You wait," said Farnsworth, emptying his beer.

"Sure. You with a fucked-up leg and me banned in half the goddamned cities in the league. We'll be playin' with ourselves, that's who we'll be playin' with."

"My leg will get better and so will your reputation."

"Your Achilles tendon may be easier to fix than my image," said Enderle, an uncertain frown covering his wide face. His nose, once straight and tall-sided, had been mashed flat across the bridge and a shiny half moon of scar tissue underlined his left eye. Grapefruit-sized biceps peeked from the sleeves of a loose blue-and-white pullover. Around his short, broad neck hung a leather thong that supported an Alaskan brown bear's incisor. His Levi's stretched skin-tight across his giant thighs and his bare feet had the rough contours and leathery texture of baseball fielder's gloves.

He was a defensive end, a position he had played since starring on the grimy high school fields of Wilkes-Barre. A number of colleges tried to recruit him, and he finally accepted an athletic scholarship from the University of Missouri after a St. Louis alumnus had surreptitiously offered him three hundred dollars a month spending money and the loan of a Jaguar XKE. He was expelled during spring practice of his sophomore year for punching an assistant coach. Marked as a misfit by the major-college athletic establishment, he drifted into construction work in Tampa before being lured to Benjamin Harrison College in southwestern Indiana. Midway through his first season, with Harrison on a four-game winning streak, he beat up a campus security guard and two students in a dispute over a parking space. Then he hooked on with the Youngstown, Ohio, Hardhats, where he played two seasons before being picked up by the Philadelphia Eagles in one of those mass-meat-market tryout camps that pro teams run when the drafting gets thin. After playing sporadically two years for the Eagles, he feuded with the coaching staff and was traded to the Browns. There he earned a starting role and established a reputation as a fine pass rusher, but weak in defending against wide sweeps. During this time he and Farnsworth roomed together on road trips and became close friends. Enderle's future seemed relatively secure until a few weeks prior to the close of the 1975 season. A young, tough-talking columnist on the Cleveland *Plain Dealer* had been chiding him in print for his failure to shut off the opposition's running for weeks, and after a game against the Buffalo Bills, when the great veteran O. J. Simpson had swept his end for nearly a hundred yards, the writer accused him of giving up and feigning a groin injury to cover up his inept play. Two days later, Enderle barged into the *Plain Dealer*'s sports department and broke the writer's right wrist and the index finger and thumb of his left hand. Although the writer did not bring criminal charges—thanks to a substantial settlement by the Browns' management—the National Football League Commissioner, Roger L. DeVoe, had given Enderle an indefinite suspension.

"Don't worry, Whitby will get you that deal in Canada or the WFL. Those guys are dying for quality players," Farnsworth said confidently.

"Yeah, I know, but I want to play in the NFL. I've got something to prove, especially to that asshole DeVoe."

"This is the first time since I can remember that it was late July and I wasn't in the middle of football practice," said Farnsworth, grasping a small ridge of flab around his waist. "Here we are, drinkin' beer and jerkin' off when we ought to be getting in shape. I feel like a tub of shit."

"You look like a tub of shit, Farnsworth," Enderle hooted, lounging back with his feet on the Bertram's windscreen.

Farnsworth laughed at first. Then the sound died away, leaving a stiff, mechanical grin on his tanned face. He pushed a wad of sun-bleached hair from his eyes, and his face, with its strong chin and small, almost dainty nose, turned somber for a moment. He wished that Roy hadn't started talking about football. He wished that he did not know that four hundred miles to the west, at Cleveland's Municipal Stadium, the Browns were at that moment completing their warm-ups for the game with Oakland. He wanted to forget that. After the doctors at the Shaker Medical Center in Cleveland had told him he would miss the first half of the 1976 season, he bought the *Red Dog* and went to the St. Lawrence to fish and drink his way through the summer. He knew the river from his childhood. His father had often taken him on fishing trips in search of the burly, jut-jawed muskellunge that prowled the waters around the Thousand Islands, and he believed it would be a good place for erasing football from his mind.

His Achilles tendon had torn loose from its mountings in a particularly nasty "mop-end" tear, as the orthopedic surgeons had called it. Farnsworth's injury had come one March afternoon during a pickup basketball game in the New Salerno, New York, YMCA. He had spent the off season working in his father's ceramics factory—a business that had produced substantial riches for three generations of Farnsworths and had made them the first family of the pleasant but ordinary upstate town of New Salerno. He had done it out of habit. He found no particular satisfaction in the manufacture of dinnerware for the restaurant industry, but it was the easy thing to do: to wander back to New Salerno and to loaf through a menial job in the shipping department, where he enjoyed the physical labor and the company of the tough, straight-talking Italians and Irishmen who worked with him.

It had always been easy for Pancho Farnsworth. Like his older brother Jud, who, as a somber and scrubbed old man of thirty-four, was immersed in the litanies of the family business—the heir to a throne of plates and saucers—Pancho had been a New Salerno high school star in football, basketball, and baseball. Jud had been too light-framed for big-time athletics and after graduating from Hobart College—a distant upstate asteroid in the Ivy League universe with long and lucrative Farnsworth family connections—and from the Wharton School of Finance and Commerce, he had married a stiff, dull-eyed blonde from Summit, New Jersey, who talked through her teeth. Jud had then blanketed himself in upper-middle-class mediocrity. Pancho also enrolled at Hobart, although several midwestern universities—front-line jock factories—had been intrigued with his speed and size. As in high school, he faked and feinted his way through college, using his facile but untested intelligence and his growing athletic charisma as substitutes for hard work. By his junior year, his genes had expanded him into an imposing figure. He grew too big and too strong for small-college football, and in testimony to his skills, he was named a Little All-American as fullback on offense and a middle linebacker on defense. Unimpressed by such obscure feats, the Cleveland Browns diffidently selected him in the fifteenth round of the 1974 draft, and he nearly ignored their modest offer. His mother and father, rooted as they were in Edwardian ideals of amateurism in sport, believed that their son's participation in games played for money was below his station and encouraged him to enter graduate school. But Farnsworth, having grown increasingly restless at home, traveled to the Browns' rookie camp at Hiram College near Cleveland and produced joyful disbelief among the coaching staff. He was swift and smooth in the forty-yard dash; he had excellent lateral movement; he was a sure, brutal tackler; and he was an intelligent reader of plays. As the 1976 season opened, the Cleveland Browns were being mentioned as Super Bowl contenders, thanks in part to a reinforced defense built around their second-year all-pro candidate from a tiny college in upstate New York. Then had come the slip while fighting for a rebound in the New Salerno YMCA and the giddy little jaunt that had been his life up to then was over. For the first time in his memory, Pancho Farnsworth was flawed, and he didn't like thinking about it.

JESSUP'S PIER SIX lay on the edge of a small cove a few miles downstream from Alexandria Bay. A rococo, multi-gabled mansion built in the 1880's, it had operated as a saloon and quasi-nightclub for as long as anybody could remember. During Prohibition, Jessup's had been a popular speakeasy and an active port of entry for bargeloads of Canadian whiskey that moved across the river in regular shipments. It stood on a low headland flanked by thick marshes and its shoreline faced a patchwork of docks attached to rotting pilings. The old structure's main floor had been altered by the addition of a flat-roofed, concrete-block annex that jutted from one side.

As Farnsworth and Enderle idled the *Red Dog* into the cove, the final hint of sunlight silhouetted the jumbled shape of the old building against the horizon. A few bare light bulbs hung from loose wires near the docks and a neon sign blinked the word "Schlitz" from an upper-story window. On the shore side of the building a cluster of mercury-vapor lamps played off the roofs of automobiles spread across the parking lot. As they tied the boat to a sagging pier, a jumble of voices and hard-driving music came at them through the open doors and windows. They climbed a series of stairs up from the docks—Enderle in the lead with Farnsworth hobbling a few steps behind. A noisy kitchen fan blasted them with a hot, greasy cloud.

"I wonder if that asshole's here tonight," said Enderle as he swung open the battered screen door. He was referring to an unidentified member of the management. A few nights before, Enderle had been telling loud jokes and accompanying the punch lines with thumps of his fist on the bar when a rangy man had appeared and told him to lower his voice. He had been wearing an expensive sport shirt and his razor-styled hair had seemed almost glued into place. The man had been skinny— much too frail for Enderle to assault—and while Roy had tensed at the affront, he had relaxed more in shock than submission while he'd listened to the rebuke. Speaking calmly, the man had told Enderle that unless he behaved, he would have to get out. He had then drifted away through the crowd.

Tonight would be different. No one would get Roy Enderle out of Jessup's Pier Six until the precise moment he was ready to depart. They entered a low-ceilinged room, the concrete-block extension to the old building. It was nearly dark. Bartender's lamps showed beneath the large circular bar that dominated the center of the cavern. Light played off several crude nautical wall motifs composed of oars, netting, and a few dried starfish. Three harsh spots lit up the empty bandstand in one corner. Tables, filled with shadowy forms, clogged all the available space. Young men milled around the bar, many cruising in solemn isolation. Girls, the energizers of saloons, were everywhere. With the band in a break, a tape system was pumping deafening music through the loudspeakers. Enderle and Farnsworth shoved their way toward the bar. They ordered two Cream Ales and turned to survey the scene. Their eyes had adjusted to the darkness and during a lull in the sound Enderle said, "Lotsa snatch." Farnsworth nodded.

They drank in silence for a few more minutes, still scanning the room, and then Farnsworth felt Enderle's mallet-sized elbow bang against his ribs. "I just fell in love!"

"Which one?" Farnsworth asked, gaping into the darkness.

"That big black-headed one over there. Right there, next to that doggy blonde with all the teeth." Enderle was eying a creamy-faced brunette sitting at a corner table with two other girls and a small man in a denim jacket. "She looks pretty good from here," said Farnsworth. "Doesn't look like she's with anybody," he added.

"Who cares? She's gonna dance with me either way when the band comes back," said Enderle, squinting his eyes.

As the bartender, a gregarious man in his mid-twenties, poured two more ales, Enderle asked him, "What's with the dark-haired chick in the corner?" The bartender sought the source of the question, a mildly curious expression on his face. Then his face turned firm and his gaze locked with Enderle's.

"Watch that stuff, man. It's trouble."

"Whaddya mean?"

"She belongs to Vince."

"Who the fuck is Vince?"

"Vince Scarpatti. He's one of the owners. He's also the bouncer."

Enderle's mouth opened in a wide grin. Then it closed again and his eyes brightened. "The bouncer? So what's that got to do with me?"

The bartender regarded Enderle carefully. "With you, maybe nothing. But nobody around here fucks with him."

"But I ain't a nobody from around here. So what are you trying to tell me?"

"Man, I'm not trying to tell you anything. I'm just telling you, that's all." The bartender stepped back, shrugged, and moved away.

They drank some more, letting the tide of bodies ebb and flow around them. Finally the band straggled back to the stand. A drummer seated himself behind a battery of basses, snares, cymbals, and a large electronic console. A tenor saxophonist and three vocalist/guitar players gathered around him. They were wearing bib overalls and red-checkered shirts, and displayed drooping, Wyatt Earp-style mustaches. Battering-ram rhythms swelled inside the room. The dance floor immediately filled with swirling, swiveling shapes. "Watch this," said Enderle, setting down his glass and thrusting into the crowd.

Farnsworth leaned against the bar and watched the giant form shamble across the room toward the girl. He knew Enderle and understood that somehow he would egg the man Vince into a battle for supremacy, not only over the girl but over the entire saloon. Farnsworth considered himself a good fighter. When the time was right, he enjoyed slugging somebody, and he recalled the time when he, Enderle, and three other Browns had taken on a pack of drunken fans in the parking lot at Love Field in Dallas during his rookie season. It had been kept out of the papers, mainly because one of the participants, a prominent Texas real estate broker, had drawn a .38 Smith & Wesson Special moments before the police arrived. There had been that beautiful split second just before Farnsworth heard the sirens when a red-faced man in a flowered shirt had swung wildly at him and he'd countered with a hooking right that had pitched the man, cold as a smelt, into the bed of an El Camino pickup. Farnsworth had always enjoyed feeling bodies cave in under the force of his blocks and tackles on the field, but there was something exquisitely predatory about smashing another man in the face with a bare fist and seeing him crumble like a tower of supermarket canned goods. He was sure that he would fight again this night, and propelled by the alcohol and a gnawing frustration, he relished the prospect. But he wondered how effective he would be with only one good leg.

He saw Enderle reach the table and the girl's face turn upward to him. She was stony-eyed, and her full lips did not move as she listened. Farnsworth, viewing the confrontation in pantomime, saw Enderle gesture, then plunge his hands into his pockets. Then the girl's lips moved and she placed a cigarette to her mouth, took a long drag, and turned her attention to the blonde beside her. Everyone at the table laughed. Enderle stood for a moment, said something, then turned back through the crowd toward the bar. The girl followed his retreat with a fierce glare for a few steps, then twisted her head away for good.

"Fuckin' bitch," growled Enderle as he regained his place at the bar.

"Looked like you got shot square in the ass," said Farnsworth, smiling.

"Fuckin' bitch. You know what she said? I asked her to dance, see. Just kind of rolled up there and asked her to dance. She doesn't say a word; just sat there frigid as a nun. She just looks at me and right out of the blue she asks, 'You got a big cock?' "

Farnsworth broke into loud laughter. "What'd you say to that, Slick?"

Enderle shrugged and tried a weak smile. "What the hell could I say? I hadda tell her the truth."

"So . . ."

"So she says, 'If it's so long, why don't you go screw yourself?' Can you imagine some chick saying that? The dirty bitch. But I got in the last shot. I called her boy friend a fag. That oughta get us a little action."

Farnsworth and Enderle were getting smashed. The babble of voices, the jumble of laughter, the rattle of glassware, the clang of cash registers, and the pulsing rhythms of the band combined to drown coherent speech or thought. Saloon smells assaulted their noses: the reek of spilled beer, the biting aroma of pot and tobacco, the fumes of cheap perfume, and the sharp odor of sweat. Finally Farnsworth picked up his glass and moved away from the bar. "Let's play a few games of air hockey," he suggested.

They entered a connecting room, beside the stage, where four air-hockey tables were arranged in a rectangle. They waited their turn, then Farnsworth challenged a barefoot, pimpled youth in cut-off jeans. Even the heavy intake of ale had not seriously impaired his reflexes and he overwhelmed his opponent with a murderous attack, driving the puck at him in a series of blinding shots. Enderle, now challenging Farnsworth, was about to insert a half-dollar into the coin slot when a large man came into the room and touched him on the elbow. He was perhaps two inches over six feet, and he moved with the easy confidence of a man who knew he was a hardnose in any company. He carried his hands with the fingers spread apart and the thumbs splayed out, like a gunfighter ready to yank a pair of Colts from his gun belt. His nose was on straight and he had no scars. He was no has-been wrestler or punched-out pug hired by the hour. The soft leather jacket that concealed his ample torso and long arms had been custom-tailored to accommodate his thick biceps and powerful shoulders. Farnsworth had seen him first but said nothing as he approached. It had to be Vince. Farnsworth figured that he had to know karate or have some other gimmick of combat. Otherwise, he would not move in on a man as massive as Enderle.

"Pack it up and get out," Vince said, his voice seeking to sound routine.

Enderle turned and regarded the man who had spoken. "You speakin' to me?"

The charade had begun.

"Who's it look like I'm speakin' to, that fuckin' wall? Move out," said Vince again, softly.

Enderle eyed him for a moment, then reached down and shoved the coin into the air-hockey table. He was ignoring him.

Farnsworth noticed a small crowd beginning to gather. Enderle was leaning on the low table, his arms stiff and spread wide. Thoughts of the game had ceased, but he refused to turn around. His eyes had a faraway look. The music blared in from the nearby band, but all talking had stopped. Without moving his head, Enderle said, "Nobody's movin' nowhere." Then his gaze locked briefly with Farnsworth's and a smirk drifted over his lips.

Two other men shoved their way into the room. One was short and wide; his hair was combed forward over a prematurely balding forehead. The other was the one with the razor-cut hair who'd told Enderle and Farnsworth to quiet down on their earlier visit. Now he looked apprehensive and slightly disheveled. The short man, inexplicably wearing a raincoat, moved near Vince, while the other sidled in closer to Farnsworth. In the front row of the thickening crowd Pancho sighted the brunette. Vince's girl had come to watch judgment day.

"Look, motherfucker . . ." said Vince.

Enderle turned and rose up to his full height. Reflexively, Vince began a step backward, then caught himself. His right hand slipped easily, almost casually, into his pocket. In this fight, there would be few preliminaries—none of the standard rooster preening and posturing that precedes most physical confrontations. Blows would come with blinding speed and it would be over quickly.

"When you call somebody a motherfucker, you better mean it, greaseball." Enderle said the words slowly and deliberately and everyone in the room tensed. Farnsworth spread his legs, trying to distribute his weight as effectively as possible.

It was a quick, fluid movement, introduced by a brief feint as Vince appeared to turn and move away. His right hand, bearing a short black rod, lashed toward Enderle's chin. A blackjack! The room was filled with gasps and screams of shock and delight. Enderle's left arm shot up to fend off the blow, and he emitted an angry yelp of pain as the leather-bound bludgeon thwacked against his wrist. Slightly off balance, he brought his right fist upward and sent it crashing into Vince's midsection, bending the man forward. A fierce animal howl came from Enderle as he leapt forward, grabbing his stunned quarry by his arms. Vince struggled to get free, but he was powerless. Enderle raised his right hand and cuffed him, open-palmed, twice across the face, as a father might spank a baby. Then he spun him around, and holding him by the seat of his pants and the collar of his jacket, he flung him, like a sack of grain, through a gap in the crowd. Moving forward, Enderle again picked up the limp body of the bouncer and hurled it onto the stage, where it piled into the drums and microphone stands like a runaway bowling ball. For a moment the place was filled with the weird, electronically amplified discordancy of a disintegrating band— drums thudding, loudspeakers collapsing, mikes crashing to the floor, and guitar players scurrying for cover. Vince plowed through the drums and crushed the amplifier console against the wallboard backdrop. A grapefruit-sized spark welled out of the ruptured container, accompanied by the vicious crackling of short-circuited voltage. The barroom went dark. Screams, the scrape of chairs, and the rattle of harried feet filled the darkness.

Farnsworth had stepped back from the table and, like those around him, had stood frozen in place as he watched Roy hurl the bouncer into the bandstand. Although the main room had lost its lights, the bulbs in connecting rooms stayed lit, and once the impact of Enderle's colossal feat of strength penetrated their brains, the crowd began to surge, some trying to get clear, others eager for a better look at the action. "Watch it, Roy," Farnsworth shouted as the heavy man in the raincoat scuttled behind Enderle and produced what appeared to be a length of three-quarter-inch water pipe. Sensing danger, Enderle wheeled on him and snatched the shaft. The heavy man's face collapsed like a rubber mask. Rigid, he fell backward, much as a novice might begin a back dive from the edge of a swimming pool. He reeled into the arms of the first-row spectators as Enderle stood above him like an angry God. He regarded the fear-jellied man for a moment, then brought the pipe up level with his eyes. His giant body coiled and a leer crossed his face. He slammed the pipe onto the surface of the air-hockey table, ripping open a jagged fissure in its plastic surface. The crowd recoiled, somehow blown back by the sheer force of Enderle's strength and anger.

Farnsworth sensed movement on his right. The rangy man with the pretty hair was sliding against him, raising something in his right hand. The hissing sound of pressurized gas reached Farnsworth's ears. An aerosol can. Mace. He pivoted and drove his left knee toward the man's groin while groping for the weapon. For a second his entire weight was on his weak leg and it collapsed, causing his body to fall down and away from the disabling spray. His knee had missed the mark, brushing instead against the man's thigh, and he found himself tumbling off balance while his adversary was trying to backstep and remain erect. Farnsworth countered with a crude tackle, lunging forward with his superior weight and jackknifing the man, writhing and struggling, onto the floor. He scrambled on top, forcing the man into a spread-eagle position. Holding the Mace can at bay with a wrist lock, he clamped a hand over the man's head and slammed it twice—in short, brutal cadence—against the floor. Stunned, the man loosened his grip on the Mace container and Farnsworth grabbed it. For a moment he was tempted to empty it into one of the man's nostrils, but his rage was not that intense. He stood up instead, again forcing the gallery back like jittery heifers. Still holding the can, he barged up to Enderle, who seemed to be standing in a trance waiting for someone to screw up nerve for another assault. "Let's get the hell out of here," said Farnsworth.

"I just got here," said Enderle evenly, his eyes still scanning the crowd.

"Somebody *has* to have called the cops. We'll split and save ourselves a lot of trouble."

"Then I'm takin' me a souvenir," shouted Enderle as he charged into the crowd. Farnsworth heard a sharp scream. Enderle reappeared, half dragging, half carrying the brunette they knew only as Vince's girl. "She says she wants a ride on the river," he said, chuckling.

At first Farnsworth was prepared to argue, but his instincts told him it was time to leave Jessup's—to get aboard the *Red Dog* and head for open water. "O.K., O.K., whatever you say, let's just move it," he said firmly. He looked at the girl. Enderle's right arm was coiled across her bosom, and her cool, disdainful expression had been replaced by the electric image of terror. Her thick hair was jumbled and the mascara around her eyes was smeared. "You son of a bitch," she screeched. Enderle said nothing; he intensified his grip and moved toward the door.

The mob split wide to give them space. The night was moonless and still and the cool air rising off the water cleared their heads. Farnsworth led the way, although his leg was paining him greatly. He limped along as Enderle dragged his prey behind. Several times the girl began to shout, but was silenced as though a valve in her larynx had been screwed shut. The crowd stumbled out behind them, keeping a prudent distance. The man in the raincoat had recovered and was leading the pack. They crowded onto the pier, filing along beneath the bare lights. Words drifted out of their midst, fragmented, tentative words like "damages," "kidnapping," "assault," "police," but Enderle and Farnsworth kept moving until they reached the boat. Pancho unhitched the lines before scrambling aboard. The Bertram began drifting into the bay. Gathering courage, the crowd surged to the end of the dock. Two youths jumped into a fiberglass outboard tied nearby and cast off.

Farnsworth found it harder than he had expected to climb the ladder to the flying bridge and was forced to sit down once he reached the controls. Good seamanship required that he run the engine-room blowers in order to purge any explosive gasoline fumes from the bilges. But there was no time. Holding his breath as a feeble hedge against the possibility of an explosion, Farnsworth kicked over the engines. They ignited without hesitation and burbled obediently in neutral. He turned to check Enderle on the afterdeck; he was standing over the girl. She was sitting cross-legged on the deck, her head in her hands, her great black mane bobbing with sobs.

"C'mon, Roy, for Chrissakes, that chick is going to be nothing but trouble," Farnsworth said.

"We'll just take her for a quick ride around the bay."

"Leave her here. You proved your point."

Roy Enderle shrugged his shoulders. "Pancho baby, you're the captain." He looked defiantly at the mob on the dock. The little outboard had floated to within a few yards of the *Red Dog* but was not about to close the distance. Enderle reached down and scooped up the girl in an easy motion. Holding her at arm's length, he pitched her over the side. Her body hit the water in a comic, kneeling posture. She rose to the surface coughing and screaming obscenities. Farnsworth punched the throttles forward and felt the Bertram leap up on plane and scurry for open water.

11

RUNNING WIDE OPEN,
the *Red Dog* skimmed away from Jessup's and into the main
shipping channel of the St. Lawrence. Farnsworth turned east
and headed between Sister Island and Third Brother Island
shoal, where the river yawned to nearly four miles in width. On
his left the black, slightly humped form of Grenadier Island
crouched on the horizon. A scattering of cottage lights glowed
on its beach. To the south the American shoreline was blurred
in a quilt of lights and low land masses formed by the dozens of
small islands that cluttered the river. Ahead the murky vastness
of the open water was broken only by the bright, steady blink of
the channel buoy at Haskell Shoal and its flashing red mate a
half mile to the north. A blanket of clouds obscured the moon,
making the soft, warm night all the darker, and Farnsworth felt
as if he were zooming along a flat plane of outer space and the
dots of light around him were far-off stars and galaxies.

Enderle lounged on the flying bridge, letting the boat carry
him toward an unknown destination. They had laughed for a
long while after leaving the chaos at Jessup's, but now the
letdown had overtaken them and there was little talk. Farns-

worth had decided not to return to Alexandria Bay, partly because it was too early to go home—hardly past three o'clock—and partly because he was not sure what would be waiting there. Perhaps the police had been called, and even now a sheriff's or New York State Police sedan might be sitting in the parking lot at Zach Landsman's Marina, patiently awaiting their return. Rather than face that hassle in the middle of the night, Farnsworth had decided to head downriver for a while, then drop the hook along the Canadian shore, perhaps at Whitney Point or Mallorytown Landing. After a day of fishing and an exploratory phone call to Zach, they would cruise quietly back to Alexandria Bay.

"You know, we oughta just keep running," said Enderle. "Just keep this bitch pointed east until we get to Montreal. The Olympics open in three, four days and there'll be a lot of action there. Hell, Montreal swings even when there's nothing special going on. That'll be a heavy scene with the Olympics."

"We could do it in a day, if the Seaway didn't hold us up too bad. They don't open the locks for every twenty-eight-footer that shows up. Still, it's not a bad idea. Better yet, we could take your camper. We could drive it in a couple of hours, even in that shit box."

"Take the boat. No way that you and I are going to do any ballin' in the back of that camper. At least not at the same time," said Enderle.

"Maybe we should have kept that broad you got at Jessup's, after all," said Farnsworth.

"That sorry bitch," said Enderle, beginning to laugh. "You remember that splash when she hit the water. Goddamn, like a fuckin' tractor-trailer!"

"Altogether, it was a pretty bad night for her and Vince," chuckled Farnsworth.

"Sure wish I'd hear from Whitby," said Enderle, suddenly turning serious.

"Relax, he'll get you the deal. The Argos are looking for a good defensive end. That's you."

"Son of a bitch said he'd find out this week," Enderle grumbled.

"That stuff always takes fifty times longer than anyone expects. Whitby's working on it. He's a good man," said Farnsworth.

"He's O.K. It's just that I feel like such a fuckin' pawn. My whole life I've been a line on the roster. Enderle and two draft choices. Enderle on the move list. Enderle waived. You know, ever since I started playing high school ball, I've never had a really clear choice; never had the chance to exercise any clear options of my own."

"Oh, bullshit. You didn't have any options as long as you played ball is what you mean. Nobody whipped your ass to make you play ball," Farnsworth rebutted firmly. Enderle said nothing in response. He could be disputed and even mocked, but it had to be on his own clearly defined terms, terms that fit his own self-image. He permitted himself to be the butt of broad, comic contradictions implying that he was frail and timid, that he was clumsy and slow afoot, but these were safe confines for his ego. But Farnsworth had directly rebuked him, challenged him when he was seeking pity. In circumstances like these Enderle dropped out of the conversation, finding reassurance inside his own head. Farnsworth knew it was up to him to regenerate the dialogue. "What I'm saying is, you know there's just so much you can do with the system. The big shooters are in command, and we all understood that when we decided to play ball. We could have tried something else, you know."

"Maybe you. The only thing I've got is my body. My only asset. I knew it from the time I was a kid. I knew it was my only chance. Gave it the full shot. But you. You're covered. You got the name, the connections, the bread, to do anything you please. No matter what, you got your old man's business to fall back on.

You got no gamble in your body. I've got everything on the line."

"I think I'd pack it in if I couldn't play any more ball," Farnsworth said gravely.

"You say that, but you'd make it. Me, I got nothing. No degree, no training, no idea where I'd even start if I don't hook on with somebody."

Farnsworth sensed vulnerability in him. For all the time he'd known Enderle he had seemed impregnable; his defenses of fiber and grit and sinew appeared so strong that they were beyond breaching. But now he sounded almost frightened. Farnsworth wanted to say something that would ease his apprehension, but nothing sensible came into his mind. Enderle's options in major-league professional football were practically eliminated. Coaching or other perimeter jobs were out of the question. He was hardly the type to return to college or begin a conventional career in business. Farnsworth wanted to tell him that a job always awaited him at his family's firm, but that was not true. His father did not like Enderle. He considered him a crude, stupid jock—the epitome of the flesh-peddling professional athlete. It had been hard enough for him to accept his son's entry into the pros, but he had rationalized it as an adventure among the heathen, Burton's secret hegira to Mecca—that sort of thing. Farnsworth's father felt that Roy was using his son while simultaneously corrupting and barbarizing him. No, there was no job waiting for him in New Salerno.

They angled northeast across the wide waters, passing Dark Island, then cutting near the American shore at Chippewa Point. Enderle had fallen silent again and Farnsworth assumed he was dozing. The warmth, rich with moisture, was persisting, even in the middle of the river. The wind was little more than an occasional wheeze of humid air and the water seemed to have turned into a thick glaze of smooth asphalt. Farnsworth decided that the oppressive heat wave would be broken only by the sharp blow of a low-pressure system swooping in from the west with its murderous spikes of lightning and its bulldozer winds. When the storm came, it would sweep down from Georgian Bay and across Lake Ontario, where it would gain velocity before funneling up the sluiceway of the St. Lawrence.

He was musing about the seaworthiness of the Bertram, with its deep-vee hull design bred from the dangerous and difficult sport of ocean powerboat racing. To the north, perhaps a mile and a half away, a few meek lights peered out from Whitney Point on the Canadian mainland. He planned to run east to clear the last shoals surrounding a cluster of small mid-river islands, then turn northward across the international boundary and make for a quiet anchorage. At first the silhouette of the ship meant nothing to him. But as he examined it, standing perhaps a half mile away, he became aware of several rather curious details. It was smaller than the oceangoing vessels and lake freighters that plied the river, and it was well out of the regular shipping lane. Most unusual of all, it seemed to be dead in the water.

"Hey, look at that," said Farnsworth, nudging Enderle.

"Huh . . ."

"That ship. Just sitting there. Kind of weird."

Enderle sat up and peered in the direction in which Farnsworth was pointing. The dull glow of the instrument panel playing on his high cheeks and prominent brow produced an ominous, abstract study of light and shadow. As Farnsworth eased back the engines, Enderle's eyes focused on the tall, rather stubby profile of what appeared to be an oceangoing trawler, perhaps eighty-five feet in length. Its superstructure was entirely aft, topped by a bridge and pilothouse forward of a squat stack and a mizzenmast intended to carry a steadying sail in heavy weather. Its main foredeck was open, except for a single, cargo-rigged mainmast. It was a grim, shadowy object, with no lights showing. No movement, either on its decks or by its own hull in the placid water, was evident. "Hardly looks real," said Enderle absently.

"What's strange is that she's got no lights. No running lights. No anchor lights. She's supposed to have one or the other," said Farnsworth, lifting a pair of 7 × 50 binoculars from a gear locker. "Doesn't make any sense."

"See anything?" asked Enderle, still only mildly interested.

"Yeah, a couple of guys on deck and maybe a few more on the bridge. Too dark to see much else."

"Think they got trouble?"

"Maybe. Might have lost power," said Farnsworth.

"Wouldn't have lost the whole freakin' mess, would they? I mean, they must have auxiliary generators or something for lights. Don't seem like the complete boat would quit all at once," said Enderle.

"It just doesn't follow for a ship that size. If she was in real trouble, somebody would be firing a flare or something." Farnsworth put the binoculars to his face once more. "She's pointed upstream, which is the way she'd swing on an anchor— her bow aimed into the current. But I can't see any anchor chain."

"Want to go over and take a look?" asked Enderle.

"You?"

"I don't care. Nothing else is going on."

"Why the hell not?" said Farnsworth, throwing the wheel over and adding power. Within a few minutes the *Red Dog* had closed the distance and Farnsworth cut its throttles as they hove to fifty yards off the trawler's port bow.

"The thing looks deserted," said Enderle, squinting in the darkness.

"At least it doesn't look like it's sinking. And I can hear something running inside," added Farnsworth. He could make out no movement on the trawler, but there was the unmistakable sound of life within the ship—the distant moan of blowers, compressors, and pumps that pulsed through the decks and bulkheads to give its steel-and-iron innards the quality of a living organism. Then a man walked out on the port wing of the bridge. He was slight and narrow-shouldered and was wearing pants and a shirt of such a dark color as to make him practically invisible.

"Hey, you guys need any help?" Farnsworth shouted to the shape on the bridge.

"Stay clear! Stay clear!" yelled the small man in a high-pitched voice.

"The guy sounds like a Frog," said Enderle. "What's a Frog trawler doing in the middle of the St. Lawrence?"

"He might be French-Canadian," said Farnsworth. "Either way, he sure as hell doesn't sound like he needs any help."

"Let him sink," said Enderle.

"This whole thing is weird, man. They're doing something with that ship, and it sure as hell ain't fishing," said Farnsworth quietly.

"Move away. You will foul our nets!" the voice from the bridge shouted.

"Nets, your ass!" countered Farnsworth. "What're you guys doing out here?" He waited a few moments for a reply, then shouted in grave, officious tones, "C'mon, speak up, or we'll call the Coast Guard!" He then turned to Enderle and, chuckling quietly, said, "That'll pull their chain a little bit."

The small man on the bridge stood rigid, his hands resting on the iron railing. He said nothing, but stared at the boat and its two tormentors. A larger, rather hunched man joined him. They appeared to confer in a series of cryptic sentences before the taller man turned and disappeared through the door of the pilothouse. The small man in the dark clothes stood where he was and maintained his gaze.

"You know what? I just spotted something," said Farnsworth. "See that forward cargo boom. It's hanging over the starboard side of the ship. Those bastards are loading or unloading something off the other side."

"Let's take a look," said Enderle.

Farnsworth shoved the Bertram's clutches into gear and

turned the boat in a tight loop. He passed under the bow of the trawler and idled along until the dull, smooth starboard flanks of the larger ship were visible. A few yards in front of them, a sleek, mean-looking powerboat was lying against the hull of the trawler. Its low freeboard, pointed bow, and rakishly canted windshield gave it the appearance of an outsized speedboat. Five men were standing on its afterdeck and they had all turned to watch the approach of the *Red Dog*. The trawler's boom hovered over them, but no cargo was visible.

"Those sum-bitches are trying something funny," said Enderle.

A sharp voice, stronger and edged with more anger than the first which had come from the ship, yelled, "This is private business. Get clear or suffer the consequences."

"What do you think?" whispered Farnsworth.

"What the hell are they going to do? This isn't their water. Let's stick around and let 'em sweat," said Enderle defiantly.

They became mired in a kind of absurd stasis: Farnsworth and Enderle and the men on the big runabout standing frozen while the three boats drifted together. No one moved, nothing was said, and the only sound was the murmur of the *Red Dog*'s idling engines.

The shot came as a harmless crackle of sound across the water, like a stick being broken. Simultaneously Roy Enderle reeled sideways, as if he had been struck in the left breast by a mysterious energy field. A groan came from inside him, and he tumbled backward against the low seat, then spilled off the flying bridge. His limp frame landed on the deck with the dull thud of dead weight. It made no sense to Farnsworth, that prickle of noise and the gyrations of Enderle. He stood there in the darkness, his mind sprinting to catch up with reality. Somehow his tactile reserves drew him to his shirt front, which transmitted a cloying dampness to his brain. His fingers reached the spot and told him his midriff was blotched with a sticky, gelatinous liquid. Blood! It was as if an electric shock pierced his brain, driving the terror of the moment deep inside his consciousness. Facts riddled him. Enderle had been hit by a bullet and that missile had sent him careening off the bridge and had splashed part of Roy's insides, blood and tissue, against his own shirt. This became apparent to him a particle of a second before another twig snap of sound came from the ship and a shower of plastic pummeled his face. A third shot immediately followed, its report floating away across the waters. Farnsworth had instinctively turned to the aid of his friend, but had been driven back by the debris tossed up by the gunfire. He fell to his knees, seeking shelter behind the bulwarks, and crouched rigid for a few seconds, while the juices of survival pulsed through his body. More deadly crackles came from the unseen gun muzzle, coupled with the hollow moan of bullets. Enderle was sprawled awkwardly at the base of the ladder, and an attempt to reach him would mean destruction. Farnsworth knelt there, his eyeballs straining in their sockets, every gland and muscle puffed and rigid, for what seemed to be hours but was actually the slow-motion time warp of crises. The firing had stopped and another sound reached his ears: a soft mumbling in the water accompanied by scattered, indecipherable voices. Engines! The other vessel—the speedboat that had been snuggled against the side of the trawler—was starting its engines. Mechanisms of escape sent Farnsworth lurching for the controls—the wheel and the throttles that would carry him away into the openness of the river. Huddling low on the deck of the bridge, he spun the wheel to port, engaged the clutches, and crammed the chromed throttle levers full forward. The two 225-horsepower Mercruisers responded instantly, thrusting the Bertram up on her screws. The *Red Dog* leaped ahead, at the same time pivoting in a sharp veer to the left. Farnsworth heard a curt yell from nearby, and his senses told him that he had come within inches of ramming the other boat. As he powered past, with the *Red Dog* heeled hard over and her starboard prop cavitating nearly free of the water, a rapid volley of small-arms fire spewed at him. A bullet tore through the bridge's seat cushion, showering him with polyurethane snowflakes, while another bore past his head, carrying with it shards of fiberglass like the tail of a comet.

Once he had rotated his craft in a half circle and was clear of the other boats, he straightened the Red Dog on course and fled away. Rising up on his haunches, he peered out at his surroundings. Ahead lay a dark horizon speckled with a few dim lights. Behind, his boat's wake cut shimmering furrows through the black water. Receding in the distance was the outline of the trawler.

But closer, Farnsworth's eyes riveted on the foaming white bow wave of the speedboat, which was pursuing like an eyeless shark, perhaps two hundred feet behind. Something splatted against a locker door beneath the instrument panel. Another bullet. Although he could not hear the detonations over the flat-out rumble of the engines, he knew that projectiles were streaking at him through the night. He dropped once more to his knees and began to steer a jerking, zigzag course back toward Jessup's and Alexandria Bay. It seemed, as he swiveled his head for a glance at his pursuers, that they were losing ground. Grudgingly they clung to his wake, but the distance seemed to be opening a few yards at a time. He was knifing south, aiming for some kind of shelter against the American shore.

The two boats rushed through the night, with the Red Dog establishing an ever-widening gap. Then the other craft suddenly slowed, and for a moment he felt a sense of relief. But within seconds a searing lick of light arrowed out of the other boat, linking the two crafts in a solid shaft of illumination. Bathed in the brightness, Farnsworth reacted by dropping flat on the deck and yanking the wheel hard to starboard. He surmised that one final, desperate volley would be directed at him; the men in the other boat—unknown men who were trying to kill him—had stopped in order to gain a more stable shooting platform and now, having zeroed their quarry in the tube of light, were carefully sighting their broadside before the range became too great. Flat on his belly, Farnsworth reached up with his left arm and twisted the boat to port. Milliseconds later bullets rattled against the superstructure. The light went out. Farnsworth was alone.

He sped on, imagining that the boat was still behind and gobbling up the distance with renewed energy. He thought of Enderle and wanted to go to him, but fear kept him at the helm. He could see the rumpled form of his friend lying still as stone on the afterdeck. Blood seemed to be everywhere. He wanted to rewind time back to when things had been innocent and frivolous and normal. His mind was leapfrogging from the condition of Enderle to the identity of their attackers, to the trouble that awaited him at Alexandria Bay—trouble that would greet him as the skipper of a bullet-riddled craft with a wounded man aboard. He wanted it to stop, for it all to go away and to be replaced by the horseplay and games that had heretofore been the main content of his life. But there was no recovery. No instant replay to uncoil the drama and to reinstate peace.

Finally he convinced himself that his pursuers had given up the chase. He stopped *Red Dog*'s engines, bringing it sloshing to a halt in mid-river. The clouds were breaking up. Venus, the morning star, hung stark and unblinking in the velvet dome above. A barely perceptible penumbra of dawn light glazed the eastern horizon. Somewhere, far off among the foggy coves of the islands around him, the sputter of an outboard motor floated to his ears. He swung awkwardly down the ladder and went to his friend. Enderle was lying on his back, staring at the sky. But he saw nothing. Life had drained out of him through the gaping cavity in his chest and now he was dead. Farnsworth grappled with this cruel knowledge, trying to understand. He knelt above him, somehow afraid to touch the inert form. Finally he brushed his fingers across the dead man's midriff and felt for the first time in his life the stillness of eternity. He crawled away, dragging his weakened leg, and sat like an abandoned child in the middle of the deck. There he gaped at the dark waters, breathing in frantic, sucking spasms, until the tears spread over his eyes and the sobs rippled through his body like distant thunder.

III

THE BIRDS were beginning their chatterbox celebration of morning but Bernard Gannet was not listening. A buttery aura of sunlight bathed the kitchen, where he sat, silent and motionless, at a broad, bare-topped table littered with coffee cups and clogged ash trays. The room was at the back of a crumbling cut-stone house that towered above the trees and rocky outcroppings of Yellow Squaw Island. It was one of the numerous mansions that had been built during those prosperous Bull Moose years when the Thousand Islands rivaled Newport and Bar Harbor as a summer refuge for the eastern gentry. Now the place was peeled and eroded after the assaults of sixty winters and even on this gentle morning it appeared gaunt and brooding in the brightness of nature.

Gannet lifted his spare frame out of the chair and moved to a window. Birds darted through the thick stockades of silver and red maples, and down a long slope he could see the shimmering waters of the St. Lawrence. On the same rough bearing, amidst other smaller, deserted islands, the incident that was causing him such irritation had unfolded during the predawn hours. It had been a botch, that stupid outburst of shooting that now threatened to compromise the enterprise that had consumed every moment of Bernard Gannet's life for the past two years. He lit another cigarette, one of dozens he had smoked in the past few hours, and crooked his elbow against the window frame. Taking deep, compulsive drags, he absently watched a pudgy gray spider fussing in its web beyond the glass, then returned the few paces to the table and sat down again. He was scrawny and haggard. His body was draped in a pair of rumpled slacks and a knit pullover shirt. Everything about him was small and pinched except for the monster chronograph on his left wrist and his bulky, black-framed eyeglasses, which seemed to have been intended for a bigger man. His eyes, although red from exhaustion, were bright and angry. Perhaps it was the fatigue, coupled with the owlish effect of the glasses, but Bernard Gannet looked ten years older than his actual age of twenty-six. He reached for a cup of tepid coffee and drained it in one swig, twisting his lips and squinting his eyes at the bitterness.

Someone was climbing the flight of stairs from the radio and supply rooms in the basement. The steps came closer, then a man came into the kitchen. He was tall and swarthy, in his late twenties, well muscled, with a stern set to his narrow, heavily tanned face. His thin lips and short, thick hair were decidedly Arabic, and his stiff military bearing was accentuated by the short-sleeved khaki campaign shirt and matching pants.

Gafaar al-Salam, a major in the Air Force of the socialist republic of Libya, gave Gannet a harsh glance as he approached the table. Gannet barely acknowledged his appearance. Major Salam walked past Gannet and went to the window. The stiffness of the encounter indicated there was no basic friendship between them. Gafaar al-Salam regarded Gannet as a fumbling amateur revolutionary, better suited for rhetorical library battles at the university than for actual campaigns of liberation. Conversely, Gannet viewed the Libyan as a tunnel-visioned martinet, given to hyperbolic outbursts and erratic spasms of action, such as the one that had come hours earlier on the river, when during the particularly sensitive offloading operation, Salam had opened fire on the small yacht and its pair of rowdy passengers. Gannet considered it an irrational act of violence— an act that might have compromised the entire program of liberation for the Province of Quebec.

"Have you heard anything from the *Talon?*" Gannet asked in a grave voice.

"The *Talon* is maintaining radio silence, as per instructions. She has been under way now for five hours. At twelve knots that should put her well clear of the St. Lawrence and into Lake Ontario. I believe the danger is over," said Salam tightly.

"Whoever was aboard the small yacht is going to notify the authorities. It seems logical that something must develop. Something," Gannet countered.

"Our fire hit them both. The one who tried to escape may have been badly wounded and died before he could tell his story. My men are extremely accurate shots. It is unlikely that he survived," replied Salam.

"If he was so mortally wounded, how did he manage to outrun our launch? No, Major, we must assume that the second man is alive at this moment and has reported the incident. After all, how would it be possible for him to conceal or ignore the kind of assault that you and your men so imprudently unleashed on him?"

"*Imprudently?* You are describing my actions as imprudent? Let me remind you, Monsieur Gannet, that revolutions—true revolutions of the type you claim to be attempting—are not undertaken with textbooks and clandestine night tricks. There comes a time for action, for the shedding of blood. Courage, Gannet, is the soul of revolution and I am beginning to wonder if you and your FLQ associates have the stomach for such an undertaking."

"I expect to shed blood. My own, if necessary, but not in a damnably foolhardy action as gunning down a pair of idiots at the expense of compromising our entire plan! It is easy for you to defend such business. You have no basic stake in this enterprise."

"Libya has a stake in all people's revolutions. Otherwise I would not be here," Salam countered quickly. He turned to the window and stood, at loose parade rest, with his back to the French Canadian.

Bernard Gannet sagged in his chair and lit another cigarette. He thought of the days when news of strong Libyan support had been greeted with such rejoicing among the tiny ranks of the Front de Libération du Québec. The prospects for the success of their enterprise—the separation of the Province of Quebec from the Commonwealth of Canada and the creation of an independent French-Canadian socialist state—stimulated and excited him more than any other single notion in his life, but the chances of failure—now heightened by the irrational acts of his Libyan allies the night before—drove Bernard Gannet to the edge of despair.

He was an outrider of a cultural, ethnic, and political movement that had been bubbling within French Canada for more than two hundred years. Bernard Gannet believed he was on the brink of snapping a yoke of tyranny that had gripped his people from the moment they arrived in New France as soldiers, explorers, artisans, and churchmen in the ranks of the Bourbon kings. New France had been a special place from the beginning. While the English to the south busily created semi-independent colonies along the Atlantic coast, the French *habitants* lived in small bands behind stockades bordering the St. Lawrence, venturing out only to trade and trap for the bounty of fur in the endless forest. New France was operated as a military base, and settlement was limited to those who were able to advance the Crown's interest in maintaining the fur trade, expanding the borders against the rival English while controlling—and converting to the gospel of the Roman Church—the savage, capricious, crafty Hurons and Iroquois who surrounded them. This insular, isolated outpost of empire maintained itself in this fashion essentially from the settlement of the palisaded fortress at Quebec in 1608 until the English Conquest that closed the French and Indian War in 1760.

The Conquest, as it is recalled in French Canada, began on September 13, 1759, when James Wolfe's British troops defeated Montcalm's regulars and militia on the Plains of Abraham during a savage, hour-long fusillade, and ended the following year, on September 8, 1760, when the governor-general of New France, the Marquis de Vaudreuil, surrendered his stronghold of Montreal and all French claims to Canada. At that moment, sixty-five thousand men, women, and children were in New France, with nearly half of them living in the cities of Montreal, Quebec, and Three Rivers. After the capitulation, formalized by the Treaty of Paris in 1763, this tiny band of French colonials, living an agrarian, semi-feudal, church-dominated existence much like sixteenth-century Europeans, was overwhelmed by conquering Englishmen—part of the population of nearly a million and a half that had burgeoned across the British possessions during the same period the French had been trying to secure the immense acreage of Canada with their thin regiments.

The trauma of this Conquest changed New France forever. Suddenly an occupying force, speaking a different language and worshipping at the altar of the heretical Church of England, was in complete command. French-Canadian merchants found their traditional sources of capital dried up. Their old currency became hopelessly inflated and their new dependence on British shipping was tantamount to bankruptcy. The economy, based on the export of natural resources, passed into the hands of the English interlopers, and the French Canadians turned inward, trying as well as they could to preserve their pastoral, religious life style. They refused to accept the new tongue of their conquerors, and the Roman Catholic clergy, so long a power in

New France, gained strength as the French-Canadian society, in the analogy of one historian, curled around itself like a wounded caterpillar, in a purely defensive posture.

In 1839, Lord Durham—a man still despised by French Canadians—sneered, "There can hardly be conceived a nationality more destitute of all that can invigorate and elevate a people than that which is exhibited by the descendants of the French in Lower Canada, owing to their retaining their peculiar language and manners. They are a people with no history and no literature."

The French Canadians struggled onward in passive aloofness, clinging to the old ways: living out their lives in the small villages along the river as they had for generations, seldom venturing from the enclaves of the family or the Church, or working in Montreal as laborers, small merchants, and menial civil servants. Aside from a few disturbances, the French Canadians let themselves be pulled quietly into the Commonwealth Confederation in 1867—the act that gave Canada formal independence from England. The French Canadians of the nineteenth and early twentieth centuries somehow tried to remain above the cultural invasion that was going on around them. In this context, Conrad Langlois, a University of Montreal professor, commented, "After the Conquest, the French Canadians developed two psychological complexes: one of superiority, one of inferiority. They came to believe they were not good in business and industry. They became interested in agriculture, local retail trade, handicrafts, etc. They also conceived themselves to be superior in spiritual matters. In short, the French Canadians came to believe they would remain inferior economically but that they were already superior in religion, fine arts, ways of life, and human values."

Bernard Gannet's life had been consumed by this Québecois split personality. Among his earliest memories were the loud complaints of his father over the dinner table in their small, drab house in Ville Jacques-Cartier—a sprawling working-class suburb that spilled across the south bank of the St. Lawrence. His father, Gérard Gannet, carried his anger deep inside a clerk's body that made its way, during the bleak, numbing winters and steaming summers alike, by bus to its desk at La Chambre de Commerce du District de Montréal, the French Canadian's separate but equal counterpart to the Montreal Board of Trade. He was a bright, feisty man whose frustration grew out of the knowledge that he was pigeonholed for life as a second-class citizen, representing a second-class race in a second-class province. He was powerless in the face of the forces marshaled by the English Canadians and their greatest ally, the cruel and corrupt regime of Provincial Premier Maurice Duplessis. "The father of the poor and the mother of the rich," was the way Bernard Gannet could recall his father and a small circle of cronies denouncing Duplessis. Yet as leader of the powerful Union Nationale party, Duplessis cleverly counterbalanced his rural, bead-clutching, Catholic, French-Canadian constituency with the "Anglocrats" through endless amalgams of patronage, blackmail, demagoguery, and the outright harassment of his opposition.

Bernard had been born during the Duplessis regime's zenith of power, and as a little boy had on countless nights climbed the stairs to his sparse bedroom with the shrill voices of his parents spilling out of the kitchen. They argued about many things, but politics was a major issue. His father had blossomed into maturity on the nationalist, separatist writings of Canon Groulx and Henri Bourassa, and as the ice of middle age began to pack around him, his bright, working-class brain became frozen in the conviction that French Canadians would live in bondage until the yoke of the English and its allies was thrown off. He became increasingly bitter with his lot and finally began to denounce the Mother Church itself, the powerful institution of Roman Catholicism that spread into every crevice of Québecois life: into commerce, education, politics, and the very fabric of the family. His wife on the other hand, the melancholic, soft-faced

Annette, was an unreconstructed child of the Church. Her life was wrapped up in the parish, and its awesome mixture of love and terror charted her every waking moment. Annette was prepared to spend her days in the service of her specially fashioned, French-Canadian God and the secular structures which served Him best. Her husband's carping about what she considered to be the adequate governance of Duplessis and his followers made her furious. After all, had not the lives of most Québecois improved under Duplessis? Which in turn meant, she reasoned, that he had reached some proper accord with God and His Church. This argument of hers, recited in rote fashion whenever politics was discussed in the Gannet household, drove her husband to the outer limits of his temper. Gérard Gannet knew otherwise: that he, as a Québecois working-class member, was being cheated and robbed of his rightful share of his own land's riches by a cynical cabal of English and American interlopers, guileful churchmen, and, worst of all, the thieving, traitorous *curés* of his own blood.

Bernard now thought of his father, dead eleven years, and his mother, perhaps at this very moment trudging off to morning mass at St. Thérèse's. He believed that somewhere, somehow, his father sanctioned his enterprise—this bold strike to create a legitimate and pure people's revolution in Quebec. Until a few hours earlier and the foolishness of the Libyans, the plan was building strength, possessed of an inner energy that would rattle through the foundations of the province like an earthquake, bringing the greedy, decadent power structures tumbling to dust. But now there was a serious emergency. His mind fogged with fatigue, he groped for solutions, yet his reasoning kept spiraling back to one central fact: he *did not know* what had happened. Only one thing was clear: During the offloading in mid-river a motor yacht had appeared out of the darkness and had been fired on in contravention of his strict orders. The yacht had fled, presumably in the direction of Alexandria Bay. Now Gannet was huddled on his island, cut off from all knowledge of subsequent events. Had both men aboard died and their craft conveniently sunk to the bottom without a trace? Hardly likely. It had to be assumed that *some* kind of police agency now knew of the incident and presumably was taking action or at least conducting an investigation. The continued radio silence of the *Talon* indicated that its voyage toward Toronto was not being interfered with, which further implied that its role in the shooting incident had not been discovered. Or had it, and was it merely being shadowed until it completed its journey across the lake? Such mysteries alarmed Gannet. Provisions for the unexpected had been studied at length during the planning stages by the best strategic minds in the FLQ, and a myriad of alternative moves had been included in the overall operation, but Gannet lacked information to make proper judgments. There he was, stuck in the barren kitchen of a semi-abandoned mansion on an isolated island in the middle of the St. Lawrence, barely able to walk to the beach without fear of arousing some kind of suspicion. Major Salam's actions had diverted him from the offensive to the defensive at the very moment when precise forward movement was imperative, and now Gannet was groping for ways to get the operation back on course. There was still time. Time to cleave the citizens of Quebec away from their oppressors during the hectic hours of the Olympics opening—a time when all of the government's security systems would be marshaled against external threats such as the Black September effort at Munich and would be fragmented and unprepared for an internal assault by the FLQ. Two years of preparation had brought them to this moment and the operation could not be permitted to abort merely because some half-crazed Libyans had failed to use restraint.

There was no other choice. Gannet lifted himself away from the table and started for the door. Major Salam turned from the window and watched him, his face a placid study in sandstone. "You move like a man with a plan, Gannet," he said.

Gannet stopped and turned toward the Libyan. "Action

requires reaction, Major. We cannot sit immobilized any longer. Things are happening out there. A mile from here is the United States of America, whose anti-revolutionary zeal I do not have to describe. On the other side of us is Canada, America's lackey in such bourgeois obstructions. I can't share your rather casual optimism that our undertaking has not been affected by last night. If nothing else, police states have uncanny reflexes when it comes to unrest from the people. My plan is to take the outboard and to run to Alexandria Bay. A few inquiries should tell us how much impact our little misadventure of last night really had. That is, Major, if I dare climb into a small boat without having one of your men open fire." Then Bernard Gannet stalked out of the kitchen and headed for the boat dock.

IV

HOT BLASTS of wind were building from the southwest by the time Bernard Gannet steered his sixteen-foot outboard into the main channel of the river. It would be another overpoweringly muggy day, which would send thousands of tourists fleeing for the coolness of the water, and even at this early hour high-tiered sightseeing boats were rushing along, loaded to the gunwales with the curious. Gannet's anger rose as he headed for the city dock at Alexandria Bay. This small American river town represented to him in microcosm all the waste, decadence, and tasteless petit bourgeois lust for commerce that had ruined America and was now pouring over Quebec like lava. The masses of glittering yachts tethered like obedient cows beside the manicured summer homes lurking among the rocks and forests of the shoreline, and the leviathan shell of Boldt Castle—the never completed fantasy fortress now swarming with tourists clutching Instamatics— which loomed above the trees of an island directly across the river, represented to him the effluvia of an economic system run rampant. As a Marxist, it was Gannet's dream not only to return control of Quebec to the Québecois but to insure that their franchise on the unspoiled territories would prevent the despoiling and looting that had taken place in America.

He left his boat slapping against the municipal pier and passed the tour-boat hustlers, standing at the side of the street, bull horns in hand, trying to shanghai the unwary up their gangplanks. St. James Street was open for business. The doors of the souvenir shops were flung wide, exhibiting collections of banners, ash trays, dolls, cheap wooden carvings, glassware, plastic jewelry, and other assorted, instantly disposable junk. The exhaust of the traffic mingled with the greasy odors of the short-order restaurants and the noise—the insect buzzing of outboards, the rustling of the cars, and the snippets of jukebox music—sickened Gannet as he climbed the steps of a large corner drugstore. From the midst of the towers of sunglasses and the shelves of cosmetics he found the newsstand and bought copies of the Syracuse *Post-Standard* and the Rochester *Democrat & Chronicle*. The clerk, a chesty woman with vermilion hair, told him that the afternoon papers—the Watertown *Daily Times*, the Syracuse *Herald-Journal*, and the Rochester *Times-Union*—would arrive about four o'clock. Once outside, he quickly fingered through the two papers, seeking headlines that might report a shooting incident on the river. It was unlikely that any such news would have reached the early editions, but Gannet was looking for any sort of clue about what might have transpired. He could only assume that some kind of reaction had taken place in Alexandria Bay. It was, after all, the nearest United States community and the only thing he felt sure about was the nationality of the two men on the cruiser; their accents had been unmistakably American. It therefore seemed reasonable that reports of the incident would have reached this village.

Finding nothing, he stuffed the newspapers in a trash receptacle and turned up a side street toward the offices of the Alexandria Bay *Recorder*, the weekly journal that was printed in the basement of the Odd Fellows Hall. A camper truck pulled up to the curb. It was a sparkling new model, loaded with accessories. Its wide doors exploded open and three noisy children spilled onto the pavement. A tired-looking man wearing clip-on sunglasses emerged and unfolded a baby's stroller. A lumpy woman, in her late twenties, her hair wired on with bulbous curlers, stepped out last with an infant in her arms. Their vehicle was carrying Quebec license plates. They spoke English as they gathered up and headed toward the business section. Gannet watched them until they disappeared around a corner, despising them for their crudeness, their gluttonous, bourgeois tastes, and their undesirable representation of his native land.

The *Recorder* office was dark and cool and smelled of ink and solvents. A young man appeared from the back room wiping black smudges from his pale hands and forearms. "I'd like to place a classified advertisement in your next issue," said Gannet. The young man slipped a hand beneath the counter, snatched out a tablet of forms, and handed them to Gannet. He began scribbling the details of an imaginary outboard motorboat and trailer he was selling, quoting a price so high that no replies would be forthcoming to a fake post-office box in nearby Clayton. "What's all the excitement in town?" Gannet probed idly as he wrote.

"Excitement? Nuthin' ever happens here. Same old scene," said the youth.

"Yeah, I know what you mean. It's just that I thought I saw a couple of police cars . . ." Gannet bluffed.

"I don't know what that's all about. Something about somebody gettin' killed on the river last night, but it's supposed to be hush-hush. My boss is down there now. He's a stringer for the Syracuse paper and he's trying to get a story." The youth paused. "Where'd you hear about it?"

"I hadn't heard. Some people in the restaurant were just commenting about all the police cars in town," Gannet lied. "Who knows, maybe you'll get a little excitement after all," he said as he paid for the classified and stepped back into the sunlight. He walked quickly back toward St. James Street, knowing he was on the scent. His supposition had been correct. The unknown yacht had returned to Alexandria Bay, and if the youth was right, there had been a survivor. Around the corner from the city dock was a small barroom, off the main tourist track. It was a local gathering place for marina workers, fishing guides, and tour-boat crews. Two older men were sitting at the bar when Gannet entered. They were nursing draft beers and watching the traffic through a large, flyspecked window scarred with a battered venetian blind. The bartender was a stooped, florid-faced man who had opened for business in a clean white shirt with the cuffs rolled up, but had not bothered to shave or install his lower plate. Gannet ordered a beer—one of those American brands with the light body and bitter taste of chilled urine—and lit a cigarette. He sat in silence for a while, on the chance that if anything was known of the shooting, it would surely pass through this saloon.

"There goes another one!" announced the more wrinkled of the two men on watch at the window. "Third one in an hour. Must have every goddamn sheriff's car in the county in town."

"About time them sum-bitches did some work," said the bartender. "All they been doing is running them speed traps. Everywhere you go there's a goddamn radar. My sister-in-law, she's been picked up three times in the last year, and hell, she never drives over thirty. If they'd spend their time haulin' in those dope addicts and niggers that are all the time raisin' hell, then you wouldn't be so goddamn sore about payin' all them taxes. But catchin' your sister-in-law in a fuckin' radar trap ain't my idea of enforcing the law."

"That was a bad thing about that shooting," Gannet cast into the conversation.

"Goddamnedest thing," replied the other old man, his straw hat yanked down over his eyes to fend off the glaring sun. "They say that fella took a high-powered slug right through the chest. I know that ambulance siren woke me up, got me right out of a sound sleep. Must have been about four-thirty. Went by my damn house like a banshee. First thing I thought, my house is on fire."

"Wasn't no use in hurrying. He was gone long before they got him up to the hospital," said the bartender.

"Have they got any idea how it happened?" asked Gannet.

"Something to do with a bar fight, I heard," replied one of the old men. "Couple of young guys got into it at one of those dives up the river. They're all the time fightin' anyway. Only this time one of 'em went too far."

"I guess they got the other guy in jail down in Watertown," added the bartender. "They say he's a pro football player. Big mother. I mean, those guys get paid to knock each other's heads off."

Bar fight? Pro football player? Gannet groped with this news, trying to dovetail it with his knowledge of the situation. Could this be another incident entirely? Based on what he was hearing, the facts bore no relationship to what he knew to have actually happened.

"I just had breakfast over at the Antlers Manor. A guy told me that the shooting was on a boat. Somewhere in the river," Gannet submitted. "Did you hear it that way?"

"Naw, it happened in one of them night spots," said the old man in the straw hat.

"Bullshit, Alvin!" countered the bartender. "It happened in the river. On a cruiser."

"You're crazy. Lawrence Pickering told me . . ."

"I don't give a goddamn what Pickering said. It happened on a boat. What do you think they got all the cops down at Landsman's Marina for? The damn boat's down there, that's why!"

"You're both wrong," said the other old man. "My cousin's daughter is a nurse's aide at the hospital. She was on duty when they brought the body in. One of the deputies said he got shot on Wellesley Island and they brought him in by boat. It was some kind of hunting accident."

"Hunting accident! Oh, for Christ's sake, what kind of crap is that?" shouted the bartender. "What in the hell is anybody hunting in the middle of the night on Wellesley? Your cousin's daughter is full of shit and you can tell her I said so!"

The argument was rising in pitch and intensity as Gannet dropped a cluster of small change on the bar and headed for the door. It was a matter of serious personal guilt for him that he did not feel more comfortable in places like that. Those men were, after all, members of the proletariat—the very workers to whom he had dedicated his life. Yet he found their attitudes perverse and difficult to understand. During his years at the University of Montreal, eagerly inhaling the heady vapors of revolutionary rhetoric, his images of the common man were clear: they stood in the slums of St. Jacques in stately but ragged formations, their dignity cloaked in the tatters of the oppressed. As a student, Gannet had visions of the proletariat in the romantic postures of Russian revolutionary posters. But when in actual contact with such people, he found them to be narrow and banal, often hostile to the liberal thinking that was most sympathetic to their cause. His first shock had come as a student when he had turned out to march in favor of the railroad workers during a long and difficult strike. He had driven with a group of friends to Ottawa, where they had unfurled red flags and mounted the steps of Parliament, only to be pummeled and cursed by the strikers themselves. Such disappointments had in no way dampened his ardor for the masses, but deep inside him it troubled him that he, a son of the proletariat, could not more effectively communicate with his kin. Various union leaders, right-wing Social Crédistes, and intellectuals had charged that the FLQ were patronizing elitists devoid of gut affinities with the people. Gannet would have felt better equipped to answer this indictment if he, as a man, had known himself to be *un gars bien ordinaire.*

Squinting against the fierce sun, he walked toward the main street of Alexandria Bay. He sighted the boxy red-and-white Ford police cruiser with the crest of the Jefferson County Sheriff's Department painted on its door. It was headed for the east end of town—probably toward Landsman's Marina. Gannet followed with long, determined strides, checking his chronograph as he approached what surely would be another clue in the riddle. He had been in Alexandria Bay for three and a half hours. So far he had confirmed his guess that the shooting victims had taken refuge there. Sifting through the rumors that he had heard, one thing appeared to be certain: Gafaar al-Salam's gunfire had struck but one of the two men. He was probably dead or, at the very least, badly injured. The identity and the general condition of the survivor were unknown, except that the presence of the police confirmed his worst fears—the authorities knew of the incident and their snooping had already begun.

Landsman's Marina lay on a spit of land that could be reached only by a lane paved with loose stones and bordered by scrub pines growing amidst goiters of brown granite. Ahead Gannet could see the pale-blue wall of the maintenance shop, but his path was blocked by a sheriff's patrol car skewed crosswise in the lane. A deputy with a large nose lolled against the driver's door, his wide-brimmed straw hat canted over his brow. He watched Gannet approach without visible reaction. "I'm sorry, but the marina is closed, unless you've got business in there," he said mechanically.

"But my friends have a boat tied up there. I'm a guest. I'm expected," Gannet said, improvising.

"What's the name of the boat?" asked the deputy, reaching for a clipboard on the hood of the Ford.

"Er . . . I believe it's called . . . the *Louise* . . . yes, something like the *Louise* . . . it's my first time on board and . . ."

The deputy was flipping through the sheaf of papers on the clipboard. "No *Louise* tied up here. This is a list of all the boats in the marina and there's no boat by that name on it."

"That's strange. How old is your list? My friends just arrived this morning and their boat may not be included. What's more, I see no reason why . . ."

"This place is shut down," the deputy interrupted. "There is a criminal investigation being carried on here and no one except boat owners are being allowed inside. If you've got business in there, you can go back into town and call the marina. They can check with this here *Louise* and if her people say it's O.K. for you to come inside, someone will come out and escort you in. Otherwise you can't enter."

There was a spikiness in the deputy's voice that intimidated Gannet. The man was a yeoman carrying out simple, rigid orders and there was no deceiving him. What's more, he did not want to press the issue to a point where he elicited suspicion about himself. Repelled, but at least certain that he was zeroing in on a source of information, Gannet left the deputy leaning against the Ford's fender and returned to the city dock. In a few moments the husky Evinrude was shoving his boat into the river. He looped around the shoreline of the village, weaving through the fishermen and the tour boats and the water skiers and the cruisers, until he reached the narrow entrance of the marina. Behind the breakwall he could see the burnished white super-structures of giant yachts: Chris-Craft Constellations, Trojans, Roamers, and Pacemakers, their stubby masts cluttered with flapping pennants. Beyond were the long, barnlike covered docks with corrugated-metal roofs glowing in the sunlight. He approached the gas dock, letting the boat nudge against the padded pilings. A tanned boy in his late teens, clad in a white shirt and shorts, came out of a small, glass-fronted house near the pumps and helped him tie up.

"I wonder if I might fill my gas tank," said Gannet.

"Sure, but you can't go any farther into the marina. It's closed for the day," replied the attendant.

"Of course. The shooting," said Gannet. "I heard that there was trouble. That's no problem for me. I just need some gas, and I'll be on my way."

"Word gets around fast," said the boy, plunging the nozzle into the gas tank. "The sheriff and everybody has been trying to keep the whole deal quiet, but in a small town like this everybody knows everything."

Gannet, sensing he had found a lode of information, made his big parlay. "That's really something. There's never much excitement like this around here. You know, with people getting shot and all. And a pro football player . . . that's the part that is wild."

"You mean Farnsworth or Enderle?" asked the boy. "They both played pro ball."

Names. Gannet quivered as he heard the names he had been seeking float easily from the kid's lips. "Well, I was thinking of Enderle . . ." Gannet tossed out.

"He was dead when he got here. He was a good guy. Really a funny guy. He and Farnsworth cracked this place up. A lot of the boat owners are older . . . kind of straight. Their idea of a good time is to sit on deck boozin' until they pass out, but those two dudes were always getting into some kind of shit. We had a fine time when they were around. It's really too bad."

"I still don't understand how it happened. You hear all sorts of rumors in town. Talk about a bar fight and things like that," added Gannet.

"Nobody really knows, I guess. Oh, maybe the cops, but they're not saying. They had Pancho down at Watertown for questioning, but one of the other guys just came in and said they'd brought him back. I think he's over on Mr. Landsman's Hatteras, probably trying to get his head sorted out."

"Pancho? Who's Pancho?" Gannet asked.

"Farnsworth. Pancho Farnsworth. What's the matter, aren't you into pro football?"

"Not too much. Spend most of my time fishing. Do they know how it happened . . . I mean, the shooting?" asked Gannet.

"Beats me. All I know is that the guy who spends the night here—kind of the watchman—said that the Sheriff's Department was here in the middle of the night looking for Farnsworth's boat before he got back. That Bertram of his came in here looking like it had been in a war. Bullet holes all over it." The youth pointed into the rows of boats under the canopies. "You can just see its transom sticking out next to that big, blue-hulled houseboat. The *Red Dog*. That's the boat."

Forcing back the urge to ask more questions, Gannet paid the attendant for the gas and pulled away, saying, "I'm heading back to the islands. There's too much excitement here. I didn't take a vacation to worry about murders and football players. The only thing I'm interested in killing is a big, nasty muskie." Once clear of the marina, he raced his boat flat out back to the city dock and pounced ashore like a homesick sailor. Within minutes he was back in the drugstore, prowling the magazine counter. He bought three magazines: the current issue of *Sports Illustrated*, *Street and Smith's Official Pro Football Yearbook*, and the *All-Pro, All-American Gridiron Guide*. He slipped into a nearby coffee shop, full of chattering tourists and the angry hum of air conditioners fighting a holding action against the heat. Finding a quiet booth at the back, he ordered a glass of iced tea and a club sandwich and began leafing through the magazines. Each of the National Football League teams was given a three-page rundown, including their predicted finishes in the 1976 standings, top draft choices, major personalities, and several grainy publicity-handout photos of their stars. Most important to Gannet were the agate-type rosters which listed alphabetically both the veterans and the rookies on each club. He began with the first team in the magazine, the Buffalo Bills of the American

Conference, who were predicted to finish first in their five-team division. Scanning quickly, his eyes briefly focused on Farley of the Bills, Fernandez of the Miami Dolphins, and Federspeil of the New York Jets, then rushed onward. He found his man on page 38. There, listed under the veterans' roster of the Cleveland Browns, was the following line:

"Farnsworth, Pancho, LB, 6'3", 235, age 24, Hobart."

The accompanying story stated that the Browns' defense pivoted around Farnsworth and described him as having the potential to play middle linebacker as well as Butkus, Schmidt, and Nitschke. The *All-Pro, All-American Gridiron Guide* said much the same thing, although a picture of Farnsworth was included in the Browns section. Gannet leaned closer to the page, peering hard at the murky halftone. Returning his gaze was a high-cheeked, smiling face topped with a furry mat of light-brown hair. The quality of the picture, coupled with the pose that had Farnsworth woodenly appear to be fending off a mass of blockers, gave Gannet only a minuscule impression of the nature of the man who had suddenly become an important influence in his own life. He searched for Farnsworth's name in the block of copy about the Browns and found him being hailed as one of the finest athletes ever to be produced by a small eastern college and noting his intelligence and leadership ability.

There was no mention of Farnsworth or the Cleveland Browns in *Sports Illustrated*. Gannet had little interest in athletics, aside from casual support of the Montreal Canadiens, and he found the publications spread before him a terrible bore. He fingered through the pages, finding stories on hang gliding, a paean to snow geese, sport fishing in Borneo, a bicycle race in Capetown, South Africa, and a profile on a San Francisco architect who'd just won the World's Roque Championship. The only story related to pro football was a two-page color spread about a Kansas City Chiefs halfback's recipe for cherries jubilee.

Gannet was able to consume nearly two hours drinking iced

tea, gobbling cigarettes, and fingering the three magazines. It was nearly four o'clock when he left the coffee shop and elbowed his way along the crowded street to the drugstore. "You sure do read a lot," chattered the vermilion-haired woman as he paid for the afternoon papers that he had snatched off the fresh piles. Gannet nodded in nervous agreement and fled outside to search the pages. Because Watertown was the closest of the three cities, he checked its edition first. It was the second lead story. It reported:

Alexandria Bay: The Jefferson County Sheriff's Department is holding for investigation a prominent professional football player in connection with the death of a friend on his yacht early Saturday morning.

Geoffrey R. Farnsworth III, 24, of New Salerno, New York, better known as "Pancho" Farnsworth, star middle line-backer of the Cleveland Browns, is being questioned by Undersheriff Vito LaStarza about the shooting death of Roy C. Enderle, 26, of Cleveland, Ohio.

Undersheriff LaStarza said Farnsworth returned his 28-foot yacht to Landsman's Marina in Alexandria Bay at about 4 o'clock Saturday morning with Enderle on board suffering a massive gunshot wound in the chest. Enderle, also a professional football player, with the Cleveland Browns and the Philadelphia Eagles, was pronounced dead on arrival at the Edward John Noble Hospital in Alexandria Bay. No formal charges have been placed against Farnsworth, although a Sheriff's Department spokesman said the death may be related to a brawl earlier in the evening at Jessup's Pier Six, a nightclub on South Shore Road, in which the two men were reportedly involved.

The Undersheriff would not comment on the investigation, other than to say, "There are a number of contradictory points to the case which have to be clarified before any formal charges are brought." He refused to state whether or not Enderle's death was being viewed as a murder or accidental and stated that a more complete statement will be forthcoming as soon as practical.

Sources at Landsman's Marina have reported that Farnsworth's boat, a cruiser fitted out for fishing, appeared to have several bullet holes in its hull and superstructure when it returned from the river. It is believed that Farnsworth and Enderle had been vacationing in the Thousand Islands for several weeks.

Enderle was born and raised in Wilkes-Barre, Pennsylvania, and attended the University of Missouri and Benjamin Harrison College. He is survived by a sister, Mrs. Artesia Tuttle of Florence, South Carolina.

Jefferson County Coroner, Dr. Marshall Winston of Antwerp, said that a certificate of death will be issued pending the results of a complete autopsy that is presently under way.

Both the Syracuse and Rochester papers carried the same Associated Press dispatch, which added nothing to the information contained in the Watertown *Daily Times* report. Gannet's confusion was escalating. Much of the story jibed with what he knew: two men on a yacht, gunshot wounds, early-morning hours, etc. But the talk of a barroom brawl—as had been mentioned during his saloon conversation earlier—baffled him. Worse yet, he did not like the undersheriff's cryptic mention of "contradictory points." Could Farnsworth have identified the *Talon*, which in turn was being investigated? Would this account for the fact that no formal charges had been placed in what was clearly a case of murder?

Gannet walked to the end of the village dock and slumped against a light pole, smoking and thinking. He *had* to know how much of the Farnsworth case centered on the *Talon* before he could make the necessary adjustment in the overall operation. Somehow he had to penetrate the barrier that had been thrown up around the investigation. He idly watched the small boats pulverizing the harbor waters while his mind scrambled for a solution. His own usefulness here seemed to be ended. He had flitted around the perimeters of the situation in Alexandria Bay and had gathered no more intelligence than could be found in the local newspaper racks. Yet more inquiries on his part would certainly arouse suspicion. Someone else would have to penetrate the police lines; someone within the movement who could reach Farnsworth and find out his side of the story without diverting any attention to the countdown toward Quebec's moment of destiny. Gannet snapped upright, away from the post, as if repelled by a magnetic field. "Of course!" he muttered, flinging the cigarette into the water and stepping off in quick steps toward shore. He veered around the drugstore corner, bouncing crazily off two grunting men trying to wrestle a console television into the trunk of a car, and broke into a sprint toward the brick telephone office behind a row of parked automobiles on the other side of the street. His face was covered with an expression of pleasant anticipation, like a soldier rushing into a battle he was sure to win. As a youth, Gannet had dreamed of his people's revolution crackling across the landscape like a human forest fire, with ideas of freedom fueling the action like pure oxygen. But now that naïve notion of poverty and frustration among the masses exploding by spontaneous combustion had given way to the conviction that revolutions had to be kindled with the care of a woodsman using his last match; that each twig must be perfectly placed before the fire was lit. This meant tiny knots of men moving with prodigious care and patience, constructing complicated infrastructures that would insure complete burning once the spark was struck. As he stepped off the final paces leading to the pair of aluminum phone booths that stood like sentry boxes outside the telephone office, he thought of Pierre Vallières, the French-Canadian revolutionary philosopher whose writings had provided such a powerful ideological thrust during his university days, and who had once described the French Canadians as the "white niggers of America." Gannet had committed many of Vallières' passages to memory, but at this moment he comforted himself with the thinker's tough reminder: *Il n'y aura pas des miracles, mais il y aura la guerre.* There will be no miracles, but there will be war.

Letting a fistful of change clatter onto the tray beneath the telephone, Gannet dropped in an American dime and began to direct-dial a phone number in New York City.

V

AIR CANADA'S Madison Avenue branch office appeared to be in a state of partial burial on the street level of a graceless, glass and white-brick office building bordering the noisy ravine. Around the corner loomed the sooty-gray bulk of St. Patrick's Cathedral, its elegant spires miniaturized among the surrounding escarpments of concrete. As a child in the distant Quebec town of St. Laurier, the sight of such a magnificent church would have buckled Agnes DePere's knees and sent her fumbling for her rosary beads, but now, liberated from what she considered to be the superstitions and secular manipulations of Catholicism, she passed the cathedral each morning with proud defiance. It had been four years since that bleak morning in Montreal when she had timorously wrapped her Bible, prayer missals, catechisms, and crucifix in a weighted paper package and flung the lot—the relics of twenty years of faith—off the Cartier Bridge and into the currents of the St. Lawrence River. Her experiences in Montreal had forced major changes in many of her attitudes, including those concerning the Church. The attendant distractions of being darkly beautiful had filled her teen-age years with an endless string of eager males. Agnes DePere had responded, partly in search of pleasure, partly for ego gratification, and partly out of boredom, because there was little else to do in the isolated, snow-swept pulp and paper manufacturing outpost of St. Laurier. Her father, a once proud, liberal lawyer, had fled from Montreal in the late forties, his career ruined by the ruthless pressures of the Duplessis regime. Now he carried on, a bitter, feeble, alcoholic husk, quivering with hatred for the interloper Americans, the barbaric invading Englishmen, and their French-Canadian lackeys whom he believed had conspired to drive him into exile. His wife, the mother of his three children, had died during childbirth, when Agnes was nine. For nearly a decade Agnes suffered in grief, until finally, amid clouds of doubt, her older brothers—one a mining engineer in the ore region of Rouyn-Noranda to the west, the other a student at the University of Montreal—convinced her that the Church's refusal to permit the abortion of a breech-birth stillborn baby had caused her mother's death.

Returning home to St. Laurier on brief visits reinforced the claims of her radical Montreal friends. She had seen a French-Canadian work force pitifully clinging to the Province's proud but toothless motto, *"Je me souviens,"* while as many as sixty-five percent of them were unemployed and on welfare. Most of the mills and factories were owned or dominated by Americans. There was strong support for the separatist Parti Québecois and its outspoken leader, René Levesque, who advocated the independence of the Province through political means, much as Canada had gained autonomy from England. It was Levesque who constantly hammered home the realities of the latent power held by the Québecois: their land mass was nearly *twice* the size of Texas and almost as large as Mexico. It was endowed with a great reserve of natural resources, ranging from wood to iron to oil and precious metals. Quebec straddled the St. Lawrence Seaway, giving it immense leverage over the economic life of the entire Great Lakes industrial basin. Yet this wealth was not owned by the *habitants,* but by powerful American interests on Wall Street and by English-speaking Canadians in the elegant new skyscrapers rising above Toronto to the West.

The special relationship of Quebec—"L'Etat de Québec"—to the Canadian Confederation had been the subject of great concern in the capital of Ottawa for years. From the day in the nineteenth century when Quebec had been allowed to retain Napoleonic law as its legal base while the rest of Canada operated with English common law, to the endless, gnawing arguments about bilingualism in schools and government and the dualism of the Catholic and secular education system, it was obvious that Quebec stood apart. To many of its critics it was a spoiler, a naysayer *("le trouble fêté"),* always sprawled crosswise to the natural flow of Canada's fortunes. Yet the release of Quebec from the Confederation was unthinkable. It was too rich, too strategically positioned to be permitted to slice itself away. The national government—like the Americans in 1861— would fight to the death to maintain the continuity of the nation. What's more, the consequences of independence for Quebec might spread beyond "La Belle Province" itself, lighting fires of separatism in Labrador, New Brunswick, and parts of Ontario. Many political experts speculated that if Quebec became an independent nation, great pressures for autonomy would arise in the west, especially in British Columbia, the loss of which would leave Canada as a land-locked, ice-bound version of a banana republic.

For these reasons, Quebec separatism transcended most political problems in Canada, causing nerves to be frayed in Ottawa like no other issue. Pierre Elliott Trudeau, the former Prime Minister, who as a young intellectual had fought for greater autonomy for Quebec within the Confederation, had reacted with understandable federalist severity in the great October 1970 crisis. It was then that the FLQ had made its first major thrust for attention by kidnapping James Richard Cross, the British Trade Minister to the City of Montreal, and Pierre Laporte, the Minister of Labour and Immigration and the Deputy Minister of the Province of Quebec. Cross was snatched from his Mount Royal home as he was dressing for work on the morning of October 5, 1970. In return for his release, the Liberation Cell of the FLQ—at that time a loose, highly secretive collection of twenty-two cells containing no more than a hundred and fifty hard-core activists—made six demands: The release of twenty-three political prisoners and their removal to either Algeria or Cuba; the payment of $500,000 in gold bullion as a "voluntary tax"; the revealing of the identity of a police informer who had infiltrated the FLQ ranks; the use of radio and television media for the promulgation of a manifesto articulating the aims of the FLQ; the reinstatement of several hundred postal workers who had been laid off; and the guarantee by the authorities that all investigation of the Cross kidnapping would cease.

This daring act of political terror by the FLQ simultaneously fascinated and shocked the generally passive Canadian popu-lace. The FLQ, having formed and re-formed in a variety of permutations, had been heretofore known as a tiny claque of lunatics who skulked around hiding bombs in the mailboxes of the wealthy "Anglais" suburbs. But now they were declaring themselves as a serious group of organized urban revolutionary guerrillas committed to the establishment of a socialist-anarchist state of Quebec.

Agnes DePere had been a willful schoolgirl of eighteen at the beginning of the October crisis, more concerned with her blossoming sexuality than politics, yet she watched with her father the broadcasts of the FLQ manifesto—a concession made by the government two days after Cross had disappeared. She watched announcer Gaetan Montreuil face the cameras and mechanically read the words that would ultimately change her life: "The Front de Libération du Québec wants the total independence of Quebeckers, united in a free society, purged forever of the clique of voracious sharks, the patronizing big bosses and their henchmen who have made Quebec their hunting preserve for cheap labor and unscrupulous exploitation. . . . We have had our fill, as have more and more Quebeckers, of a government which performs a thousand and one acrobatics to charm American millionaires into investing in Quebec, La Belle Province, where thousands and thousands of square miles of forests, full of game and well-stocked lakes, are the exclusive preserve of the powerful twentieth-century seigneurs. . . . We have had our fill of promises of jobs and prosperity while we always remain the cowering servants and bootlickers of the big shots who live in Westmount, Town of Mount Royal, Hampstead, and Outremont, all of the fortresses of high finance on St. James Street and Wall Street, while we, the Quebeckers, have not used all our means, including arms and dynamite, to rid ourselves of these economic and political bosses who continue to oppress us. . . . We are the workers of Quebec and we will go to the end. We want to replace the slave society with a free society, functioning by itself and for itself. An open society to the world. Our struggle can only be victorious. You cannot hold back an awakening people. Long live free Quebec. Long live the Quebec revolution. Long live the Front de Libération du Québec."

These words articulated much that her father and brothers had been complaining about for as long as she could remember. The statements being woodenly recited by Montreuil took on a startling personal connotation.

The crisis stabilized for five days, with the government refusing to accede to more of the Front's demands. Then the Chénier Cell of the FLQ kidnapped Pierre Laporte from the front lawn of his St. Lambert home while he was tossing a football with his eighteen-year-old nephew. At forty-nine, Laporte was the second-ranking politician in the Quebec provincial government and a popular, highly motivated man. As a crusading parliamentary journalist for *Le Devoir*, he had been one of the few newspapermen to butt heads with Duplessis. It had been his efforts in reporting a major cabinet scandal that had assisted in the destruction of the corrupt Union Nationale. Laporte's capture stunned Quebec. He was, after all, one of their own countrymen (although radical separatists despised him, like anyone who worked within the federal system, as a quisling for the Anglo-Saxons), and they fumbled for reasons why the FLQ would have chosen to take such a respected political figure.

Eleven days after James Cross disappeared, Pierre Elliott Trudeau rocked Canada by invoking the Emergency War Measures Act, a long-forgotten law of World War I vintage that permitted the government to suspend civil liberties in the face of internal crisis. While his opponents stammered in protest at Trudeau's harsh action, nearly thirteen thousand policemen took to the streets in the early morning hours of October 16 to round up every known terrorist, FLQ sympathizer, and outspoken separatist in the Province. The act gave the government carte blanche; it had absolute power, aside from being able to dissolve Parliament. Search and seizure without warrant and imprisonment without charges for twenty-one days or ninety days without bond before trial were two of its more salient features that would affect the immediate crisis in Quebec. And Agnes DePere as well. That evening, as she returned from school, her father, slumped at his desk in a helpless, alcoholic fury, reported that Guy, her younger brother, had been snatched from his apartment by a unit of CAT—the Combined Anti-Terrorist Squad—and was behind bars without a specific charge, for an indefinite period.

Before the arrests stopped, nearly five hundred Quebec residents had been tossed in jail, including Pierre Vallières and his associate Charles Gagnon—the two most visible figures in the FLQ—Robert Lemieux, a radical young lawyer known for his defense of radicals in the Province; the vocal left-wing labor leader Michel Chartrand; singer Pauline Julien; self-proclaimed Marxist Stanley Gray, a former political science lecturer at

stuffy, conservative McGill University; and Dr. Henry Belle-
mare, a specialist working with a Montreal health clinic. The
following morning Agnes DePere took her father's aged Austin
Marina and rushed southward down Highway 11, through the
russet forests and around the eroded humps of the once mighty
Laurentians, headed for Montreal. Shocked and panicked at her
brother's trouble, yet stimulated by this high-voltage charge of
adventure passing through her life, she felt compelled to be near
him.

Friends of her brother helped her get temporary lodgings with
a cab driver and his wife who were deeply involved in the FLQ
but had been left untouched by the dragnet. At first, when she
was around, their conversations were guarded, except for some
grandiose pronouncements about the benefits that were bound
to accrue from the kidnappings and predictions of bloody
retaliation for Trudeau's harsh countermeasures. They were
right. A day later Pierre Laporte's strangled, lacerated body was
discovered in the trunk of a 1968 Chevrolet parked in a desolate
corner of the St. Hubert Canadian Army Base.

Canada reeled from the deathblow. Unused to violence, she
had watched the urban uprisings of the American blacks and the
antiwar riots with a certain smugness, sure that her own maturity
and spirit of civil libertarianism would prevent any such
unpleasantness within her own borders. Then came Laporte,
murdered by men who were now acting like the hard-core
revolutionaries of Cuba, Algeria, South Vietnam, and Northern
Ireland. Agnes DePere spent those incredible days in a state of
dazed fascination. It was as if her face had been pressed against a
plate-glass window, where she could watch the drama but could
not take part, much less understand the dialogue of the participants. Grim young men slipped in and out of the apartment,
muttering in subdued tones. Paul, the cab driver, spent the
entire Sunday after Laporte's death in deep conversation with
four men in the bedroom of their small apartment on Des
Récollets Street in Montreal North, a working-class residential

district. His wife, Marie, had smoked three packs of Gauloises while standing watch at the front window overlooking the street. When the men emerged from the room, Agnes was introduced. She paid particular attention to a wiry, unshaven student named Bernard Gannet. Another of the group also impressed her, but in a rather ominous way. Paul Rose shambled out of the bedroom to confront her, his face framed in a scraggly, Castro-style beard and his left eye glazed with a thick cataract. An unemployed technical school teacher, Rose was a prime suspect in the Laporte kidnapping and narrowly escaped arrest on several occasions. (He would be captured eleven weeks later.) Mumbling a cursory greeting, he checked the street and slipped down a back stairway to a waiting car.

She also received several telephone messages from a shadowy figure in the movement known as Pierre Boutette. His quick and forceful voice intrigued her. He always called with cryptic instructions for Paul, but when he spoke with Agnes, his conversation lapsed into brief flurries of small talk. Amid the growing boredom of her self-imposed isolation, the calls from Pierre Boutette represented to her a connection with a more dynamic and clearly defined element of the movement, an element about which she wanted to know more.

In the fifth week, she learned the details of their mission. Two blocks away, in a brick and stone-faced triplex on Des Récollets Street, members of the Liberation Cell of the FLQ were holding James Cross. He was reported to be in good health, subsisting on a steady diet of soup, spaghetti, peanut-butter toast, and stupefying hours of French-language television. Each day the danger of being captured by the police increased. Finally Agnes, simply by being present, was assimilated into the Ravachol Cell of the FLQ. Named for a late-nineteenth-century French anarchist who, on July 11, 1892, was guillotined for terrorist acts of bombing and murder, the cell had chosen to use as a byword one of Ravachol's statements at his trial: "My object was to terrorize so as to force society to look attentively at those who suffer." They also favored a couplet that came from a street song that had swept French socialist circles after Ravachol's death. It had claimed:

> It will come, it will come,
> Every bourgeois will have his bomb.

Marie and Paul seldom left their apartment, choosing instead to watch television, read paperback pornography, and agonize over the fortunes of the Montreal Canadiens. The cell's mission was to operate as an outer picket for the kidnappers: to patrol the local streets in search of police snoopers, to operate as messengers, and, if necessary, to serve as a diversionary fortress in the event the Cross hiding place came under direct siege. Four Canadian military FN-C1 7.62mm automatic rifles and six boxes of ammunition had been stored behind a false panel in the bedroom. Two alternate rooftop escape routes had been planned.

Agnes found Marie to be an evil-tempered woman, devoid of trust for any human being. Her husband was superficially pleasant, but constant exposure revealed him to be a chronic whiner, whose revolutionary philosophies seemed to have been distilled into homicidal hatred of Anglo-Saxons. A Frenchman by birth, he had been a member of the OAS—the Organization *de l'Armée Secrète*—the right-wing terrorist group which had fought the government's policy to give Algeria its independence, before he emigrated to Canada. When drunk or stoned on the bitter grass that found its way into the apartment, Paul bragged about his role in the ill-fated 1964 holdup of Montreal's International Firearms Shop. After training in a secret Laurentian camp under the supervision of François Schirm, a former Foreign Legion noncom, a small terrorist group had tried to hold up the store to steal armaments. The assault had been botched and two store employees had been killed and most of the terrorists had been arrested. Paul had escaped. The other members of the Ravachol Cell came from the vast, acrimonious, politically conscious University of Montreal community. A few were students, more were outriders who were floating on the choppy waters of the university's separatist activities, impatient for action. Despite their activist instincts, they were a boring lot, given to lounging around the apartment, swilling cheap wine, and arguing about the theories of Marx and Marcuse. Only Bernard Gannet was different, and it was his inner fiber that made him interesting to her. She speculated that the resolves of at least half of these revolutionaries would split apart, like spoiled pumpkins, when the first steel-jacketed, high-velocity ammunition began to smash against the walls, but she knew from the start that Bernard Gannet would stand his ground. He had a wry, fatalistic sense of humor and a trenchant brand of sarcasm. His hunger to establish a sound philosophical basis for his actions increased, in turn, her appetite for reading. He brought with him from the university packages of frayed paperbacks and much-read hardbounds: the essays of Marx, Régis Debray, Engels, Merleau-Ponty, Mounier, Frantz Fanon, and the complicated, systematic philosophies of Husserl and Heidegger, the novels of Camus, Sartre, Dostoevski, Tolstoi, and the separatist polemics of Vallières and Gagnon plus numerous tracts and articles from small intellectual papers such as *Cité Libre, Parti Pris*, and the official journal of the FLQ, *La Cognée (The Hatchet)*.

It is no rare irony that jailers often become imprisoned by their prisoners, and such was the case with two FLQ cells and their captive, James Cross. Agnes DePere had found herself bound by this circumstance, and save for neighborhood reconnaissances and trips to the grocer's, she stayed huddled in her small bedroom, isolated from the droning television, and read the piles of literature supplied to her by Gannet. She found that the classic novelists—Dostoevski, Tolstoi—offered lucid insights into the nature of man, and she saw countless parallels between the Russian peasants and workers and the Quebeckers she had known in St. Laurier. The philosophers, for the most part, left her drowsy after a few minutes' scanning, but the writings of Pierre Vallières, especially his *White Niggers of America: The Precocious Autobiography of the Quebec "Terrorist,"* electrified her with his angry but often bathetic denunciations of the Quebec power structure.

Gannet's return from the university each evening triggered in her new urges for discussion. Armed with fresh ideas from her day's reading, she eagerly engaged with him in good-natured debates about politics, literature, and economics. She tended to be vigorously utopian, which clashed with Gannet's growing pragmatism. He had been through the same stage of naïveté as she, which prompted him to treat her on occasion with the patronizing affability of an aging professor. This infuriated her, and he generally apologized. The relationship was strong and contentious, full of lusty peaks and valleys of love and anger, and it created in Bernard Gannet a sense of disbelief. This beautiful, passionate woman had appeared in his life at a time when he believed that the liberation of Quebec required a self-imposed celibacy—made easier by the dismal fact that the female recruits to the movement tended to be lank, humorless, and flat-chested, with bad complexions and chain smoker's halitosis.

But Agnes, with her facile brain and splendid, small-hipped body, lithe and creamy-skinned, topped by a mane of anthracite hair, produced in him urges that he had not felt since he was a teen-ager, and on many autumn evenings—when chill spikes of wind sent herds of dry leaves scuffing along the quiet streets—he found himself in a boyish sprint over the last half mile from the bus stop to the apartment. In the third month, he began sleeping with her, their pliant bodies crushed together on the daybed in Agnes' room, making joyful love while the television squawked and their cellmates argued and stood watch beyond the thin partition.

One night they were coiled together after their lovemaking, their minds in contented repose. They were smoking, and the two rosy pinpoints of light from their cigarettes were the only illumination in the dark room. There had been a long silence. "You know, I was reading a quote of Fidel Castro's," she said softly. "He began his Cuban revolution with eighty-two men, but he said that if he had to do it again, he would depend on ten or fifteen men and absolute faith. He said it doesn't matter how small you are if you have faith and a plan of action."

"Faith is for women," he replied disdainfully. He felt her body go rigid and he knew that he had said the wrong thing.

"You fatuous pig! Tell me that when you are half the man Fidel Castro is!" she barked, cuffing him with a pillow and leaping out of bed. She dressed quickly and left the room, leaving Gannet to chuckle in quiet resignation and to muse over his good fortune.

The second of December arrived cold and bleak. A few streaks of snow were being driven down Des Récollets Street by a gusty west wind. Paul left the apartment before dawn, to drive the early cab shift, leaving his wife to sleep until mid-morning. Gannet awakened at six o'clock and crawled out of the snug bed he shared with Agnes and dressed quickly in the cold room. It was his assignment to scout the area before leaving for classes. The zeal for round-the-clock watches had long since wheezed away and Agnes and Marie would be left to handle the sentry duties during the day. Half dozing, Gannet staggered out of the bedroom to routinely check the front window before heading for the bathroom. He expected the standard sights: a few swathed and muffled pedestrians boring, heads down, into the wind and a small squadron of automobiles, their exhausts condensing gouts of white vapor, sputtering toward mid-city.

Instead he saw three figures, standing alone in an otherwise empty street. They were wearing woolen greatcoats and burnished steel helmets. Slung in their arms were automatic rifles with stubby bayonets clinging to the muzzles.

"Jesus Christ, the Army!" Gannet blurted out, diving for cover. "Agnes, get out of bed, the Army's in the street!" Agnes rushed into the room naked, her body radiating a porcelain sheen in the half light. "No, no, for God's sake, get dressed!" Gannet yelled. "The Army. It's the Army!" She disappeared for a moment and returned yanking a wool sweater over her head and buttoning a pair of jeans into place. Marie spilled out the other door, half dragging, half carrying a brace of automatic rifles to the window. Gannet took a final look, then crawled across the floor to the phone. He frantically dialed the apartment where Cross was being held, expecting to reach Marc Carbonneau, like Paul a cab driver, or his cohort Jacques Lanctot. A throaty male voice answered after a single ring. It had a strange, rather stiff cadence that generated immediate alarm within Gannet. "Marc is not here right now," said the voice slowly and deliberately. "Wait a minute, and I'll see when he'll be back." The line went silent. Gannet held the circuit open for a few seconds, then crashed the phone against the cradle as if it had become molten hot in his hands.

"What's the matter?" asked Agnes.

"I don't know, but I don't like it. Somebody answered who I've never heard before. All of a sudden it hit me that it might be the police, that they've intercepted the line, that they were trying to trace my call."

He looked up upon hearing the harsh, metallic clank of one of the automatic rifles being cocked and saw Marie, a freshly lit Gauloise stuffed between her teeth, raising the weapon for a volley out the window. "No, Jesus, no!" Gannet shouted, stumbling over the low table as he flung himself at Marie. Snatching the weapon from her hands, he grabbed her arm, at first with manic firmness, then with a diminishing grip that turned into a soothing rub. "We've got to wait. It would be insane for us to open fire now. They may need us down the street. Let's not reveal our position until we can do some good." Gannet spoke in a calm, reasoning tone. Marie slumped back into the couch and took a long, lung-filling drag on her cigarette. Agnes stood near the window, her left arm draped around her midsection like a sash, her right hand pressed nervously against her lips.

Gannet went to the coat rack by the door and pulled down his khaki, down-lined winter jacket. "I'll try to see what's going on. Just stay cool until I get back," he said. Taking two steps at a time, he reached the lobby in a matter of seconds, which was empty and silent except for the clatter of a steam pipe somewhere deep in the building. He cracked the front door and the wind lashed against his face like frigid surf. Checking in both directions, he was still able to see the three soldiers—paratroopers, he speculated—standing at the curb. He paused for a particle of a second, as a man about to depart a high diving board, and then stepped routinely out the door. He bounded to the bottom step before he heard a voice—the mechanical tones of the nearest soldier, speaking in French. "Excuse me, sir, this area has been blocked off. There is a civil emergency. No one is allowed on the street. You will have to return to your home until further notice."

"Civil emergency? What is this? Hey, I've got to get to work. I'm late already," Gannet said, taking two steps toward the soldier.

"No farther. No one is permitted in this area. I have orders." The soldier spoke sharply.

"O.K., O.K., I only hope you'll explain this to my boss," Gannet said resignedly as he turned and climbed the stairs to the apartment entrance. As he stepped through the doorway he looked back at the soldier—a young man, like himself in his early twenties, and what was worse, a French Canadian. The madness of it all, Gannet thought, that at this point in the revolution most of his own comrades remained duped into serving their Anglo-Saxon masters. Yes, much consciousness raising lies ahead, he mused as he climbed the stairway, headed for the rooftop. A narrow iron ladder led to a trapdoor that opened onto the roof. Gannet had been up there many times in the past months, checking escape routes and choosing sniper positions. He had barely poked his head above the coaming of the hatch when he sighted two figures on the next roof. One was a military man, a warrant officer in the paratroopers, who was holding a walkie-talkie. The other was wearing civilian clothes but had a high-powered hunting rifle with a telescopic sight gripped loosely in his gloved hands. Four more men, all armed, were on the rooftops across the street.

Gannet half slipped, half slid through the hatch and to the base of the ladder. He crouched on the floor like a cornered animal for a few moments before he regained his composure and returned to the apartment to report to the two women that they were surrounded and trapped. Dramatically, he walked into Paul and Marie's bedroom and hauled out their mattress and laid it against the front window. Then he instructed Marie to fill all the available containers with water and loaded the other two rifles.

They waited. No movement came from the street, aside from an occasional police car or light military vehicle speeding past. None of the soldiers seemed to be paying any attention to their apartment. Isolated and ignored, they turned on the radio and switched back and forth between CKLM and CKAC, the two major French-language radio stations, to find out what was happening in their own crisis. As Gannet expected, the Cross hiding place had been discovered and a four-square-block area—which included them—had been cordoned off by troops and police. Marie snapped on her television to receive confirming information. They sat there with the clammy realization that the authorities were utterly ignorant of their existence. On the one hand, it was a relief to know that the armament in the street would not be directed at them—and on the other, a disappointment. They had after all prepared themselves to enter the battle and were poised to play pivotal roles in the climax of the Cross affair, but now they had to face the fact that the police didn't know—or, God forbid, didn't give a damn—that they even existed.

Paul called at mid-morning from a public phone booth in the West End. "Can't you do something? Three fucking months cooped up in that rotten cubbyhole, living like goats, and now they are in the streets, beneath your noses, and you're powerless! You've got guns. Start shooting!" he screamed, slamming down the phone. Gannet held the humming receiver for a moment and stared grimly out of the window. To begin a scatter-shot barrage would mean nothing. According to the radio and television, so many regiments of troops had swarmed into the neighborhood that no amount of shooting could have diverted attention from the other cell and their hostage. Gannet was prepared to die for the liberation of Quebec, but to fall in a suicidal gesture of defiance seemed to him senseless.

By mid-afternoon, Marie had drunk herself into a surly, word-slurring stupor. She turned melancholic, rambling through disjointed laments over the failure of the kidnapping, the absence of Paul, and their inability to influence the events around them. "Goddammit, we're like mice in a hole. Where's Paul? If Paul was here, we'd have something. We'd have a man here. A man who would take action. You let us sit here while the government tears the rest of them apart. You have no balls, Gannet." She lifted herself out of the upright chair where she had been teetering and lurched toward him. He maintained his watch at the window, trying to ignore her. "Balls! Gannet, where are your balls?" she screamed at him from close range, where he could feel and smell her warm, rancid breath oozing around his face. He tried to restrain himself, then his rage gave way and he smashed her across her damp mouth with an open palm, sending her tumbling against a small dresser on the opposite side of the room. Blood dripping from her lower lip, she lay there in dazed repose, then, mumbling obscenities, staggered into the bedroom and flopped onto the bare steel spiderwork of the mattress springs, to plunge into a deep, heavy-breathing slumber.

The crisis passed by early evening. Carbonneau, Jacques Lanctot, his wife and infant son, another kidnapper, Pierre

Seguin, plus Lanctot's sister and her husband, Jacques Cossette-Trudel, agreed to return Cross in exchange for exile in Cuba. Night fell over Montreal, a Canadian Air Force Yukon military transport lifted off the runway of the international airport at Dorval, headed for Havana, while James R. Cross gained his freedom. "I feel as if I've been a witness to my own funeral," Gannet said to Agnes as he turned off the radio and they headed for a long, aimless walk through the newly vibrant, light-bathed streets of the city.

NEARLY SIX YEARS had passed since Agnes DePere's first meeting with Bernard Gannet in that apartment on Des Récollets Street. They lived together for nearly three years after that. It was a period of consolidation. Her brother Guy was released from prison soon after Cross had been found, and he returned to his studies. He was now living in Dijon, France, where he was active in left-wing politics. Paul regarded his blunted influence in the Cross affair as a shameful emasculation and he steadily stirred up the inner councils of the FLQ until late 1973, when he led a raid on the Royal Canadian Mounted Police Headquarters in Westmount. On the way to the target, the car, driven by a young accomplice, was stopped for speeding by a Montreal police patrol car. Infuriated, Paul attempted to use the sawed-off Ithaca 12-gauge shotgun concealed beneath the front seat. He was killed by a single round in the solar plexus from officer Maurice O'Neil's .38-caliber service revolver. Marie was never heard from again.

The relationship between Agnes and Bernard suffered a slow erosion. Endless planning sessions, impeded by niggling disputes over tactical details and political orthodoxy, consumed more and more of Gannet's time, and as the months passed, he burrowed inside himself, becoming increasingly distant and introspective. His humor and sarcasm were gradually buried beneath his growing gravity of purpose—a purpose that reduced her presence to the status of a mere physical trinket. She took a job as a waitress in an evil-smelling restaurant near the university, where she had enrolled as a student. But life with Bernard, centered in a seamy one-room apartment, had lost its joy. She tried to inject her new political awareness into his thinking, but as the intensity of his own thoughts increased, he turned off her intellect like a leaky faucet and contented himself with her sexuality.

"I think you remember your mother too well," she said one day after a long argument.

"What do you mean by that?"

"Your mother is timid and obedient. She knows her place and keeps it well. In your heart you are afraid of women who do otherwise."

"My mother is hypnotized by beads and candles and other superstitions of the Church. She is a fool."

"You like that. You want all women to be fools. I am not like that. Someday you will understand."

They celebrated her twentieth birthday with a modest meal in a quiet restaurant and an embarrassingly bourgeois hand-holding session at a double feature. That evening he told her that he was leaving for France. From there he would pick up a false passport and fly to Tripoli, where he would meet with Pierre Boutette, who was operating as the FLQ's emissary to the Libyan government. They hoped to conclude an agreement for armaments and money, plus expert military advisers, to support a war of liberation. He told her that the revolution would be coordinated with the opening of the Olympic Games in Montreal three years hence.

When Bernard Gannet returned from Libya, blossoming with hope, he found their apartment empty. Agnes DePere had gone.

She had driven to New York with a medical student named Cavielli. The pace of Manhattan proved to be an effective antitoxin for the dark, high-pressure closet life with Gannet and the FLQ, and she quickly decided to stay. After working briefly as cashier in a midtown Nedick's, she got a job as a salesclerk at the Tailored Women on Fifth Avenue, where her ability to speak French (albeit the colloquial "Jouval" of Montreal) as well as English, plus her striking looks, made her an instant success. But the crisp, rather aloof clerk was a split woman—a conventional bourgeois child of commerce by day, a seeker of change by night. Finding a basement apartment on West Fourth Street, she enrolled in non-credit evening classes at New York University's Washington Square campus, and through her selection of courses—The Origins of Anarchism; North American Communist Movements, 1820–1929; and Leon Trotsky, His Post-Revolution Correspondence—she was thrust into contact with the radical student community which orbited the university. She flirted briefly with an organization known as the Worker's Provisional Coalition, but found it to be dominated by yappy, spoiled middle-class youths who recited revolutionary rhetoric as if tape cassettes had been implanted in their heads. They had no hard knowledge of liberation movements, and her experiences with the FLQ—about which she said nothing—were the source of her rising disdain for them. She was briefly intrigued with one of the members, a tough-talking graduate student named Isaac Silverman, until she discovered that he maintained himself exclusively on the largesse of his father, who was an orthodontist in Far Rockaway, Long Island. Other men drifted into her life, but were of no meaning.

Agnes wrote to Bernard in the fourth month, telling him about her job and academic undertakings. She was becoming active in the Women's Liberation Movement, she said, and was concentrating on a NOW splinter group's efforts to break the sex barrier with train crews of the New York Transit Authority. Her letter was long and rather chatty, but made no mention of her sudden departure from Montreal. Gannet came to New York the next week, having borrowed a friend's car and rushing south along New York's Northway and Thruway in a nonstop drive to see her. He found her more resolute, more sure of herself, and because of this, even more attractive than before. Her new confidence permitted her to see Bernard Gannet in a better light as well. He was no longer an amalgam of an older brother and student adviser, but a male she could meet on equal terms. He tried hard to persuade her to return to Montreal, but she resisted firmly, telling him that her job—which paid her well—and her studies made such a move impossible. He visited her many times thereafter, finding their bond maturing in direct relation to her burgeoning independence. They remained infrequent but enthusiastic lovers and the intensity of their physical unions seemed to offset a widening emotional gap. Agnes was able now to treat him in a more casual fashion—generally pleased with his company, but inclined to release him from her thoughts when he was not around. She had become increasingly aware of his flaws: his inclination to ruminate over the most trivial problems without reaching a decision, and his sometimes irritating failure to forget that she was not his exclusive property. Yet he was the only man she had ever known whose motives she did not suspect, who she felt cared for her humanity and in no way threatened her rising consciousness of unfettered womanhood. Absence had diluted her involvement with the FLQ, although she still fancied herself a soldier for the revolution.

Seeking to stimulate her involvement in the movement, Gannet had arranged—through sympathizers within the airline —for her to become a ticket agent with Air Canada in New York. There she worked as a part-time operative for the FLQ, carrying out a multitude of routine chores, primarily greasing the passage for various members, emissaries, and allies entering and leaving North America—an operation which was considerably easier through Kennedy International Airport than at Toronto or Montreal. One of those travelers was Pierre Boutette, who was in the ascendancy in the FLQ. His trips to Europe brought him through New York with increasing frequency and it was not uncommon for him to add an extra day to his schedule in order to have dinner with Agnes DePere. She found him to be a striking, rather fearsome man, full of contradictions. He was superficially relaxed and harmless chatter welled out of him with great ease. But when he began to talk of the movement, his deep, clear voice hardened and he spoke of death and retribution with the self-righteous ferocity of an avenging angel. He told her little of his background and he remained to her a mysterious, but strangely compelling, itinerant who simultaneously elicited fright and fascination.

WHEN GANNET had called her at Air Canada's Madison Avenue office on that lazy Saturday afternoon, she had cringed slightly at the sound of his voice. Her mind had been on preparations for an amusing evening, and she knew—from the timing of the call—that Gannet's message might interfere with her plans. She reached for a pencil to copy the prearranged code Gannet was reciting: "My name is Alexander, initial B. I want to book a flight from New York to Calgary tomorrow afternoon— as close to three o'clock as possible. I cannot wait for you to check the schedules and reservations at this time. Please call me back as soon as possible. I will be at 482-8991."

"I am sorry, Mr. Alexander, but we are not permitted to make calls regarding future flights. However, I will be glad to check availability and perhaps you can call me back. Please ask for Ms. DePere."

"Thank you, Miss—er, Ms. DePere, I will return the call."

"Thank you . . . Mr. Alexander."

Quietly cursing the development, Agnes slipped down the long counter, where the only other agent on duty, a round man named Ralph with shiny hair, was booking a flight to London for an elderly couple. She walked briskly to the employees' lounge, where a public telephone hung on the wall. Groping through her handbag, she removed a heavy, gold-plated cigarette case. She unscrewed the base, and a miniature container with a black-satin finish and a tiny keyboard of buttons on one surface appeared in her hand. When Gannet had given it to her and had demonstrated its ability to make unrecorded, toll-free telephone calls anywhere on earth, he had called it a "Blue Box." She lifted the receiver, dropped a dime in the box, and dialed 800-335-6667, a toll-free number to the admissions office of Sparks Technical Institute, a small, struggling private college in Topeka, Kansas. Once the automatic equipment had penetrated—through the trunk lines—to the open, vulnerable heart of the telephone dialing system, Agnes held the Blue Box to the mouthpiece and punched out the number she desired on the keyboard. Emitting soft, subtle tonal frequencies, the Blue Box triggered the proper relays and soon Agnes heard the cadenced drone of a telephone ringing. She had known, from prior calls, that Bernard was waiting in a public booth in Alexandria Bay. All of his calls came from a scattering of public phones on both sides of the river to eliminate the risk of detection from the island—which did not have a telephone.

A familiar voice answered. "Yes."

"Mr. Alexander. I have your reservation."

"O.K., Agnes, it's me," said Gannet over the street traffic in the background.

"Bernard, this is a bad time. What do you need?"

"I'm sorry, Agnes. We are in trouble. The operation is in danger. We had a shooting last night. On the river, while the *Talon* was unloading. An American was killed. It's very complicated, and I don't really understand what happened myself, but the American authorities are holding another man . . . not one of ours. He's some kind of professional football player. . . ."

"A what?"

"A football player. His name is Farnsworth."

"So what's that got to do with me?"

"It's complicated, but you can help. We need you."

"Bernard," she said with mild impatience. She was thinking about the evening—a show and a dinner with a wealthy, quick-witted advertising executive named Jamie Lysle. It was a turnabout for her—to be seeing a frivolous man like Lysle, a man she had met while he was picking out a birthday present for his wife—but she viewed it as a relief from the increasingly grim and earnest commitments to school and the women's movement. "Bernard, I'm really busy."

Gannet paused for a moment, then spoke deliberately, as if he was trying to maintain his composure. "You've got to come to Alexandria Bay."

"What . . . ? I can't come to Alexandria Bay. My job. I've got other things. I just can't. . . ."

"Take a vacation, call in sick, just don't show up for work. I don't care, Agnes, how you work it out. It doesn't make any difference to me, Agnes, just get up *here!*" His voice turned hard and the last words crackled out of the earpiece like a straight razor whipping across a leather strap.

"All right, all right, I'll be there," she said resignedly. "But what do you want?"

"Get a flight to Syracuse. Serge Boucher—the fellow from Newfoundland—he will meet you and give you final details. Basically I want you to get to talk with this guy Farnsworth and find out what he knows. Once we know that, we can alter our plans accordingly. The police have him boxed in completely. It's impossible for me to break through without risking attracting attention. But you . . . a woman ought to be able to make it. Oh yes, remember those press credentials for the Toronto *Globe & Mail* we had made up for you? Bring them along. They might get you past the cops."

At first the idea of traveling to upstate New York to interview an arrested football player sounded like the height of idiocy. A waste of time. Her mind filed through a series of reasons why she should not go. Then she began to think of her father, now in his grave two years, and the angry men in Montreal who were preparing for the great struggle. And Bernard Gannet. Who was ready. "I'll be there in the morning, Bernard. You know that," she said firmly.

VI

THERE WAS an intrinsic uselessness about boats like Zach Landsman's fifty-three-foot Hatteras motor yacht. Too large to be operated easily and gracefully, yet too small to provide the space generally associated with luxurious living quarters, the craft—like all middle-sized cruisers of its type—looked as big as the *Scharnhorst* tied up in its slip but in reality could not accommodate many more people than could a PT boat. Jarvis Whitby had set up operations in the dark, cool main cabin, where the mahogany paneling shimmered like Hershey bars and the air was filled with the firm aromas of polishing wax, woolen broadloom, Cuban cigars, and expensive gin. Somewhere an air conditioner whispered and the syrupy tones of stereo music drifted through the compartment. Whitby's custom leather briefcase yawned open on a chair, its letter pouch revealing his passport, a Pocket Flight Guide, a Hertz car rental contract issued at the Jakarta, Indonesia, office, a pit credential from the German Grand Prix, a reservation confirmation from the Century Plaza in Los Angeles, and other visible documentation that its owner was a hard-running, high-rolling, globe-trotting All-American stud.

Jarvis Whitby lounged on the couch, his feet resting on the coffee table, which held a half-finished bloody mary. His brawny hands fiddled absently with a matchbox while he supported a telephone receiver between his chin and shoulder. His large, combative eyes were following the exquisite rump of a brunette who was polishing the handrail of a Chris-Craft tied in the next berth. He was talking to Father Christopher Ludens of St. Bartholomew's Catholic Church in Shaker Heights, Ohio. It had fallen on Whitby to patch together arrangements for Roy Enderle's burial. Enderle's sister, he had discovered, was working in a massage parlor in Florence, South Carolina, and hadn't seen her brother in seven years. She had neither the money nor the desire to attend his funeral. "He was never nuthin' to me and I was never nuthin' to him when he was alive, so why change it now that he's gone?" she had asked before hanging up the phone. Father Ludens had been a regular of the Browns' locker-room retinue and had tried hard to smooth the rough edges of Enderle's personality with the pumice of God's word. He had not been particularly successful, other than to persuade him to assist in some summer youth programs in the Cleveland ghetto and to speak at the parish's annual sports banquet. He had been distressed at the news of Enderle's passing and assured Whitby that he would arrange for a funeral and proper burial in consecrated ground as soon as the Jefferson County pathologist had finished with the autopsy and issued a certificate of death.

"Father, I can't tell you how much we appreciate this," said Whitby in a clear, confident voice. "I know that Pancho will be especially grateful, and I'd really like to bring him to the phone, but he's asleep right now. He's had a rough time of it. After Roy was shot, the police grilled him pretty hard about what happened. The poor guy is not only really shaken about the incident, but he's just plain exhausted. We've given him a couple of sleeping pills and have him in bed right now. When he gets some rest and a little clearer picture of what's going on, I'm sure he'll be in touch. The league and the Browns' front office are all shook up and the newspapers are driving us nuts. Fortunately, the guy who owns the marina where Pancho has been keeping his boat is letting us live aboard his yacht, which gives us plenty of privacy. I just got in here this morning. I went to a party after the game—by the way, I thought the team looked pretty good; whenever you can score thirty-one points on that Oakland defense, even in an exhibition game, things can't be all bad—and didn't get home until late. Then Pancho calls me at five-fifteen this morning and tells me he's in jail in Alexandria Bay, New York, on suspicion of murder. Fortunately, I managed to charter a Lear and got up here before nine and arranged bail and all that sort of thing. It's a strange deal, Father, very strange deal. But anyway, I can't thank you enough for your kindness in this particularly difficult time, and I know Pancho will be in touch with you before the funeral—which we'll of course attend, providing we get this thing straightened out with the police."

Jarvis Whitby hung the phone on its cradle and slumped back into the soft couch, watching the girl's soft, rounded bottom move across the windowpane, gliding from one window of the Hatteras to the next, like a split-image film. He shook his head and whispered to himself, smiling, "That's about all I need. Yes, Lord, just about all I need." He was a tanned, brawny man in his mid-thirties, with a shock of styled, mildly thinning hair combed into shaggy bangs over his forehead. He had the bulldozer body of a halfback and the tender, manicured hands of a scholar. He had been raised in a small, windswept town on Michigan's Upper Peninsula, where his father ran the biggest bank in the area. After graduating from the University of Michigan, he spent two years as an artillery observer in Vietnam and returned home with the Purple Heart—awarded for a compressed spinal disk suffered in a drunken tumble out of a Saigon taxicab. Jarvis Whitby received his law degree from Harvard, where he first recognized that he had an uncanny ability to talk. Words spurted out of him like bullets from a machine gun—lucid, cogent strings of words spitting forth in perfect formation with the ease of exhaling. He found that his speech centers seemed to work faster than his mind, that his glibness permitted him to converse on subjects about which he knew nothing, and with people he did not know or care about. His gift gave him a kind of artificial propulsion system. When he encountered an obstacle, he merely accelerated his chatter, burying the trouble in piles of words. This skill gave him substantial powers as a trial lawyer, although he often entered court shabbily prepared, ignoring legal scholarship in favor of his ability to pummel the witnesses and spellbind the jury.

Jarvis Whitby was never down. It was his native enthusiasm and compulsive urge to persuade that veered his career away from pure law and into the hectic, high-dollar business of sports marketing. After serving as corporation counsel for a large sporting-goods conglomerate that produced ski gear and golfing equipment, he took a job with International Management, the Cleveland firm run by Mark McCormack, the lawyer who managed the careers of Arnold Palmer and a multitude of other superstars. Whitby then broke away from the McCormack organization to form his own operation with a nucleus of young clients. Whereas McCormack concentrated on established sports heroes with maximum earning capacity, Whitby geared his operation to handle youthful men whose greatest years lay ahead. He signed Pancho Farnsworth after his first season with the Browns, when it had become apparent that he was a future All-Pro. The same reasoning had prompted him to represent Toby Trevis, the nineteen-year-old surprise winner of the 1975 U. S. Open; Billy Joe Priddle, the stock-car-racing sensation; James McKenzie, the fast-rising Australian Grand Prix driver; and Dieter Kreitz, the Austrian gold-medal winner in the giant slalom and downhill at the recently concluded Winter Olympics. For these five men, Jarvis Whitby acted as manager, legal adviser, accountant, father-confessor and sometime wet nurse— all for twenty percent of their gross incomes. It was a good thing, this management business, despite the constant travel, the chaotic home life, and the occasional unpleasantness such as the present Farnsworth problem.

He had closed his eyes for a moment when Zach Landsman entered the cabin. He was dressed in a pair of faded Levi's and a blue pullover. His face was puffy and there was a grim set to his mouth. "Oh, shit, if I'd known this was going to happen, I'd have laid off that booze last night." He shuffled across the cabin to the bar. "You want another bloody mary?" he asked Whitby.

"No, thanks. I need a clear head. But you go right ahead, Zach. One more will fix you right up."

"Oh, shit, why do I do this to my body?" asked Landsman as he stirred up a bloody mary.

"I think we've got the funeral arrangements about worked out," said Whitby.

"I cannot believe it. I mean, I just absolutely cannot believe that this thing has happened," said Landsman, collapsing into a chair. He sat inert for a minute, gazing at the brunette on the Chris-Craft. "Goddamn, that's nice stuff. She belongs to a big real estate developer in Toronto. He keeps her and the boat down here all summer."

"Maybe when I get Pancho straightened out . . ." said Whitby.

"Forget it. She's got a setup like you wouldn't believe. Untouchable. Un-fucking-touchable, I guarantee. Every guy in this marina has taken a shot at her. Nothing. Absolutely zero. Anyway, what's going on . . . I mean with Pancho?"

Jarvis Whitby regarded Zach Landsman for a moment before he replied. Zach was the classic case of a screw-up son whose family had bought him a commission in the boondocks. He'd been a junior investment counselor in the family's Wall Street brokerage firm after barely squeezing out of Brown and spending twenty-four months as a lieutenant in the United States Marine Corps. He had lasted four ragged years in the brokerage business before his older brothers had finally induced him—

through some rather heavy investment—to open a ski area in New Hampshire with an old prep school pal. A pair of warm winters had wrecked that venture, along with his marriage (complicated by the involvement of a young schoolteacher from Franconia), and he'd drifted—again buoyed by family money—into the marina operation at Alexandria Bay.

Whitby was prepared to accept him as an ally during this crisis. Landsman had made a substantial contribution to the search for a solution to the shooting. He had observed that all commercial Seaway traffic was monitored from Montreal to all points on the Great Lakes. If the ship that had fired on Farnsworth and Enderle had been a freighter of some sort, he had reasoned, it would have cleared Canadian customs and immigration at Montreal before entering the Seaway and a record of its position in the Seaway would exist.

This proposition had made sense to Whitby, and he had called a friend from Harvard Law who was working with the Maritime Commission in Washington. He had caught Randy Starkweather at his home in Arlington as he had been dressing for his regular Saturday-morning golf game and, using his vaunted powers of persuasion, had enlisted his aid. His friend had promised to use commission channels to check with Canadian authorities on the whereabouts of all small trawler-type vessels or oceangoing yachts fitting Farnsworth's rather ragged description that might be plying the St. Lawrence waters.

"Not much is happening," Whitby said to Landsman. "I'm waiting for a call from my buddy in Washington. With any luck at all, he might have a couple of leads. If that doesn't work out, or if the cops don't come up with something, we've got trouble. I've got Pancho loose on a simple disorderly charge for the time being, but there's no way I can keep it away from a grand jury unless we get more developments. A man is dead by gunshot and the people are going to demand that someone pay. Right now the only candidate is Pancho."

"Everybody knows he didn't do it."

"You and I know he didn't do it. And LaStarza knows. I mean, LaStarza is a sharp man. He is a smart policeman. But he's the undersheriff of this county and someday he's going to run for sheriff and you *know* he can't afford to let this thing drift away. There's no way he'll just close the books and let Pancho go. Unless something breaks, he'll just sling it to the grand jury and let them play with the case. And quite frankly, he'll get an indictment."

"How can that be? The boat was riddled with bullets! Pancho didn't shoot those at his own boat!"

"Who's to prove in a court of law that Pancho didn't land the boat on some island and blast it to make it look like an external attack, *after* he'd shot Roy?"

"Smugglers."

"Huh?"

"Smugglers. I know goddamn well Roy and Pancho got mixed up with smugglers. There's always been smugglers on this river. They say that during Prohibition the place looked like New York Harbor, with all the rumrunners roaring back and forth. Now there's some illegal Chinese sneaking in, and the drugs and only God knows what else. They tangled with some bad-asses, and they got shot at. If they'd been able to chase Pancho down, they could have simply sunk the boat and Roy and Pancho would have just faded off the face of the earth."

"Don't get me wrong, I believe they got shot at from another boat, and your theory about smuggling makes sense. After all, they didn't open fire because our guys disturbed their ride on Moonlight Bay. I only wish Pancho had used his radio sooner. Then somebody might have been able to run down that freakin' mystery boat before it disappeared."

"Like Pancho explained, the radio is located at the lower control station. He just didn't dare try to reach it while he was being chased. Then when he discovered Roy was dead, he was just too shaken to think."

"I know, I know," said Whitby. "I can understand why. I just wish it had been different." The phone rang; its sound was gobbled by the deep carpeting of the cabin. "That's Washington," he said, snatching the receiver from the hook. "Whitby," his voice crackled. He listened for a moment and then he bared his teeth and rolled his eyes in a signal of mock disaster. Placing his hand over the receiver, he whispered to Landsman, "It's Roger DeVoe, the NFL Commissioner . . . a complete jerk." Then he returned to the call. "Hi, Roger! Goddamn, it's good to hear from you! How the hell are you? It's been a while. . . . Well, Roger, I can understand your concern," said Whitby after a long pause. "But frankly, the image of the NFL is a secondary concern to me right now. We've got to accept the reality that Pancho is facing criminal charges that are considerably more important to his personal well-being than the aspects of pro football's image. There's nothing we can do about that until I succeed in getting him cleared. . . . No, no, Roger, we don't think he shot Enderle, nor do the police really seriously consider that possibility, although that could change. But the situation is extremely fluid and . . . Sure, Roger, I understand your position, but I'd advise caution on your part. Premature action before any conviction could cause you some serious problems, especially if Pancho's career was ruined. . . . Sure, Roger, we'll be in touch."

Whitby flung the phone onto its carriage. "That asshole! That stupid stuffed shirt! Pancho gets himself in trouble and that clown is on the phone telling me he's considering suspending him to protect the image of the NFL. Image? For Christ's sake, with all the inside betting action, half the guys zonked on uppers, and all the other screwing around that goes on in that business, and that fool is going to unload Farnsworth to protect pro football's image. I'll tell you something, if he so much as suggests that in public, I'll bang a suit on him so fast he'll think he was in the Six-Day War."

The phone rang again. It was Randy Starkweather. He reported that a check with Canadian and American Seaway authorities had revealed nothing. Although nearly two dozen large ships had cleared the Seaway, headed both inland and toward the Atlantic, in the past twenty-four hours, none seemed to fit Farnsworth's description of a small, trawler-like vessel. Moreover, no serious attempt to monitor the movements of private yachts and small craft was made because of the great traffic density. Starkweather did mention that all commercial traffic on the Seaway was controlled and the location of every ship was known at all times. During the early morning hours of Saturday, only two ships were in the Alexandria Bay area: the *Auguste Schulte*, a 409-foot diesel freighter owned by the Pjell–Fred Olsen Lines of Oslo, Norway, and the *J. N. McWatters*, a 730-foot bulk carrier owned by Scott Misener Steamships, Inc., of St. Catherines, Ontario. "No matter how smashed he was, Pancho couldn't have mistaken either one of those monsters for a freaking trawler," Whitby observed. Starkweather suggested that *Lloyd's Register of Yachts* might offer a clue, but Whitby noted that as long as the name of the ship was unknown, such research would be futile.

Zach was mixing another bloody mary as Whitby ended the conversation and said, "Make me one of those things while you're at it. I might as well get drunk right along with you." He rose from the couch and walked to the cabin window. The girl had moved to the forward deck of the Chris-Craft, where she was hosing down the main cabin top. "She doesn't look so tough," he said absently.

"Don't say I didn't warn you," Landsman said, handing him a fresh drink.

"Good God, one o'clock in the afternoon," said Whitby, glancing at his gold Rolex. "We ought to start thinking about getting the boy wonder out of bed. That guy from the *Plain Dealer* and Wallace from the *Times* and Cosell . . . I can't hold 'em off forever. Sooner or later we're going to have to surface and face the press."

"We ought to let him sleep a little longer. After all, the poor guy has been through a lot."

"Unfortunately, Zach, my man, Pancho hasn't been through enough," said Whitby testily. "Life has been spoon-fed to him since he was born. The Achilles-tendon thing and this deal are the first problems, at least to my knowledge, that he has encountered in his entire twenty-four years. I don't think the son of a bitch has had even a bad dream or a runny nose. I mean, he is totally, one hundred percent, unprepared for this kind of adversity. If it's the kind of trouble you can knock down with a blitz on third and long or a weak-side overshift, he's dynamite. Absolute dynamite. But this kind of toughness is foreign to him. That's overstating it; not really fair to the guy. Nobody can play the kind of game he plays and be a wimp. No, I'm not being fair. Pancho's a good kid and I really like him. Yeah, maybe he can get tough now that he's facing some serious challenges."

"I've never subscribed to the trial-by-fire theory of growing up," said Landsman.

"I can see that," said Whitby, but he caromed off the subject before Landsman could retort, and refixed his gaze on the girl. "What's that broad's name?" he asked, letting Farnsworth slip out of his thoughts. "She just doesn't look that tough."

VII

THE HUSHED compartments of the Hatteras had become as confining as a cell for Farnsworth. In fact, there had been moments, especially during the numerous phone calls from his father, when he would have opted for Undersheriff LaStarza's brand of hospitality. LaStarza had been aboard that morning, having driven up from Watertown after early mass, and had clambered on deck as the bells of Alexandria Bay's First Methodist Church tolled morning services. He was a brusque, intelligent lawman, with eighteen years' service with the New York State Police in its crack Bureau of Criminal Investigation before leaving to become undersheriff in Jefferson County—a job he knew would lead to the sheriff's position as soon as that bloated old politico Arthur J. Kruetter retired. From there LaStarza planned to build a power base and run for the state legislature, a place where he believed his hard-nosed honesty would quickly illuminate him on the dull, hidebound Albany political landscape.

Vito LaStarza had investigated dozens of murders in his career and he was supremely proud that few of them had gone unsolved. He took no personal credit for this record, for he believed law enforcement was a plodding team operation devoid of the inspirational sleuthing found in mystery novels. "Things are generally what they seem to be," he was fond of saying to those who suggested that crimes involved the bizarre and the unexpected. He had seen too many murders to know that more often than not they were menial, grubby excesses of cruelty committed with butcher knives and blunt instruments in nickel-and-dime robberies and sick spasms of passion. No, Vito LaStarza was far from convinced that Pancho Farnsworth and his friend had been involved in some madcap mid-river adventure with international brigands. His gut instincts told him that Farnsworth was lying. "You will be a successful and long-lived police officer if you accept the fact that eighty percent of anything that anybody tells you in the line of duty is a lie," he counseled all the recruits to his force.

He had sat in the main cabin for an hour that Sunday morning, quietly listening to Whitby's argument that an obscure smuggling operation had brought about Enderle's death. Farnsworth contributed little to the conversation, only repeating, with irritating consistency, the story he had been telling from the beginning. LaStarza did not particularly admire either of these men. Whitby was too glib, too cocksure, too eager to tilt reality to his advantage to be trusted. Farnsworth was distant and close-mouthed, and this troubled LaStarza. The act of lying, he had found, was generally accompanied by an attitude of seeming forthrightness, by a professed urge to cooperate in the search for truth. That Farnsworth was not operating in this fashion in no way relieved LaStarza's suspicions, but it did generate in him a grudging respect for his firm refusal to alter his story.

This was a bad case for Vito LaStarza. While he was pleased that Sheriff Kruetter was attending the annual New York State Sheriffs' Conference in the Catskills, which would neutralize the old hack as well as allow LaStarza to steal the headlines, he knew that unsolved murders—especially those that attracted the national media—had a way of nibbling at a man's career like moths in a blanket. One imprudent statement, one false arrest, one indication that Farnsworth was being treated any differently than other citizens, might mean political ruin. Therefore he chose to be cautious and to trust his basic notions about men: that whatever guile they possessed would be employed not in the commission of crimes but in their concealment. He would hold Farnsworth at bay while he and his staff sorted through a series of simple leads, primarily centered on the participants in the Jessup's Pier Six scuffle. Vito LaStarza was convinced that Enderle's death was directly connected with that incident. While there had been illegal alien traffic, in some cases involving mainland Chinese crossing the unpatrolled wilderness borders between Quebec and the states of New York and Vermont, and substantial movement of drugs, and other contraband along the St. Lawrence frontier, he was inclined to discount the hostile-smuggler theory. When LaStarza left Landsman's yacht to drive the few miles up the shore to Vince Scarpatti's rented summer cottage, he believed he was approaching the source of the trouble. With a record that included a suspended sentence for assault with a deadly weapon and strong but unproved links to an auto-theft ring in the Buffalo area, Scarpatti stood tall on LaStarza's list of suspects. His humiliation by Enderle in front of the clientele at Jessup's might have triggered deadly instincts for revenge, suspected LaStarza. To the point that Pancho Farnsworth denied any role in his friend's death, LaStarza tended to accept his story. If there was a killer among the cast, it was Vince Scarpatti.

"THAT LASTARZA really gets inside my head. He's a tough dude to reason with," said Farnsworth as the undersheriff disappeared in the clutter of yachts.

"He figures we're holding something back, it's that simple," said Whitby.

"He's got to know I didn't kill Roy."

"No question about that. If he thought you'd done it, you'd be in the slammer now. And there'd be no way I could bail you out. No, he just thinks something is fishy. He doesn't want to buy your boat story."

"What else can I say? It's the goddamn truth," growled Farnsworth.

"I only wish we could get some kind of a handle on that big boat," said Whitby, leaning back and gaping at the cabin's overhead.

"But the cops should be doing that."

"What the cops should be doing and what they are doing are two different things. These guys are civil servants. They believe in what is called 'solid police work,' which is grinding away toward the most simple-minded solution imaginable. Subtlety is not LaStarza's long suit, and it may be beyond his capacity to imagine this case as anything more than some kind of grudge killing resulting from that saloon fight."

"So where does that put us?" Farnsworth asked.

"You heard LaStarza say it. He claims he's notified the Canadian authorities and the immigration guys and the Coast Guard and the Seaway people, and I'm inclined to believe him. But imagine you're sitting in some Ontario Provincial Police station across the river and here comes this notice from Alexandria Bay that says, in effect, 'Hey, we've had a murder here which may have—according to one of the prime suspects—involved a large, completely unidentified yacht. Please be on the lookout.' You know what the cops over there are going to do with that? Bang, right in the old shit can, that's what they're going to do. The problem is this, Pancho: The Thousand Islands are full of big yachts. That thing could be tied up at any one of hundreds of private slips or in dozens of ports here or in Canada or be floating around somewhere in Lake Ontario or have slipped through the Seaway and be halfway to the Atlantic by now. If we had maybe the *name*, we'd at least be somewhere, but with what we've got to work on, LaStarza's got us by the short hairs."

"The son of a bitch better find that yacht, that's all I've got to say," said Farnsworth as he shredded the label from an empty beer bottle.

"You know what worries me?" said Whitby. "What really worries me is that LaStarza is going to jerk around with this case for a while, until he can't find anything out about the boat and the local folks start to get on his ass about making some arrests. Then he'll do something like charging you with third-degree murder or manslaughter and just tossing it in the lap of the district attorney. Landsman says the guy has political ambitions and you know there's no way he's going to let this case get in his way. LaStarza's been around for a while, and he knows what can help him and what can hurt him. You can hurt him, and he isn't going to let that happen."

Farnsworth stared in silence at Whitby, his eyes unblinking. "There's no way I'm going to sit here and let that happen," he said.

"You haven't got much choice. Just consider yourself lucky you're here and not in a cell in Watertown."

"That's easy enough for you to say—you haven't got any real stake in this."

"You crazy, man? What do you mean, no stake? I've got you, haven't I?" Whitby said sharply.

"Simple bucks, Jarvis. I get in trouble and you lose your meal ticket. So you figure your best gamble is to cool it while LaStarza sniffs around. That way we don't make any waves, although if it works out the wrong way, I'm the one who's in the can, not you."

"Come on, Pancho, this whole deal is getting to you. You know I'm concerned about you—as a friend as well as a client."

"Don't blow smoke up my ass. I don't need it right now."

Jarvis Whitby leaned back on the couch once again and said nothing. The murmur of idling engines entered the cabin. An aged Richardson was heading for its slip. The sharp-edged shouts of playing children were coming from far away. The rhythmic clanging of a hammerhead against steel drifted across the water from the boatyard. He toyed with a ball-point pen, then turned his gaze toward Farnsworth, who was hunched forward on his chair, his head arched downward. "Take it any way you want to, Pancho, but I'm telling you the best strategy right now is to sit tight. Anything you try on your own not only is guaranteed to piss off LaStarza but will probably get even more of the press on us. And believe me, about all we need is more publicity on this thing. I'll bet Arnold Libermann has heard about it already."

"Arnold Libermann?"

"The guy from Mark Ruby Cosmetics—their ad director—the guy we're going to do that deal with, the deal for Ice Man deodorant commercials. You want to show up in those or on the CBS Evening News?"

Zach Landsman appeared at the cabin door, looking grave.

"Hey, I'm sorry about the interruption, but there's somebody outside who wants to see you."

"We aren't seeing anybody, Zach, you know that," snapped Whitby.

"Yeah, but this may be different. A broad from the Toronto *Globe & Mail*."

"Aw, come on, for Christ's sake, Zach, *especially* newspaper people. You know we aren't seeing any of them."

"I know, I know, but she says she's from the area. Somehow I think she can help. Believe me, she isn't your average fat-ass-reporter type."

"Help? How do you mean, help?" asked Whitby.

"She seems to know quite a bit about us already. The way she talks, she seems pretty plugged in to what goes on around the river. I think she may be able to give us a line on the ship. At least it's worth a try, why don't you let me bring her past the guard."

Whitby butted out a cigarette and rubbed his eyes. He inhaled heavily in resignation and looked at Farnsworth, who was staring at Zach. "God, I don't know," he said. "Sooner or later we're going to have to come out of our den and face the world. This chick may be as good a way to start as any. Especially if she's got some information to offer. What do you think?"

"You're the big shooter with the media. Do as you like," said Farnsworth heavily.

Agnes DePere's attitude had improved since leaving New York. Her passage from the summer inferno of the city to the clean, sunny St. Lawrence country had helped to ease her irritation. On the drive northward from the Syracuse airport, her contact, Serge Boucher, a stern, humorless youth with scraggly hair and a knobby, well-muscled body, had given her the meager details of her mission. The dossier on Farnsworth consisted of a single page torn from *Street and Smith's Official Pro Football Yearbook* and the newspaper clippings. Using her false credentials, he told her, she was to pose as a *Globe & Mail* correspondent to gain an interview with Farnsworth and to extract as much information as possible from him. The idea intrigued her, and she had looked hard at the husky, open face that stared at her from the wrinkled page of the sports magazine. When Serge had stopped the rented Ford Maverick near Landsman's Marina, she had eagerly stepped into the street. The warm wind nibbled at her hair as she entered the arena of yachts. Whereas Gannet had been repelled by their opulence, she found them appealing, lithe creatures lolling at their berths.

Zach Landsman returned from the Hatteras and approached her on the dock. "O.K., I've got it set up, but you probably should get it over with as quickly as possible. You know how it is."

"Of course. I'll be brief," she said crisply.

"Follow me, Miss Fitzsimmons," said Landsman, moving toward the yacht. "By the way," he said over his shoulder, "what's your first name? You know us Americans and first names."

"Sarah."

"I swear I hear some French somewhere in you," he said.

"My mother was French, my father was Irish. I was raised in Hull," she answered.

"I'd give anything to be bilingual," he said idly. "Hey, that reminds me," he said, turning to face her. "Pancho thinks he heard some French voices on that ship he ran into last night—he'll explain the whole thing—but maybe you can help. I tell you, it's strange. The whole thing is absolutely weird."

"Why would the Toronto *Globe & Mail* be interested in this story, Miss Fitzsimmons?" asked Jarvis Whitby as he mixed himself another bloody mary. Farnsworth had remained seated during the introductions, trying to remain unmoved by Agnes' arrival, but he found it increasingly difficult to ignore her. She was dressed in a pair of brown slacks made from a slippery material that clung to her. The matching blouse was low-cut.

"We've got a large circulation in the St. Lawrence region, and interest in professional football is quite high in Canada," she answered quickly in level, confident tones. "So my editors decided it was worth having me take some time away from my vacation and come over."

"Over? From where?" asked Farnsworth flatly, without enthusiasm.

"Across the river. With some friends. Near Gananoque. You know where that is?"

"Yeah. Roy and I . . . Roy, he's my buddy who was shot . . . we tried some muskie fishing near Howe Island a couple of days ago." She watched him as he spoke, finding him more physically imposing than she had expected. His eyes, deep-set, contained the same liquid fierceness that was in his picture, but they softened easily, as did his mobile mouth.

"It's ironic that you're from a Canadian paper," said Whitby. "I almost had a deal for poor ol' Roy to play with the Hamilton Tiger Cats. That might give you a local angle for your story. Roy was a helluva guy. A real gentleman. He would have been very popular in Canada."

Farnsworth listened to Whitby's chatter, knowing that he had actually found Roy cranky and uncooperative. He wished that Jarvis Whitby would stop treating everyone around him like merchandise in a fire sale. "Exactly what do you want to know about this thing, Sarah?" he asked, slicing into Whitby's ramblings, which were escalating toward a full-blown eulogy for Roy Enderle.

Agnes turned to confront Farnsworth. He was staring at her, obviously impatient to get on with what he considered to be a conventional interview. "Everything you're prepared to tell me, *Mr.* Farnsworth," she countered spikily, reaching into her handbag for a stenographer's note pad. He answered her questions automatically, covering the affair more or less accurately, except to dismiss the brawl at Jessup's as a brief shoving match.

"You have no idea of the identity of the ship?" she probed.

"If we did, we wouldn't be here wondering what these hick cops are going to do," said Whitby.

"Like I said, it looked like some kind of a commercial trawler. Who was on it, I haven't the vaguest idea. Except that one of them talked like a Frog."

"A what?" asked Agnes.

"A Frog. A Frenchie, you know. One of the guys sounded French. Maybe French-Canadian or something," said Farnsworth.

"Jeeesus Christ! I just thought of something. Christ yes!" yelled Whitby, leaning forward and banging the heel of his hand on the glass-covered coffee table. "Why didn't we think of this before?" Farnsworth and Agnes DePere watched him as he rose up and paced toward the window. "I'll think of their name. Give me a minute. Just a minute. . . . The French Canadians. They've got some creeps up there who are always raisin' hell. Kidnapping guys, sticking bombs in mailboxes. Yeah, that was their big trick, bombs in mailboxes. Now who in the hell are they?"

"Yeah, I know who you mean," said Farnsworth. "Terrorists. They've got some hard on against Canada. Who are those creeps?" he said, turning toward Agnes.

She had stiffened at the exchange. "Do you mean the Front de Libération du Québec . . . the revolutionary army that advocates a free and independent nation of Quebec?" she asked coldly.

"Those are the guys," said Whitby, turning to Farnsworth. "They might be the ones. They're about due for another cuckoo try to bust up the system in Canada. We ought to call LaStarza about that."

"It's unlikely that the FLQ is involved," said Agnes. "They are a very small organization and quite disorganized, I've heard. I'd hardly think they could afford even a rowboat."

"Yeah, maybe. But tomorrow I'll mention it to LaStarza. Maybe he can get something going in Canada. We're getting mighty tired of being locked up on this ship, Sarah, believe me," said Whitby.

"I'm sure it's difficult," she agreed, with a faint suggestion of sarcasm lining her voice. Then she put her notebook away and stood up. "Thank you, both, for your time."

"Stick around, Sarah, and have a drink," Whitby said, moving toward the bar, carrying his own empty glass.

"Thank you, but no. I've got to file my story, which will take some time. And the drive back to Gananoque. Some other time, perhaps." Brushing aside Whitby's mild protests, Agnes left the cabin and was about to step ashore when Farnsworth appeared behind her.

"Sarah, did we say something wrong? About the French? All of a sudden I sensed that maybe you were sore. It was nothing personal. I want you to know that."

"It's nothing. My mother was French. Sometimes it's a sore point, but nothing important. Don't be concerned, it's something that is only serious to Canadians. Americans just don't understand."

"Hey, I'm sorry, really sorry. And I was going to ask you about tonight. You know, nothing is going on here, and I was figuring that after you got your story written you could come back and we could sneak over to the Pine Tree Point Club or maybe cook a couple of steaks on board. You know, just kind of sit around and waste some time."

She looked up at him; his position on the deck above her made him appear colossal in size. She found a certain restless vitality about him that appealed to her physically, but there was little about his attitude that was attractive. "Not tonight. I've got the story and then I'll be busy. No, I'm sorry."

"I'm sorry too. I'd just like to talk to somebody new for a while. To get my mind off this other thing. It's beginning to get me crazy."

"I know what you mean."

He shrugged a signal of modest defeat and said, "Listen, if your plans change, give me a call. Just ask for Zach Landsman's private line. I'll be here, I'll guarantee that." He watched her nod an acknowledgment and turn away down the dock.

Jarvis Whitby came to the cabin door and stood in silence as she disappeared among the jumble of superstructures. Farnsworth heard him light a cigarette and inhale deeply. "Goddamn, that's heavy stuff. Heavy stuff," Whitby said quietly. "You put a move on her?"

"Half-assed. I tried to get her over here for dinner."

"Yeah?"

"Said she was busy."

"Too bad."

"I think we pissed her off."

"Why?"

"That talk about the Frogs."

"So what?"

"Her mother's French."

"Tough shit."

"Yeah, for me and her."

BERNARD GANNET was squatting, guru-like, on the large double bed that overwhelmed the cramped motel room. An air conditioner hanging precariously from the sill of the single rear window filled the space with a cacophony of humming fans and gears. An ash tray beside him overflowed with mangled cigarette butts. He was trying to assess the information that Agnes had brought him. She was sitting in a blond-wood lounge chair beside the bed, half watching a blurred black-and-white telecast of an aged Elvis Presley movie. Serge leaned against the door, keeping an eye on outside movements through the window and snatching glances at the television. He had laid a Spanish-made Llama XI 9mm automatic on the small desk top—an act Agnes viewed as low melodrama.

"You're absolutely positive this Farnsworth had no idea of the *Talon*'s identity?" Gannet asked slowly.

"For the fourth time, Bernard, they don't have the vaguest notion," she said impatiently.

"Their speculations about the FLQ. I don't like that."

"It was idle chatter. Nothing more."

"Tomorrow they talk to the sheriff. That could lead to something," Gannet said, frowning.

"I don't see what could come of it. What can an American

sheriff do? And besides, in a few more hours it will be too late for them."

"Never sell the police short. They generally know a great deal more than we give them credit for. One call to Ottawa could trigger Canadian security forces, and for all we know, they've got the *Talon* under surveillance. You just can't take those things for granted. Goddamnit, Serge, turn that television off!" he shouted.

Serge Boucher looked at Gannet with contempt and stepped to the television set. He punched a button and the screen went blank. "Hold on to your nerves, Gannet, the real tension hasn't begun yet," he said, smiling.

Gannet caught Boucher's eyes in an unblinking stare. "When it starts, we'll see whose hands tremble first," he said. "Now get outside and sit in the car." Boucher glowered at Gannet before edging to the desk, where he scooped up his automatic. Stuffing it in his pocket, he went outside.

Gannet rested his head in his hands, saying nothing. Agnes sat in the chair recalling their small apartment in Montreal, where she had also waited for Bernard Gannet. "What kind of man is this Pancho Farnsworth?" he asked idly.

"Why do you want to know?" she asked.

"I'm curious. I sense that you found him intriguing."

"He's a big he-man type, obsessed with his own masculinity. Very basic, Bernard, very basic."

"Can you handle him?"

"Handle him?"

"You know, get him to do what you want?"

"I really never thought about it. Despite your baroque view of women, I don't go around evaluating my sexual influence on every man I encounter."

"O.K., O.K., let's not get into that," said Gannet hastily. "I was just wondering about using you to neutralize him."

"Neutralize? What do you mean by that?"

Gannet got up from the bed and went to the window. Pausing until he had completed tucking his wrinkled shirt into his pants, he said, "I want Farnsworth out of action . . . neutralized until the operation is over."

"For a minute I thought you meant you wanted him killed."

"Hopefully, that won't be necessary, although there are those of us who would find that a more satisfactory alternative."

"Meaning what?"

"Meaning that there are a lot of angry men around us. Like Serge out there. He hungers to kill somebody. As if other men's deaths will bring him more life. Our friend Boutette is another. Boutette is the most bloodthirsty man I know."

"I think it is mostly talk with him," she said.

"Maybe, maybe not. We'll know shortly," he replied.

"So what about Farnsworth?"

"You say he invited you over there tonight?"

"Sort of, it was nothing serious."

"Whatever, but I want you to accept. I want you to get him to the island."

"What can that do for us?"

"It injects a powerful element of confusion. If he disappears, the American authorities will become obsessed with finding him. It will distract them from us, especially since he is their prime suspect. Cops work in straight lines, believe me."

"Listen, Bernard, I have done this small thing for you. A small thing for the revolution. But now I want to go home. I want to take a long shower, have a quiet meal, and go to bed. In the morning I'll catch a bus to Syracuse and fly to New York. I've played my part."

"You don't mean that," he said firmly.

"Well, I mean it if all you expect me to do is play some idiotic Mata Hari role. I believe in the cause as much as you—as much as anyone on earth—but I'll be damned if I'll take part in some fool charade. If you have something worthwhile for me to do, I'll stay. Otherwise I'm going."

"Agnes, this is worthwhile. The revolution needs you. I need you." His voice was deep and firm, yet as he looked at her a curious softness crossed his face, and he appeared more vulnerable to her than she could remember. "This is the beginning, not the end. There are other things. Better things for us." He reached for her hand, gripping it hard. She closed her eyes and returned the firmness of his grasp, while nodding a silent acquiescence. She would stay. And she would do her part to neutralize Pancho Farnsworth.

BY THE TIME the woman he knew as Sarah Fitzsimmons had returned, Pancho Farnsworth had downed three double scotches. After the surprising call from her, he had bustled around the cabin, trying to brush up the rubble he and Whitby had accumulated. He had laid two T-bones out for broiling, had uncorked an inexpensive bottle of California Cabernet Sauvignon, and had selected from Zach's meager collection of stereo tapes an eight-track collection of famous movie theme songs by Hugo Montenegro as the best compromise for mood music. Whitby had, as he predicted, made good his liaison with the girl from the Chris-Craft. Zach had departed to a cocktail party in Clayton, leaving the Hatteras to Farnsworth. He wanted to be cool, to move slowly and deliberately with Sarah, to play down his head-crusher jock image and to work on his somewhat tarnished skills as a gentleman. He had decided this while mixing his second scotch, with the Montenegro theme from *Hang 'Em High* whispering in the background.

Dinner unfolded with a certain awkward rapport. She smiled in the right places, but seemed a trifle rigid—a state which he decided to counter by standing off himself, rather than trying a risky, now-or-never kamikaze move to get her into his stateroom. Agnes was softening in the face of what she had expected to be an ordeal. His persistence in maintaining perfect behavior reminded her of a naughty little boy trying to curry favor with a teacher, and she was amused by it. He was not stupid—she discovered that early in the going—and the glancing blows they made at politics and the arts indicated that he was an aware individual, at least in the limited context of conventional social numbness. It made it easier this way.

A pair of plates spread with steak bones and gristle lay in the galley sink. The empty bottle of wine stood guard nearby. He rummaged through Zach's liquor cabinet and removed a bottle of Rémy Martin VSOP. Unable to find the proper glasses, he pulled a pair of water tumblers out of a cupboard and poured two inches of cognac into each. "There, I knew you'd figure I was a bum sooner or later. At least this is better than serving it out of the bottle with a couple of straws."

"You've done well up to now," she said, smiling. He plunged into a chair near her and propped his feet on the coffee table. He held his water glass in front of him in a toast. "Hey, I'm glad you decided to come," he said gently.

She caught his gaze, could not hold it, dropped her eyes to the rug, and raised her glass. "Frankly, I didn't know what to expect."

"Given half a chance, even us jocks can act like human beings," he said easily. "Depends on the company," he added, draining away several ounces of the bittersweet liquid.

The alcohol was beginning to work on Agnes. The hard edges of her resolve were eroding. The appeal of the man near her was intensifying, and she warned herself that she had better get on with the mission before more psychosexual relays in her brain began to snap closed. "Pancho," she said hesitantly, "this may sound weird, but I've got something to talk to you about. Something that may help your . . . your situation."

"Like what?" he asked absently.

"Like the shooting. I don't know, but it could have a bearing."

"C'mon, we haven't talked about that all night. Let's leave it be."

"Let me just tell you about one thing. Then we'll drop it."

"It better be good," he said in mock threat.

"This guy at the paper in Toronto. He's sort of a friend. When I filed my story I chatted with him about your case. He's been doing some investigative reporting on contraband shipments between Canada and the States. He told me he's come across a very active smuggling operation in the St. Lawrence involving Cuban cigars."

"So?"

"So they may have been the people who shot at you."

"Come on, will you, Sarah."

"No, I'm serious. I know it sounds silly, but this guy says it's really big business."

"How in hell can it be serious business? We've got trade with Cuba again. You can buy Cuban cigars in your local drugstore."

"Yes, but they're very expensive. He says the American tobacco interests forced extremely high tariffs when diplomatic relations were restored. So there's a terrific profit if they're smuggled through the Seaway and into the States. I'm just telling you what he said."

Farnsworth slipped back in his chair, eying a table lamp across the room through the amber liquid in the bottom of his glass. "Roy got shot by guys sneaking cigars into the country? Christ, that's even too weird for me to handle."

"One more thing this guy told me."

"Go ahead. After the cigars, I'll believe anything," he said.

"There's an island. It's somewhere near here, he says. It's known to the American and Canadian customs authorities, and they've raided it twice but found nothing. Yet his sources say it's still being used."

"An island? That might explain the base for the launch. Could be. Yeah, it could be," he said, rising from his chair. "This guy mention any names . . . names of any islands?"

"Yeah," she said slowly. "He called it . . . Yellow Squaw . . . in the Amateur Islands."

"*Amateur* Islands? Never heard of 'em, but let's see if we can find 'em on Zach's charts." He went up the ladder leading to the pilothouse and yanked open the chart drawer. Lifting out a batch of Lake Survey charts of the St. Lawrence, he returned to the main cabin and spread them out on the coffee table in front of Agnes. They scanned several, with Agnes feigning intense effort in the search, before Farnsworth began running his finger over the smooth parchment surface of L.S. 114: "Butternut Bay, Ontario, to Ironsides Island, N.Y." "There. The Amateur Islands!" blurted Farnsworth as his finger touched the yellow outlines of a small group of islands just north of the Canadian border in mid-river. "And you know what? Those islands are within a mile of where Roy and me got shot at. A *mile!* Sarah, that's got to be the deal. It fits. You are beautiful. We may get this thing settled, after all. Wait'll Whitby hears about this!" Farnsworth reached for the phone on the end table at his elbow.

"No! Wait!"

"But I've got to tell Whitby. We've got to get the cops and start clearing this mess up," he protested.

"Just a minute, Pancho. The thing is this: What I've told you is privileged information. I promised that I wouldn't tell anybody. What's more, the police are already aware of this thing, I think . . . at least the Canadians are . . . and it would stand to reason that if they thought it was connected with your case . . ." She made her observations hesitatingly, leaving obvious blanks for him to fill in.

"They might have checked it out," he followed. "But then again, they might not have. You know how bureaucracies work. Half the time one hand doesn't know what the other is doing. It's possible that the Jefferson County Sheriff's Department doesn't have the vaguest idea what the hell is going on with the Canadian customs guys." He rose and paced to the far side of the cabin, in deep thought.

After a long pause, Agnes spoke. "You know what we could do? We could go have a look for ourselves."

"Ourselves? What good would that do?" he asked.

"I know it sounds a bit bizarre, but it might produce a couple of things. First of all, we could scout the islands—on the map, er, chart, it looks as if there are only a few in the general area—on the off chance the ship you saw is there."

"That's impossible. Those guys had to bail out once they finished shooting. The chance was too great that I'd identified them," countered Farnsworth.

"Perhaps, but it would still give us something concrete to go on. At least you could say to the authorities, 'Look, on So-and-So Island there is a suspected smuggling operation that has to be investigated,' " she replied.

"Why can't the cops do that? All we have to do is call them up."

"You forget one thing, Pancho. I'm a journalist. My story would be a hundred times stronger if I was actually involved, if I had actually been on the scene. That gives me a first-person approach that I might otherwise miss."

"Yeah, but I'm under a kind of house arrest. LaStarza would have my ass if I went anywhere."

"You've still got your boat. . . ."

"The poor thing looks like it went through the Tet offensive."

"It'll still float, won't it?"

"Hell, it'll run like Jack the Bear."

"Well, then," she said with an impish smile crossing her face, "how could the sheriff mind you taking a girl for a boat ride?"

He looked at the girl coiled on the couch, her face coy but open. He thought of a quiet cove and the vee berths of the *Red Dog*, where there was no chance of intrusions from Zach or Jarvis. He drained his glass and stood up.

VIII

STILL TATTERED from the attack, the *Red Dog* had been removed from beneath its tarpaulin shroud, its engines had been fired up, and now it was planing across the St. Lawrence with Alexandria Bay's splattering of lights disappearing behind the bulk of East Mary Island. Farnsworth, once again sitting tall on the bridge beside the girl he knew as Sarah, was heading the Bertram downstream, on course through the main shipping channel of the Seaway. The night was warm and the gusty southwesterly winds had whipped the St. Lawrence into a substantial chop.

He felt better than he had since the shooting. It had been difficult for him to reboard the *Red Dog* and tread the deck where the life had spilled from his friend. The boat had been swabbed down by Landsman's crew and the only signs of the attack were the pockmarks of the bullets and the badly gnawed windshield. He forced this into the back of his mind, concentrating on the lights of the channel buoys, the fragrance of the woman, and the uncertainty of the night that lay ahead.

As the moment of betrayal came closer, guilt was beginning to envelop Agnes. Until now her relationship with Pancho Farnsworth had been pleasant enough, and she was beginning to find a certain charm in his innocence. But now her role in this scenario was beginning to prey on her conscience. Her other duties for the FLQ had been pranks compared to this enterprise —an enterprise of such seriousness that she imagined it might cost this man his life. Yet it was the very magnitude of the operation, as described by Gannet and others in the movement, that permitted her to justify the deceit. At stake was the future of Quebec, she labored to convince herself, and in that context the fortunes of a single person, herself included, mattered little.

For that reason she had been able to accept the presence of the third, concealed figure on the *Red Dog*. Had Pancho Farnsworth bothered to check the gear locker in the main cabin, he would have encountered the muzzle of a Llama 9mm automatic in the hands of Serge Boucher, who had hidden himself there before their arrival. If that had happened, Farnsworth would have been taken prisoner on the spot, which would have been riskier, according to Gannet's reasoning. Ideally, Boucher would not reveal himself until the boat neared the island, where a neater, more private capture might be executed. This was the way it was working out, although Agnes found this option more difficult than if Farnsworth had been taken, cleanly and honestly, as soon as he had stepped on board. At least that would have relieved her of the charade she was forced to go through as the *Red Dog* sped through the dark.

"This whole part of the river is loaded with shoals," said Farnsworth. "I've got to be kind of careful or we'll be swimming. You feel like a little dip?"

"I didn't bring my suit," she said tightly.

"Who said anything about a suit?" asked Farnsworth.

Agnes said nothing in response, which prompted him to ask, "Why so silent? You're acting kind of weird . . . like this isn't much fun."

"I guess it's been a long day," she replied quietly.

They rode on in silence, letting the drone of the twin Mercruisers substitute for conversation. Playing a small flashlight over L.S. chart 114, which flapped in the breeze, Farnsworth navigated to the Amateur Islands. They appeared to be deserted, save for one large outcropping of rock with a castle-like structure looming out of the trees. "That looks like the only place of any size in the whole area," said Farnsworth as he cut back on the throttles. They cruised into the lee of Yellow Squaw Island, where the protected waters were calmer. Flipping off the navigation lights to avoid detection, he idled to within a hundred yards of the shore while lifting his binoculars from the gear locker. Then he shut off the engines. "Completely dark," he said.

As the boat sloshed to a standstill, Serge Boucher unwound himself from the jumble of life preservers in the locker and slid into the cabin. Suddenly a small metallic object tumbled out of the locker and clattered onto the fiberglass deck. Boucher went rigid, fearing the sound had been heard on the bridge. When there was no sign of alarm, he reached down and retrieved the source of the noise—a small gold cigarette lighter. Seeking a place where it would cause no more disturbance, he tossed it onto the spongy surface of the vee berth in the forward cabin. After sighting the silhouette of the house, he turned to the lower control station and scanned the dimly lit instrument panel. He snapped the port and starboard engine ignition switches into the "off" position. Although they remained "on" on the flying bridge control panel above, the engines would not start unless both sets of switches were coordinated. He drew the Llama from his belt, clicked off the safety, and cocked the hammer. Then he slipped into the galley seat facing the door and laid the weapon on the table before him.

"Wait a minute . . . wait a damn minute!" Farnsworth's voice was building with urgency as he glued the binoculars against his eye sockets. "The boat house . . . yeah, there's a boat! It looks like . . . yeah, yeah! It's the same boat that chased . . . ! Those sons of bitches are moving out . . . !" He dropped the binoculars away from his face and turned toward the instrument panel. "It's time to haul ass. They're the same dudes, I know it," he said, his voice increasing in pitch. He snapped the ignition switches into place and pressed the port starter. Nothing. Deadness. He fiddled with the clutch lever, knowing that the engine would not fire unless the lever was perfectly positioned in neutral. Still nothing. Giving up on the port side, he turned to the starboard controls and found them equally inert. "Something is really screwed up." Agnes sat, stiff and silent, her eyes riveted on the approaching launch. Farnsworth jiggled the switches in a rising frenzy, then said, "They're coming, baby. We better get this thing running or our ass is a grape. The trouble's got to be down below."

She watched his immense form flow down the ladder with surprising grace, considering his lame leg. She followed him with particular attention because she believed it was likely that she would never see him again, and the thought did not appeal to her. She heard Farnsworth fling open the cabin door and waited for him to say something as, she imagined, he practically tumbled over Boucher and his waving automatic. Agonizing seconds passed with no noise whatsoever from below: no exclamations of shock, no noise of a scuffle, and, thankfully, no reports from Serge's pistol. The waves slapping the hull, the whine of the wind, and the exhaust rumble of the oncoming launch were the only sounds that reached her ears. Finally she heard his voice, now cool and modulated, drumming out words sharply filled with irony: "Hey, Sarah, it's O.K. now. Your little creep friend's got me. It's all right. And thanks . . . yeah, thanks a million, you . . . you stab-in-the-back bitch!" Then she laid her head in her arms and didn't look up until long after Farnsworth had been loaded into the launch and taken to Yellow Squaw Island.

HIS CAPTORS, four in number, including Boucher, had not broken their silence as they escorted him aboard the launch with a pair of ugly, flat-black automatic rifles aimed at his head. They bound his arms behind him with heavy nylon cord and covered his eyes with adhesive tape, held in place with a stocking cap pulled down to his neck. He was led ashore, first stumbling along a wooden dock, then up a stone walk, before descending into what felt like the dampness of a cellar. Prodded forward, he then heard a door slam behind him and a padlock click. He stood in place for many minutes, feeling his heart rattle against his rib cage and tensing against his bonds until his arms began to ache. Finally he toppled onto the dirt floor, having discovered that the simple act of sitting down was extremely complicated without sight and arms to aid in balance. He made several attempts to free himself, then capitulated. His mind groped for a hold on reality. Occasionally, he could hear the thump of feet on the flooring above, but otherwise the silence was complete. He inched around the space on his back, trying to determine the size of his cell and perhaps to find a sufficiently sharp edge with which he could fray the cords holding his wrists. He wanted badly to regain the use of his arms so that at least he could go down fighting, flailing for his freedom rather than to have his life blasted away by a pistol pressed against his sightless, unmoving skull. Farnsworth decided that he was going to die. Before that took place, he wanted to marshal his strength for one final surge against his captors, whoever they might be.

BERNARD GANNET could not determine exactly why, but he had decided he wanted to meet his new prisoner. Perhaps it was the celebrity status of this professional athlete, or perhaps it was the involvement of Agnes and the bitter convulsions of guilt she was now undergoing because of her assistance in his capture. He had ordered the man named Farnsworth brought to him—in the rude tribunal hall formed by the bare kitchen and its single, flyspecked overhead light. They thrust him through the door like a pair of small men trying to move a grand piano. Gannet unconsciously stepped back in reaction to the bulk of Farnsworth, who was blinking with anger and uncertainty. Boucher and a wiry Libyan—one of Salam's elite guerrilla force—kept a pair of AK-47 automatic rifles stuffed against his ribs until he reached a chair at the edge of the big table in the middle of the room. "Sit down, Farnsworth," said Gannet evenly.

"What the hell is this all about?" asked Farnsworth as Boucher slipped a chair beneath him.

"That's a reasonable enough question, considering your situation," said Gannet.

"Listen, you're crazy if you don't think everybody in the country isn't going to be out trying to find me in a few hours. Save yourself a lot of grief and let me go."

Gannet gave him a forbearing smile and turned away. "Pancho Farnsworth, professional football player . . ." he said absently, as if he were reading the words off a plaque. "I've never met an All-American football hero. I suppose I should ask for your autograph," he said with mild sarcasm as he slipped into a chair opposite Farnsworth.

"Listen . . ."

"No, *you* listen, Farnsworth!" barked Gannet. "This is a very serious business you have had the misfortune to involve yourself in. I'm as sorry as you are that it happened. And I might add that the last thing I wanted was the death of your friend, but sometimes the price of impulsiveness is inordinately high. If you choose to cooperate, you will avoid the same difficulty. We are not killers by desire."

"Roy Enderle would have trouble believing that," Farnsworth said bitterly.

Gannet eased back on the rear legs of the chair and lit a cigarette. He watched the bluish smoke drift in timid swirls around the light. After gathering his thoughts for a few moments, he spoke. "Have you any idea what you're doing here?"

Farnsworth shrugged his shoulders. "Does it make any difference? Cut the crap. If you want your creeps to shoot me, go ahead and get it over with," Farnsworth said.

"We don't kill prisoners of war," Gannet said firmly.

"What do you mean by that?"

"Farnsworth, have you ever heard of the Front de Libération du Québec . . . the FLQ?"

Farnsworth looked briefly puzzled, then turned grim. "The FLQ. Sure. Everybody has heard about your chicken-shit mailbox bombs."

"Very good. That's about the level of political consciousness I'd expect from a professional jock. But it doesn't matter. Frankly, I'd have been amazed if you'd have known more. The point is this, Farnsworth, you and your buddy stumbled into an extremely sensitive operation associated with an even larger enterprise . . . an enterprise that may very well affect the destiny of this hemisphere and perhaps the entire world. It is in a very strong sense a military operation, and that is why I am referring to you as a prisoner of war. Therefore, you will be treated according to conventional rules of combat."

Farnsworth watched the scrawny man across the table. His sharply featured face seemed blurred with fatigue, but the eyes behind the heavy glasses were bright and contentious. Farnsworth's mind was smeared with impressions, none of which seemed to prompt any logical responses. His game was defense, which centered on the instant decipherment of the opposition's offensive intentions and the brutal use of his body to blunt their attack. In that situation he had total freedom to roam the field of play, and because of this the other side had to view him as a major element in their plans. Not so here. The man with the glasses seemed to have no real concern for him or his potential to interfere—in whatever obscure military operation he was referring to. Farnsworth was struggling with the rising awareness that, for the first time he could remember, he was helpless. "You don't really believe that you can keep me hidden on this island, do you? People are going to start looking for me in the morning . . . maybe even now they know I'm missing," he said without conviction.

"With any luck at all your detention won't last long. As I said, we are at a critical stage of this operation, and it will reach a climax within a very short time. Once that is done you can go back to your fun and games."

"At least my fun and games don't involve shooting people in the back," Farnsworth snapped. "No wonder you assholes can't get any popular support."

"Hey, listen to that! Did you hear, Serge? Farnsworth knows all about the revolutionary movement," Gannet shouted to Boucher.

Farnsworth heard a voice from behind him speak in French, then fray into laughter. Gannet replied in French, then returned to English as he eyed his prisoner. "Farnsworth, tell me about socialist revolutions. Do you know anything about people's uprisings in Algeria, Cuba, Vietnam, or do you really figure they were just a gang of nuts sneaking around killing and kidnapping?"

"What difference does it make what I think? You've got your ideas, I've got mine."

"But I'd like to hear some of those ideas. I've never met a classic bourgeois athlete before, and I'm curious to learn what makes a man like you tick, what would prompt you to devote your life to brutalizing others for money and the accolades of the crowd."

"If you've got this operation under way that's going to change the world, how come you've got time to sit here and talk with me? I'd figure you had bigger deals to attend to than that," Farnsworth retorted.

"Believe it or not, Farnsworth, the countdown is proceeding

on schedule despite the ill-timed and unfortunate intrusion you and your associate made on the *Talon*."

"The *Talon?*"

"The *Talon*," said Gannet easily. "That's the name of the ship you blundered onto. Despite that trouble, it's safely reached Toronto, although your escape gave us some bad moments. In fact, that's why we had to send Agnes after you—to determine just how much you knew."

"*Agnes*, that bitch," said Farnsworth.

"Actually she's kind of sorry about the whole thing, if that'll make you feel any better. Her name is Agnes DePere."

"Shit," said Farnsworth.

"Back to the revolution. I'm curious. Do you have any inkling of the kind of things men like us are trying to do?" asked Gannet in a conciliatory tone.

"You're trying to wreck a perfectly good system, that's what you're trying to do."

Gannet paused, his steady eyes locked on Farnsworth's. "Do you really believe that?"

"I wouldn't say it if I didn't believe it."

"Now let me get this straight. The 'perfectly good system' you refer to is, I presume, capitalism, where we get a neat distribution of the wealth in the hands of the privileged few while the working classes support them with their labors. Is that what you mean?"

"If that's the kind of distortions you want to use while defining it—yeah, that's what I mean."

Gannet was smiling. "Does your family have any money, Farnsworth?"

"What do you mean?"

"Money, money, man! Does your family belong to the working classes?"

"Well, my old man works," snapped Farnsworth.

"He works where? How does he make his living?"

"He runs the family business . . . a ceramics factory in upstate

New York. He's a classic capitalist. He gets driven to work every morning in a long limousine, wears a top hat and striped pants, and carries two big sacks of money around with him—with dollar signs painted on the sides. And, oh yeah, I almost forgot. He always smokes big cigars."

"It's bad enough without your sorry attempt at humor," said Gannet soberly. "Your old man is rich and holds the destiny of poor workers in his hands. My father died a pauper, ground into the dirt by the exploitation of his labors. Why should there be any difference between them?"

"Maybe my old man is smarter than your old man. Did you ever think of that?"

"Not likely." Gannet paused to watch Farnsworth hunch forward in his chair and begin to vibrate with bitter laughter. "What's the matter with you? Where do you see the humor?"

"This is so goddamn crazy, I can't even believe it," said Farnsworth, a wide smile covering his face.

"How do you mean?"

"I mean, I'm sitting here, with a couple of creeps sticking guns in my head, and with you, who's raving about a grubby little revolution that has killed an innocent bystander—my friend—and we're arguing about whose old man is better. My old man can beat up your old man. That's insane. Let's get on with it. If you're going to kill me, kill me. But cut the rhetorical crap." Farnsworth's voice had turned hard and defiant.

Gannet leaned back in his chair. He began to speak in firm, patient, almost condescending tones. "There is a great tide of history sweeping around us, Farnsworth. Everywhere on this planet, workers, peasants, students, honest intellectuals, and young people of all kinds are rising up to destroy the aged, corrupt power structure your old man represents and to replace it with an order of human cohesion—a cohesion that will be the vital force of a new, classless society replacing the present system based on the exploitation of man by man. You ought to pay more attention, Farnsworth. Things are happening in the world—many more important things than carrying a goddamn leather ball up and down a grass field or peddling dinnerware. One of the major problems of the entire American system is that you've got your priorities so fucked up that you probably think what you and your family do is worthwhile. That's a sorry comment."

"What I do, I do well. Can you say the same thing?"

"Doing well—achieving—in the context of men playing little boys' games is so ludicrous, so isolated from reality as to be unworthy of comment," said Gannet. "It is like bragging that you can eat your dinner without dribbling on your shirt."

"O.K., let's agree for the sake of argument that professional football is a lot of overcommercialized nonsense. Now you tell me what's better about what you're doing—about killing innocent citizens and kidnapping and terrorizing and tearing up a system that has brought more good to more people than anything in history. Is that leading to some greater good? Bitching is understandable if you can't cope."

"You might bitch too, Farnsworth, if you'd seen what some of us have seen. You have no more understanding of what it means to be a Québecois than you have of living on Mars. How would you know what it's like to be a second-class citizen—a white nigger as some have called us?"

"White niggers? What kind of pathetic nonsense is that?" asked Farnsworth with disdain.

"Spoken like a true American," said Gannet. "That is precisely the brand of arrogance that will cause your downfall. 'White nigger,' in case you haven't heard, is a perfectly precise term for the Québecois. Like the American black, he was brought to a foreign land as a labor force to be exploited. After three hundred years their conditions remain essentially the same: both are second-class citizens, excluded from the power structure, harbored in filthy ghettos, and treated with sickening, patronizing liberal charity, as a child feeds and grooms a puppy. Your blacks are 'niggers' and 'spades' and 'spear chuckers' and 'jungle bunnies.' We are 'Frenchies,' 'Frogs,' and 'Pepsies,' *les maudis peps's*, to the Anglo imperialists who occupy our homeland with as much ruthlessness and cruel racism as the Nazis occupied Poland. Except our occupation has lasted insufferably long and our patience has ended. For years and years, Farnsworth, my ancestors lived with the 'English fact,' as they called it, and contented themselves with more cosmic satisfactions—with accomplishments in farming and simple crafts while clinging to the black frocks of the Church. Yes, those sorry, submissive fools permitted the English and American imperialists to literally steal their country while they listened to the soothing litanies of the Catholic Church and their superstitions about St. John the Baptist, sacred hearts, and blood from wine. The Church was, is, and always will be the handmaiden of aristocratic power, capitalism, and fascism! It was the Church which hoodwinked the people into clinging to the old ways—'the past our master,' *'Je me souviens,'* and all that rot—which blinded them to the thievery and exploitation going on around them. The *future* is our master, Farnsworth. Oh yes, we may complain, but we have plenty to bitch about. What if you had been raised in a homeland where a foreign gang of interlopers had imposed their own political system and their own language over that of the rightful owners? What if your state of New York had two official languages—say, for the sake of argument, English and Chinese—and you, as a native, could not think of advancement in business or politics without being fluent not only in your mother tongue—the tongue of your ancestors for a thousand years—but also in the language of the Chinese invaders? It may sound absurd to you, but that is a curse that we have lived with for centuries."

"Now wait a minute." Farnsworth paused. "You . . . I don't even know your name . . . how can I talk to you if I don't know what you're called?"

"My name and what I am called are two different things," Gannet said, smiling. "After all, they call you 'Pancho'—which I am sure is an amusing bit of frivolity for your Anglo friends, but might be construed as a gratuitous racial slur by other semi-American citizens, namely the oppressed Chicanos. Farnsworth, why not call me 'nigger'? That would probably make you most comfortable."

"You know, you guys are so far out of touch that it's almost funny. You talk about me being out of the real world; maybe you ought to get off your asses and quit reciting polemics to each other and find out what the hell is going on out there. I don't know about you 'niggers,' but I'll bet most of the brothers I play football with would laugh in your face."

Normally, Gannet would have dismissed a man like Farnsworth as a conventional, bullheaded American, but now, with a surplus of time, he found a certain satisfaction in sparring with a representative of the old order. "Again, that confusion of athletics with reality," he said calmly. "The white power structure has cleverly deluded the oppressed into thinking success in sports is the avenue to equality. The black man's distraction with games keeps him from playing with guns. The same is true of hockey in Quebec, where boys chase a puck and dream of fame and riches with the Canadiens. There racism is present too—the implication that our old penchant for grace and pacifism makes us more adroit than tough on the ice. You may have heard the saying that French hockey players can skate but they can't fight."

"Yeah, I've heard that. But why don't you finish the statement? It might sound a little more balanced that way. The correct saying is: 'Frenchmen can skate, but they can't fight. Englishmen can fight, but they can't skate.' Does that make the Englishman any better? It implies that he's a clumsy, belligerent oaf. C'mon, nigger, if you're going to feel sorry for yourself, at least be accurate," Farnsworth shot back.

"Fair enough. It makes little difference. Sport cannot be mistaken for life, and as long as it is, it will serve as a sedative for the masses." Gannet shrugged. "Take that great sham of commercialism, the Olympics. It opens in a few days within walking distance of many poor Québecois neighborhoods, and most of the people won't have enough money to attend! Why is this? Because Quebec's assets are being siphoned off by American and Anglo-Canadian corporations. Those things we mean to get back, Farnsworth, just as your colonial ancestors snatched your country away from the British exploiters and gangsters who were draining the wealth for the power of England. Do you get my point?"

"You make it sound as if the French Canadians are living in concentration camps. What about the separatist party? I read the papers too. Every time you have an election, you get your ass kicked in. And what about Drapeau and Trudeau? Weren't they French Canadians? Didn't they rise to power?"

"The separatist party—the Parti Québecois—plays into the hands of the establishment by trying to gain power through parliamentary means. Dreams for such a peaceful solution are naïve beyond comprehension. And even if such a thing did happen, do you think the Anglo-American imperialists would stand by without a response? Did ITT and the copper companies let poor Allende return his nation to its native population? What a joke! As much a joke as to call Trudeau a Québecois. That traitorous whore. At least we know where this new Prime Minister, the racist Tory from Alberta, Alva McClelland, stands on the question. Trudeau was a shifting, shadowy target, but we can identify McClelland, who at least is honest about his hatreds. We prefer him to the slippery liberals who speak out of both sides of their mouths."

"So what are you going to do about it? What kind of a big play have you got in mind?" Farnsworth asked.

"What are we going to do about it? We are going to overthrow the system, throw out the corruption and the imperialism, and return Quebec to its rightful owners!"

"Talk is cheap. It'll take more than murders and kidnappings."

"Farnsworth, how old are you?"

"Twenty-four."

"I'm two years older, but we are contemporaries. You and I will live to see Quebec join the family of nations as a free state. But before that happens, we will have guerrilla war in North America. Armed conflict is inevitable. America won't stand by while one of her major fiefdoms slips away. Hell, American troops were marshaled on the border during the Cross-Laporte crisis, and we weren't about to launch a full-blown revolution then. Now we are ready."

Farnsworth, finding a certain comfort in the hopelessness of his situation, presented Gannet with a comic leer. "You are so full of shit that I can't stand it," he said evenly.

Gannet collared his temper and replied carefully, "You know, Farnsworth, you exhibit a fascinating consistency with the American character—irreverence, defiance, ribald humor, and, sadly, a myopic disregard for truth. I suppose it's understandable in your case. You have every reason to play the fool. After all, your life has been fat so far. Wealthy family, good schooling, athletic heroism, a strong body, and plenty of screwing."

"I get my share."

"I'd be surprised if you didn't. But you should try it with a single faded dress shirt, shiny pants, and run-down shoes. You would quickly find out what kind of a stud you really are without a dime to spend."

"What are you trying to say?"

"I'm saying that you're soft. Under that muscle there is a punky center—as with all Americans. It was what enabled Agnes to sucker you here and in the end will enable us, the working classes of the world, to bury the petite bourgeoisie. That's you, Farnsworth."

"Are you telling me you wouldn't be quite so militant if you could get more ass?"

"You arrogant bastard! The day will come when the FLQ and men like us and women like Agnes DePere will be marching toward a new world and you and your stupid football games and your, your *dishware* factories, will be buried in the dust of revolution. One by one we are weak and poor—no match for your massive bodies and bank accounts—but there are more of us and our zeal is greater than you can imagine. We're the fleas of the earth, but our numbers and our minuscule size give us the advantage. One day soon you fat dogs will feel the blood draining away, and then you'll know it's too late."

IN FRUSTRATION, Gannet dropped the microphone onto the bench in front of the RF 1550 100-watt VHF-FM transceiver. For twenty minutes he had been trying to reach the launch. His message was simple: return immediately to the island.

He was in a corner of the basement of the old house, surrounded by radio gear. Looming beside him was the RF 745 10-kilowatt, high-frequency, single-sideband transmitter with power enough to ring the world with messages. It was this radio, coupled with an RF 505A receiver and a Russian-built speech scrambler, that enabled the FLQ unit on Yellow Squaw Island to maintain communications with other operations in Quebec, Newfoundland, and Labrador and with a special Libyan revolutionary support group centered in a desert village south of Murzuch in southwestern Libya. Operating on a shifting, prearranged series of frequencies between 2 and 30 megacycles, in terse coded and scrambled messages, Gannet's station was part of a secret radio network designed to coordinate the upcoming operation. The gear had been produced in Rochester, a hundred and ten miles to the southwest, and had been part of a large order of electronic equipment delivered to the Libyan Army in the summer of 1975. After it had been shipped to Tripoli and officially accepted by Libyan military officials, it had been stored in a government warehouse for seven months until its delivery to the FLQ had been arranged by Paul Boutette.

The Libyan government, inspired by the Muslim zealot Colonel Mummar el-Qaddafi, had been supporting a variety of insurrectionist movements around the world ever since his seizure of power in 1969. Shipments of arms and money had reached the Sudanese rebels, Al Fatah, other fedayeen guerrilla groups (including Black September), the American Black Liberation Movement, the Irish Republican Army, and the FLQ, despite protests from a variety of governments and the United Nations. But Qaddafi, whose disregard for Libya's international reputation increased in direct proportion to the staggering profits pouring forth from its nationalized oil industry, continued the aid. In 1973 British authorities had intercepted a German tramp steamer off the Irish coast laden with Russian-built arms bound for the IRA. The weapons had been loaded aboard in Tripoli. No such shipments to the FLQ had been detected. Two ships—9800-ton motorships of Liberian registry, owned by a syndicate of Lebanese businessmen operating out of Accra, Ghana, and crewed by Arabs—had made regular passages to Canadian Great Lakes ports carrying Egyptian cotton fabrics, cotton yarn, and rice. Since they sailed according to a carefully timed schedule that placed them in the Seaway near Yellow Squaw Island in the predawn hours, it had been a simple matter to offload, while still under way, a series of well-disguised, floatable containers full of arms and matériel. Those waterproof crates had been lashed together and towed ashore by the FLQ launch. The smuggling system had worked until early 1975, when agents inside the government had indicated that suspicion was rising within Canadian customs about the movements of the two motorships. A warning of plans for a search by authorities in Montreal was passed to the FLQ while one of the ships, the

Qara Su, was in mid-Atlantic. Receiving a signal from the radio on Yellow Squaw Island, the *Qara Su*'s crew jettisoned the contraband—several thousand Russian Kalashnikov automatic rifles, two tons of Belgian-made ammunition, a batch of American rocket launchers, and twenty of the ultra-secret French SR-101 rapid-fire 90mm mortars with five hundred rounds of companion projectiles. The ship arrived in Canada with a legal cargo. However, additional shipments had to be rerouted through Cuba, then to Miami on small boats, and up the east coast by truck to a furniture factory in Barre, Vermont, from where they were flown the final few miles into Quebec by light planes operating from a remote airstrip.

Although efficiency had slipped badly with the new system, the arms pipeline had remained open. Because its role as a transshipment point had been largely abandoned, the Yellow Squaw Island facility had been reduced to a communications station and a place for pickup of special cargoes of contraband and personnel. That accounted for the function of the ocean-going yacht *Talon* (named for Jean Baptiste Talon, an early administrator of New France, 1665–68, 1670–72, who stimulated colonization and industry and encouraged westward movement), which, because of its compact size and noncommercial registry, could more safely undertake special missions. At least that had been the case until a few nights previous, when Farnsworth and Enderle had nearly broken up the final mission of the craft. Being offloaded at that particularly critical moment were two dozen of the latest Russian SAM-10 surface-to-surface guided missiles.

Gannet leaned forward to peer at a small card taped to the front panel of the VHF-FM transceiver. The unit was used for short-range river communications and operated within a spectrum of frequencies to avoid detection. Double-checking that for this particular date and hour of the night he should be transmitting on 159.150 megacycles—and assuming that the launch's similar radio was also tuned to the same channel—he keyed the microphone once again. "Little Willie, Little Willie, this is Big Al, Big Al: The refrigerator is broken. Over." He waited for a reply to his message, which, after descrambling and decoding, was a clear instruction to suspend operations and come back to the island as quickly as possible. The silence was broken only by the modulated hum of the loudspeaker. He tried again. No answer. Again. More silence.

"Goddamn them!" he shouted, slamming his open palm against the desk surface.

"No luck?" asked Agnes as she appeared out of the shadows and walked to his side. Her face had been cleared of makeup and her hair fell in lank, uncombed wads around her shoulders. The luminescence of her skin had been replaced by a gray smear of despair.

"They won't answer. It's that crackpot Salam. I don't know what the hell it is with those Arabs—hang-ups about their masculinity, a reaction to having to lick Western boots for so long—barbarism—I haven't any idea, but they're crazy to kill somebody. It was Salam who ordered his men to open fire on Farnsworth the first time. Then they were such bad shots they couldn't do the job properly! Now the son of a bitch has countermanded my orders and taken Farnsworth, his boat, and our launch."

"You think he'll kill him?" she asked.

"Of course he will. That's what he told Serge he was going to do. 'If you Quebecker women haven't got the stomach to get rid of this enemy of the revolution, we will,' is the way he put it. They're taking him out into the lake, where they'll shoot him and sink him and his boat in deep water. What's more, I sense the gentle hand of Pierre Boutette somewhere in this thing."

"But Pierre's in Toronto. On the *Talon*. How could he . . . ?"

"Salam spoke with him by telephone on the mainland earlier this evening. I know that. If he didn't tell Salam to eliminate Farnsworth, I'm sure he didn't object."

"You are always so eager to make Pierre seem like a homicidal maniac. Why blame Pierre?"

"Pierre Boutette is two men. Someday you will see that."

Agnes turned away from Gannet and stared blankly into a corner of the cellar. Her eyes gravitated to a small moth dodging crazily around a bare light bulb. She began to nibble on the nail of her right thumb, and her left hand fidgeted idly with the front of her blouse. "I feel like a swine. Like a Judas," she said.

"*You* feel like a swine? What about me? I told the guy we wouldn't harm him. I said we weren't killers. We had sort of a good argument. He's hopelessly bourgeois, but hardly evil. Salam will justify his action on the basis that it would have been too risky to keep Farnsworth as a prisoner, but I know better. He wants his life because he botched the job the first time."

"Bernard, if I'd known a man was going to die partly by my hand, I'd have told you to go to hell when you called me in New York," she said.

"I understand," he answered in muted tones as he pulled his glasses away from his head and rubbed his eyes. "I suppose it was my own selfishness that got you into this in the first place. I'd never ask you to knife somebody like we're doing to Farnsworth."

"It's different now."

"How do you mean?"

"Those crazy days hiding out on Des Récollets Street, they were somehow more innocent, all puffed up with rhetoric. Maybe I secretly felt the system we claimed to be trying to overthrow would actually protect us in the end."

"The stakes were high then. They are higher now," he said.

"Try the radio again."

"Could be Salam is right." He shrugged.

"In what way?"

"Maybe we're too soft," he said, leaning back in the chair and gazing at the dials in front of him.

"Too soft to be sadistic, wanton killers? No, Bernard, for the people of St. Jacques you can lash out at your enemies, like a soldier. Like a man. But to murder a prisoner? Get that idiot Arab back here before he poisons you and everything you stand for."

"There's time for a few more calls, then we've got to leave. It's two thirty-five now. We've got a four-hour drive to Toronto and by then we'll be over the brink. A lot of men are going to die today, and Farnsworth is just going to have to be listed as a casualty of the revolution. If he's the only innocent victim, we'll be lucky. The clock is ticking. In five hours the first bomb goes off, and by the time we go to sleep again, maybe this whole goddamn filthy world we've been hating so long will be gone—up in smoke. I know I'm tough enough to fight for that."

GAFAAR AL-SALAM was freezing. The wind slashing across the river was warm by Temperate Zone standards, but for a man raised on the coast of North Africa, where the Ghibli ripped off the Sahara like the breath of a volcano, it was frigid enough to raise goose bumps and make his teeth chatter. "Goddamn this climate," he muttered to Marcel Delisle, who was at the helm of the *Red Dog*.

"This is perfection for us, Major. Five months from now you'll be able to walk where we are now. This river will freeze from shore to shore," mused Delisle.

"By then I will be back in Bengasi, in a place where men can walk on warm sand and not have to wrap themselves in bearskins," he said.

"It may be too chilly for you, but the weather is ideal for our mission. The cloud cover hides the moon and the chop on the river means we'll meet no other boats at this hour."

"That much we can be thankful for. The launch is only two hundred meters behind us, and I can barely see her running lights. Is your man sure of our rendezvous?"

"It's simple. We'll meet here, at Allan Otty Shoal at the mouth of the river." Delisle, a brawny youth with an unruly wad of black curly hair, pointed a flashlight at a Canadian Hydrographic Service Chart folded on a clipboard. "The water around there is plenty deep to sink this boat and its cargo. And it's nearly four thousand meters from the nearest land, so we'll have no risk of being seen. Nor will anyone hear the grenades exploding at that range. We'll be back to the island in two hours."

"I'm proud that you and your man piloting the launch . . ."

"His name is Boucher, Major."

"Of course. You and Boucher show the kind of nerve that will make this revolution a success. I'm sorry that I can't say the same for Gannet. He seems to have no stomach for blood, which is a critical weakness in a war of liberation."

"Frankly, I've never liked the man. He substitutes arguments for action. That bores me," said Delisle.

"Revolutions are successful only when men stop thinking and start fighting," said Salam firmly. "Pierre Boutette believes that. He is your most effective leader. Your future is bright as long as he remains in power. He understands what it is all about."

"Men will fight for Pierre Boutette," said Delisle.

"I can see that," said the Libyan. "Now, enough of this cold. I'm going below to see how our oversized Yankee is facing up to his final moments." He slipped down the ladder from the flying bridge and stood for a moment in the shelter of the cabin, absently watching the foaming wake being swallowed by the darkness. He felt a great climax of pleasure rising inside him. He relished the prospect of executing Farnsworth and seeing the very deck he was standing on slide into the black water. This would be his first American victim—satisfying a yearning for reprisal that had clawed at him since he was a child. Gafaar al-Salam had grown up as the son of a dirt-poor father who had scratched out a living by raising goats and scavenging scrap metal from the litter of tanks, trucks, and matériel left by the Allies and the Germans in World War II. Later their tiny hut bordered the massive U.S. Wheelus Air Force Base near Tripoli and his first memories of Americans were of loud, obscene men prowling the land for trinkets, drink, and women. These barbarians from the West, with their monster cars, their garish clothes, and, most important, their thundering jet airplanes, which simultaneously frightened and fascinated him, seemed to violate every law of Islam. As he grew older he became a fanatic disciple of Gamal Abdel Nasser and his Pan-Arab nationalism. After a brief term in a technical school in Tripoli, his eager mind and ardent patriotism helped him to be picked for officer's training in the Libyan Army, in which he was enrolled when Mummar el-Qaddafi led the 1969 coup that replaced the creaky, pro-Western monarchy of King Idris I. While he had not directly participated in the overthrow, he, like most of the officer corps, had long been radicalized by Qaddafi's unique mixture of fundamental Islamic piety, anti-Zionism, and Arab socialism.

He quickly rose to the rank of captain in the Libyan Air Force in the fervid belief that Qaddafi would lead the Islamic world to a renaissance of the eighth-century Saracen empire that spread from Persia to Spain. After the death of his young wife from an undiagnosed intestinal disorder, Salam immersed himself in the causes of Libya. He was among the first to fly one of the hundred and ten Mirage III multipurpose military jets Qaddafi purchased from France between 1971 and 1975. Like many of his fellow aviators, he found the nuances of the sophisticated aircraft difficult to fathom. Four months after his first flight, he was on a training mission over the seacoast city of Al Khums when an instrument warning light winked red in his Mirage IIIR. Panicking, he immediately jettisoned, only to find out later, to his chagrin, that the blinker had merely indicated a malfunction in the plane's high-altitude infrared photography system. He continued in service, however, reaching a pinnacle of pride when he led a low-level flyover as part of the full military funeral Qaddafi had given for the five Black September guerrillas killed in the 1972 terrorism at the Munich Olympics. He did not participate in the aerial combat of the Yom Kippur war of 1973, but he helped train Egyptian pilots for the conflict and flew numerous reconnaissance missions over the Mediterranean. His flying career ended two years later, in the summer of 1975, while on a joint maneuver with the Egyptian Air Force high above the desolate Gilf Kebir Plateau, which straddled the Egypt-Libya border. During a complicated tactical maneuver, Salam's Mirage IIE fighter-bomber nicked the tail section of an Egyptian MIG-21, causing both aircraft to spin out of control. He managed to jettison once again, although for some unknown reason the Egyptian could not get free and crashed with his aircraft. Salam's chute failed to open completely and he fell into a rocky, arid ravine with such force that his pelvis and right leg were badly broken. He lay there for four days while search and rescue attempts were stalled by bickering between the two air forces over who was to blame for the collision. Finally, semi-conscious and hours from death, he was found by an East German geological crew working for the Egyptian government. His recovery, complicated by the effects of exposure and dehydration, took more than six months. After his release from the hospital, recurring dizzy spells, a loss of depth perception, and an erratic pulse prevented his return to flight duty.

But Gafaar al-Salam had been too loyal and zealous an officer to be relegated to a soft supporting role behind a desk. Riches had poured into Libya from her nationalized oil industry and Qaddafi had become increasingly bold about meddling in the internal affairs of other nations. His initial efforts to aid various revolutionary movements with money and armaments expanded to a point where he began, in the early winter of 1976, to send secret military advisers to assist various revolutionary groups. Two Libyans were discovered on the island of St. Croix, operating with the local black terrorists, and were expelled by the United States government. Replying to a stern American protest, Qaddafi noted that American "military advisers" had been functioning as counterrevolutionaries in numerous nations for decades and his government was merely providing the same help, except to the oppressed rather than to the oppressors. As aid to the FLQ accelerated in cadence with plans for a major insurrection prior to the 1976 Olympics, Qaddafi decided that Libyan soldiers should also be present. Nineteen guerrillas, under the command of Major Gafaar al-Salam, were given training in urban warfare, with special emphasis on mortar and surface-to-surface missile tactics, and were smuggled into Quebec by ship and through the use of false passports. Major Salam had arrived three months earlier as an attaché to the Libyan Embassy in Ottawa. But most of Salam's time was spent in Montreal, where many days were consumed in the positioning of concealed mortar and missile units—some of them mounted in specially disguised panel trucks for mobility—and zeroing in the weaponry on a variety of private and public targets in the area. He also spent many days on the island, helping to coordinate the Montreal attacks with others planned for Ottawa and Toronto and maintaining communications with the homeland. Now, as soon as he eliminated Farnsworth, he and his aide, a glowering Berber named Seif, would make the two-hour drive to a small farmhouse on a little-used road outside St. Clet, in the municipal county of Vaudreuil, which lay to the west of Montreal. St. Clet was in a unique strategic position, in that it lay near the confluence of the St. Lawrence and Ottawa rivers. Twelve miles to the east were the Pont de L'Ile aux Tourtes— the bridge that carried Autoroute 40 over the water on its way to Ottawa, a hundred miles away—and the Autoroute 20 bridge at Terrasse-Vaudreuil, which connected Montreal with the Trans-Canada Highway to Toronto. Twenty-six miles to the east was the Montreal International Airport at Dorval. All of these targets—the bridges, the autoroutes, and the airport—were in easy range of Salam's thirty-six SAM-10 missiles that had been stored, with their launchers, at the St. Clet farm. Three other missile sites, at La Plaine to the north of the city, St. Amable to the east, and St. Jacques le Mineur to the south, formed an outer offensive perimeter capable of interdictive fire to destroy the fourteen large and small bridges linking the main islands of Laval and Montreal with the mainland. This strategy was designed to isolate the city (in concert with the destruction by demolition teams of the Métro and automotive tunnels under the rivers) while an inner network of mortars—coordinated with small guerrilla assault groups—attacked government and police installations, utilities, and other targets in the city's *centre-ville*. Initial diversionary barrages would be directed at the Olympic Village in the eastern part of the city in an effort to force significant police and military detachments into protecting the thousands of visiting athletes. This was the essence of the FLQ timing: the notion that provincial and government authorities would be so preoccupied with preventing another Munich that they would not be prepared for an insurrection. Gannet and other FLQ leaders had made sure that certain well-known federation members, left-wing sympathizers, labor and student leaders, radical separatists, and others had made loud, public denunciations of the Olympics within the past few weeks and had made their movements highly visible to the authorities. In this way they hoped to delude the police into believing the FLQ was reduced to ineffectual sputtering about the worldwide event taking place in their midst.

FARNSWORTH LAY in a semi-fetal position on the port-side vee berth of the *Red Dog*. With his head wedged against the rope locker in the bow of the boat, he was able to watch his guard, Seif, who sat passively at the galley table with his AK-47 in front of him. A mysterious, desperate power was beginning to well up inside Farnsworth. His options had been reduced to a pair of alternatives: to live or to die. To remain passive would mean certain death—the tall, severe Arab had already told him that—which gave him no choice but to make one final spasm in behalf of survival. He considered a direct assault on his guard, but realized he would be cut down in the first movement from the bunk, even if his arms were free and he had two fit legs.

The cabin door opened. Farnsworth watched Salam hunch slightly to enter the compartment. He heard him say something in Arabic to the man at the table and then watched him approach. The Arab leaned over him, his eyes glinting with confidence. "Make your Christian peace. We'll see if you Americans are as tough as you think you are," he said.

"I'll manage, goat shit," said Farnsworth.

Salam stiffened and the hint of a smile that was flitting across his face disappeared. "You'll pay for that." He sneered and turned to the table, where he sat down, facing Seif, his back to Farnsworth.

While he was shifting his body to trade insults with Salam, Farnsworth's hands, still bound behind him, had slipped between the bulkhead and the berth cushions upon which he was sprawled. His left hand touched a small metal object wedged against the fiberglass. He recognized it immediately. It was Sandy's lighter. She was the creamy blonde from Atlanta who'd spent a weekend with him in late June. For a moment he could see her lovely naked body curled up in the space he now occupied, her graceful fingers lighting a cigarette between bouts of lovemaking. Since then she had written several times asking if he would search the boat once more for her cherished gold Dunhill. Now he had found it.

Farnsworth opened the lid and fired the lighter. He could feel its heat brushing along the inside of his wrists as he tried to direct the flame against the rope. Being nylon, the line smoldered for a few moments, then burst into flame. His flesh was burning too, but he clung to an agonized silence as the ugly odor of frying skin and singed hair and the acrid fumes of the rope reached his nostrils. At the moment he decided he could no longer tolerate the pain, he felt his arms break free.

"I smell smoke!" said Salam in Arabic as his head swiveled in the direction of the vee berths. He rolled away from the table and took three quick steps to the forecabin entrance. Suddenly Farnsworth's bent legs uncoiled with the force of a sledgehammer, catching Salam squarely in the stomach. He was flung backward in a ragged, loose-jointed jumble of appendages, with Farnsworth inches behind. Seif, who had also left the table to examine the source of the smoke, was caught by the flying body of his major, and both men—whose combined bulk barely exceeded that of their adversary—slammed in a heap against the cabin door. Salam, who was the larger of the two, landed on top of his cohort and he quickly raised a leg to fend off the leaping form of Farnsworth. It did him no good. The full weight of Farnsworth, propelled by awesome furies, pounded against the Arabs amid ugly cracking sounds rising from the deck. The right forearm of Farnsworth—as with all professional football players, a weapon as stout as a nightstick—landed a short, harsh blow on Salam's skull. Farnsworth leaped to his feet, pulling the inert form of Salam with him. Gripping his victim by his shirtfront, he pondered him for a second and then hurled the body against the lower control station, where it seemed to disintegrate under the terrible impact. Farnsworth turned to spot Seif scrambling to reach the AK-47, which had tumbled to the deck. He took a quick step forward and kicked the small man in the face. Then he picked up the rifle and battered Seif's head until he stood breathless and dazed above the carnage.

He heard an alarmed voice on the flying bridge, directly above him. Delisle had cut the throttles and was shouting, trying to determine what was going on in the main cabin. "Major, Major, is everything all right down there? You need any help?" Farnsworth, inhaling in great gulps, snatched the AK-47 from between the limp legs of Seif and aimed it at the overhead. He pulled the trigger. The cabin vibrated with a series of deafening detonations and from behind the haze of gases spewing from the barrel appeared a random rivetwork of bullet holes in the vinyl covering. He had pointed the automatic rifle directly upward, at the spot where he thought the pilot had been standing on the flying bridge, and its angry reports were immediately answered by a tight, high-pitched shout of fear and a loud splash beside the boat. Farnsworth flung open the cabin door and vaulted onto the open deck. A few yards off the starboard side he spotted the bobbing head of a man. The eyes, partially obscured by a thicket of drenched hair that resembled rotten sea weed, were bulging with fear. Farnsworth raised the AK-47 and lined up the head in the sights. Then he turned the rifle away and looked astern, where the launch appeared out of the night. He fired from the hip, watching the projectiles riddle the water like a shower of pebbles as they hurtled toward the boat. The man at the helm ducked and the launch stopped.

"Serge, Serge!" Delisle shouted weakly. His wide eyes were still glued on the big man holding the rifle. Farnsworth raised the AK-47 to his shoulder and aimed it once again at Delisle. "I'm giving you life, motherfucker. Life! Start swimming!" Delisle began a feverish but awkward crawl toward the idling launch. Dropping the rifle, Farnsworth scrambled back into the cabin where the two inert forms lay. Seif's face was an ugly pudding of blood and bruises. Major Salam lay on the deck beside the *Red Dog*'s shattered transceiver. He had struck the unit with sufficient force to rupture the metal shroud and, as evidenced by the awkward tilt of his head, to snap his neck in the process. Drenched in perspiration and grunting and snuffling like a giant anthropoid, Farnsworth dragged the two bodies onto the deck. Then he pitched them into the water as Delisle, who had reached the side of the launch, and Boucher, who stood inert at the helm, watched helplessly.

"Here are two more, you Pepsi bastards! And tell the nigger I'll be back. Yeah, tell the nigger that Farnsworth's after his ass!" he shouted into the night.

DAWN HAD COME as a soupy gray glow, first rimming the eastern horizon, then spreading throughout the heavy clouds until it had illuminated the white-capped water in subdued, gloomy light. He had been pressing westward along Ontario's north shore for three hours by the time the sun had made its muted appearance. The winds and the seas were slowing the *Red Dog*'s pace, although it lightly planed the six-foot rollers in a series of graceful leaps, punctuated by an occasional collision with a wave top that sent sheets of spume lacing across Farnsworth's face. Trance-like, he had gunned his boat away from the killings and set a rough course for Toronto—for Gannet had said that the *Talon* had headed for that port. If he could somehow connect that vessel with Enderle's murder, it would add legitimacy to his entire involvement, including the violent deaths of the two Arabs. At the very least, it would delay the inevitable confrontation with LaStarza and certain arrest for a variety of offenses, probably including murder.

His brain was keyed to the deaths of the Arabs as precisely as a recording loop. He would play through the incident, then make a desperate attempt to divert his thinking, but would soon find his thought processes once more marching through a perfect re-creation of those deadly moments. His entire life in sports had been constructed around mock death. The tackle, accompanied by frenzied urgings from the crowd, the coaches, and his teammates, was a symbolic assassination of the runner. Every usable word in the thesaurus relating to violence, mayhem, and brutality had been a part of his football vocabulary for as long as he could recall. Coaches did not urge their players on to simple victory; they called for an orgiastic killing of the opponents. The fans sought nothing less than complete annihilation of the enemy, which the press reported with lurid verbs otherwise reserved for massacres and air raids. Sometimes the verbal hyperbole had escalated to dangerous reality. In his junior year at Hobart he had accidentally clipped Tony Harper, Alfred's excellent halfback, and had broken his right femur and badly torn his knee ligaments. Against Dallas in his first season with the Browns he had blitzed the Cowboy's young quarterback, Jackie Hartzel, and had sent him to the hospital with three broken ribs and a hairline skull fracture. Those incidents, plus uncounted others in which bodies had collapsed and bones had shattered, had been justified since his childhood as a part of the game. But the curses, the knuckles, the knees and elbows, the bared teeth, the crushed cartilage, were nothing—a springtime frolic—compared to the horrible spasm of true death he had experienced a few hours earlier.

He was alone on the expanse of grim water and sky, a single figure at the helm of the tiny boat. Visions of three dead men tumbled through his mind. First Enderle, his midriff torn away, life leaking out, then the tall Arab, his head bobbing, and his partner with the wrecked face. "Threes. Death comes in threes," he repeated aimlessly. He felt suspended from life, as absent from humanity as the waves that romped on the visible perimeters of his earth.

His wrists, scorched vermilion by the rope fire, burned with a steady, searing pain. His damaged leg was aching, and he wondered whether he had reinjured it during the scuffle with the Arabs. His eyes were burning from exhaustion and the steady gnawing of the wind. He wanted to go below and tend to his wounds and perhaps to sleep, but the rising seas gave him no respite. He began to hum a few jerky bars of a top-forty rock tune from his college days, although he could recall neither the title nor the words. The snippet of music rattled in and out of his consciousness until his thought processes were operating in parallel and he began to reconstruct the battle and the killings to the accompaniment of the idiotic music. For a while his mind conjured up snapshot exposures of other places and people: a favorite saloon in Cleveland; a girl's bedroom in San Francisco; a rusted Mercedes-Benz 190 diesel—his first automobile; the volleyball court at the New Salerno summer place; his father, twitchy, yet trimly buttoned down, in the locker room after his last Hobart game; the missed tackle—which permitted O. J. Simpson to break a game-winning 72-yard run against the Browns in the 1975 playoffs; his mother, tanned, athletic, imperious, her right hand eternally cupped around a martini glass; and Agnes or Sarah or whatever her name. He felt like a fool. Much of his life, he decided, had centered on a fascination with the trivial, and he recalled Gannet—that strange, intense little weed of a man—telling him that beneath his layers of muscle was a punky center. But perhaps now, with the wind and the pain rising and the stakes not sanitized by Astro-Turf and referees' whistles and flags, some of that soft core might be purged from him. He bent lower over the wheel, water slipstreaming along his temples from his squinting eyes, his perfect teeth bared in urgency, and pushed the throttles with the heel of his right hand to reconfirm that the *Red Dog* was running flat out.

THE CANADIAN quarters and dimes clanked into the pay phone at Smitty's Marina in Cobourg, Ontario. Farnsworth had interrupted his rush to Toronto with a stop in the placid old coaling port to refuel his boat and to call Landsman. After rumbling at top speed up the navigation channel and leaving an angry squad of fishermen to shake their fists at his wake, he had tied up at the gas dock and stumbled below to repair himself. After swabbing wads of margarine on his wrists and swilling a half quart of milk and a tepid can of Genesee—the only potable liquids on board besides water—he had surveyed the cabin damage by light of day. The steps were cracked and the galley table was tilted at an awkward angle. The radio transceiver, lying on the deck, looked as if it had been hit by a cement truck. On the galley seat was a black metallic object—an extra thirty-round magazine (called a "banana clip" by Vietnam veterans) for the AK-47, a last reminder of his former guard. Then, as a pudgy man with a pencil-line mustache sleepily duck-gaited his way down the dock, Farnsworth had leaped ashore, ordering the attendant to fill the tanks while he found a telephone.

"Zach? Zach? This is Pancho," he said into the phone.

"Pancho! Christ, man, where are you? We've been going crazy. Jarvis just got in, and he's been trying to figure out what in the hell . . . Are you with that broad?"

"No, no! Jesus, man, this is really bad. Really bad! That bitch was one of *them*. She . . ."

"Wait a minute. One of *them*? Who's them?"

"The FLQ, man. They're the guys who got Roy and because of her they almost got me." He paused, the emotion welling inside him. "Zach, it was them or me. Them or me!"

"What do you mean?"

"I'm in deep shit," he said, forcing the words. "They had me. They were going to kill me—I *know* that, Zach, they were going to kill me, they told me that."

"Who told you that—the FLQ?"

"Oh God, it's so complicated. Those Arabs—they've got some Arabs helping them—and when they got me on this island in the river they loaded me on the *Red Dog* and were going to take me and the boat and dump me in the lake. Then I got away. I killed two of them."

"I understand. It fits together," said Zach.

"Zach, for Christ's sake, do you hear me? Don't be so freakin' cool! I just said I killed *two* men, with my bare hands. That's murder!"

"Listen, baby, you may be in something a helluva lot bigger than anything you can imagine. I'll get Whitby on the other extension and you can explain it from the beginning and then we'll try to fit the thing together with what's happening in Canada."

"What's happening in Canada? I'm in Canada right now and everything's cool. Nothing's going on here."

"Maybe where you are, but we just heard a radio bulletin. A few minutes ago, about seven-thirty, the FLQ opened up rocket attacks on the Olympic Village in Montreal. It seems that they've made an attempt to kidnap McClelland, the Prime Minister, in Toronto. If that's true, you're not involved in murder, Pancho, you're in a goddamn war."

X

GANNET HAD NEVER
claimed to be a good driver. Automobiles were like most
machines to him—mysterious, capricious gadgets to be avoided
whenever possible. He hugged the slow lane as he steered the
rickety Ford Econ-O-Line van along the commuter-clogged Don
Valley Parkway. Unfamiliar with the sloppy transmission link-
age, he missed a shift to second while climbing a slope to the
rear parking area of the Parkside Inn and stalled the Ford. "I
hope you can shoot better than you can drive," said a voice from
the rear of the truck. "If we do this right, nobody will have to
shoot anything more than a few tear-gas bombs," Gannet replied
as he restarted the engine. Seven members of the FLQ—including Gannet, Agnes, and another young woman, a sallow-faced
student named Claire, in addition to Serge Boucher and three
lean, grim men dressed in business suits and carrying luggage—
arrived outside the inn at precisely six-thirty that morning. A
warm rain began to fall, filling the air with the soft hissing of
traffic heading toward the center of Toronto a few miles to the
west. The Parkside Inn was dug into a low hill overlooking the
green hummocks of Riverdale Park in the southeastern corner of

the city. It had been built, in bold contours of preformed concrete and native hardwoods, as a luxury-hotel complex during the mid-sixties, when Toronto had reached peak acceleration in its metamorphosis from a dowdy outpost of empire to one of the most sparkling cosmopolitan centers in the world. Within the Parkside Inn's elegant confines were first-class accommodations, superb restaurants, and a number of auditoriums and conference rooms. It was in one of these facilities, the Kitchener Suite, a compact, oak-paneled private dining room, that Canadian Prime Minister Alva McClelland, the abrupt, tough-talking Progressive-Conservative party leader from Calgary, was scheduled for an informal breakfast meeting with the Industrial Resources Council of Canada.

Gannet parked the van near a rear entrance of the Inn and went inside. Slowly, at broken intervals, to avoid the spectacle of so many people offloading from a single van at one time, the rest of the crew emerged and regrouped in Room 2403, which was situated on the twenty-fourth floor of the recently completed thirty-story tower annex. At eighteen minutes to seven, about half an hour before McClelland was expected, Gannet, using a passkey, entered 2403, finding a drowsy, quite attractive woman in her middle thirties sprawled in the king-size bed. "Get up! We need this room," he said officiously as he yanked back the heavy draperies. The woman muffled a scream as she burrowed deeper into the covers and watched Gannet with rising panic. He heard the toilet flush and spun away from the window, his Colt .22 Woodsman automatic aimed at the bathroom door. A tall, sandy-haired man with sloping shoulders and a thickening midriff, naked except for a pair of orange briefs, stepped into the room.

"What the hell?" he blurted, his eyes scanning from his fear-frozen companion to Gannet's pistol.

"Keep your mouth shut and you'll be all right. One sound and you're dead," Gannet said ominously.

"If it's money you want, take it and get out," the man answered.

"What I want you can't give me—other than total silence. Now get back in bed with your lady. And roll over on your bellies and keep your faces down."

Agnes entered the room while the man, moving in mechanical slow motion, as if his joints had been congealed in a Siberian cold snap, climbed into bed. Within minutes the rest of the crew arrived. Claire came in pushing a chambermaid's cart, loaded with linens, towels, soap, plastic cups, and cleaning gear. Edmund Ballot, a well-groomed printer from Montreal, appeared in a conservative business suit bought specifically for the operation. Régis Saint-Louis, a sometime television repairman and self-professed electronics expert, burst through the door carrying two large pieces of luggage; he immediately ducked into the bathroom with one still in his hand. The last man in was Michel Ostrand, a glowering Belgian who had served in the OAS and as a mercenary in the Congo and Angola before emigrating to Canada. "Goddamn ties, I'd go crazy having to wear one of these things," he said, snatching the knot away from his neck and loosening the top shirt button.

"Take care of them," Gannet said, waving his pistol in the direction of the rigidly prone couple. Michel Ostrand lifted a large roll of heating-duct tape from a suitcase and went to the bedside with Edmund Ballot. Moments later the man and the woman were bound and gagged with the tape. Régis Saint-Louis stepped out of the bathroom dressed in a bellhop's uniform—an outfit rented from a theatrical supply house—that closely resembled the livery of the Parkside Inn. Claire shed her raincoat to reveal a white chambermaid's uniform. Ostrand returned to his bag and removed five gas masks and five tear-gas grenades. He then passed a mask and a grenade to everyone except Agnes. Finally he took a pair of olive-drab flak jackets from the bottom of the suitcase and gave one to Gannet while donning the other himself.

There was a tense silence in the room, and the group stiffened each time the corridor echoed with the chatter of guests who were arriving for the Prime Minister's speech. Gannet checked his watch once again. At precisely seven-fifteen he pulled a walkie-talkie from inside his jacket. "Unit twenty, this is base. What is your position? Over." "This is unit twenty," the radio immediately crackled, to Gannet's simultaneous delight and surprise. "I have just dropped a fare at the Royal York, am heading for my pickup. Over." The voice was that of Raymond LeBarge, an expert helicopter pilot who, while speaking like a cab driver, had been communicating from the cockpit of Hugh Twitchell's missing Bell Jet Ranger cruising over Toronto's outer harbor three miles to the south. His terse message indicated he was in position to play his critical role within the next few minutes. "The fare will be on time, unit twenty," Gannet replied quickly.

With several minutes left as a cushion, the group stood stiffly around the room, smoking cigarettes, gazing out the window, and checking gear. Ostrand made a rather ostentatious display of jamming home the thirteen-shot magazine of his Browning 9mm Parabellum and leveling it on several mock targets, including the heads of the two bound and gagged bedmates. "Remember, we want him alive," Gannet warned firmly. "Hit him only if there is no chance of getting him out and after I give the order."

Ostrand returned a tight smile and slipped the big automatic back into its shoulder holster.

Gannet found himself fiddling nervously with the guests' paraphernalia spread on the bureau top. He picked up the man's wallet and lifted out his driver's license. It read: "Arnold L. Dressler, 4185 Split Rail Lane, Bloomfield Hills, Michigan." Probing further through the wallet, he found a business card: "Arnold L. Dressler, eastern regional sales manager, Silicone Products Division, International Mitex Chemical Corporation." A picture slipped out. It was a miniature print of a formal family portrait showing Dressler seated beside a pert, long-necked brunette with eyes that appeared to have no lids, and surrounded by four scrubbed children, two boys and two girls, all woodenly baring their teeth at the camera. Gannet took another look at the woman in bed. Her hair was frosted blond, and she seemed to be larger than Dressler's wife in the picture. The blonde's black leather purse lay nearby and Gannet dug through it until he dredged out her wallet. Her driver's license had been issued by the Province of Ontario and it revealed her name as "Laura Averill, 5000 Tower Square Apartments, Sheppard Avenue East, Scarborough, Ontario." "Hey, everybody," Gannet announced in an attempt to loosen the tension, "we have stumbled into a goddamn bourgeois den of iniquity. Mr. Arnold L. Dressler, on the left, has been screwing around with Miss Laura Averill, on the right, while poor Mrs. Dressler sits around in Michigan and tends the home fires." A taut riffle of laughter filled the room.

"Claire, Edmund, Régis, it's time," Gannet said moments later. "Remember the plans. Stay cool and it will all work. Long live the Quebec revolution," he added solemnly as they slipped out. Claire, pushing her cart, stationed herself near the entrance of the Kitchener Suite, while Ballot and Saint-Louis moved in the opposite direction, where they would pose as a departing guest and bellhop near the elevator doors through which McClelland was to appear. Moments later Agnes DePere walked down an adjacent corridor to join Serge Boucher, who was posing as a repairman working on a service elevator. "You're in deeper than I wanted to get you. I'm sorry," Gannet said to her before she left.

"It's funny, when I left New York, I had this strange feeling that it would be a long time before I returned," she said in a muted, flat-toned voice as she turned away from him.

Gannet and Ostrand remained in the room with the door cracked in order to hear the flurry of activity in the lobby which would signal the Prime Minister's arrival. Ostrand slipped on his gas mask and, turning toward Dressler, saw their captive staring at him, his eyes glittering with hate. Once again Ostrand aimed the Browning at him. Dressler turned away and pressed his nose into the fluffy hair of his bed partner. Gannet's watch read seven twenty-nine. The time had come. It had been said many times that, if nothing else, Alva Garnet McClelland was the most punctual Prime Minister Canada ever had.

He liked to consider himself a self-made man, although, in truth, his grandfather, Isaiah McClelland, had left a sizable family fortune accumulated from Calgary real estate. Nevertheless, it had been his own energetic, sometimes ruthless business enterprises—McClelland Northwest Drilling, Ltd., McClelland-Durban Refining, Ltd., Alberta Petroleum Associates, Ltd., and a massive parent company, McClelland International Holdings, Ltd.—that had transformed him from a prosperous western businessman to a tycoon of the first magnitude. Alva McClelland was a late-comer to the Canadian national political scene. A distaste for Pierre Elliott Trudeau and his Liberal policies as Prime Minister prompted him first to run for Parliament from his suburban Calgary riding, then to reach for control of the Progressive-Conservative party. His fierce, business-oriented puritanism, along with his denunciations of government paternalism, welfare schemes, and bureaucracy, helped him displace the old Tory leader, Robert Stanfield—a gaunt man whose lofty goals had been shrouded in cloaks of dull caution. When the Trudeau government fell, its support washed away by a tide of inflation, unemployment, persistent welfare scandals, western resentment over natural-resources policies and rising bilingualism in government, and a general irritation over the Prime Minister's increasingly caustic and arrogant style, Alva McClelland became Prime Minister. He immediately assaulted the job with self-righteous, head-butting Anglo-Saxon vigor. His tight-money measures, coupled with severe price controls and limited price supports for industry and agriculture, had a reining effect on inflation, and his stiff reforms within the welfare bureaucracy cut down the abuses. But unemployment, especially in the industrialized eastern provinces, persisted. To labor rumblings in Quebec and Ontario, McClelland reacted with harsh words. Much of his angry rhetoric was directed at the French Canadians, who, he implied, were using their ethnic and cultural frustrations as an excuse for their province's economic and industrial difficulties. While he did not dare to denounce publicly the government's policy of bilingualism in courts of law and at all levels of the civil infrastructure, he made it clear in private interviews that French Canada would remain a weak and subordinate area until it shed what he referred to as "archaic regionalism" and made a complete link with the Anglo-Saxon heartland of the nation. In a speech to Parliament made shortly after taking office, he created an uproar in Quebec by admonishing the French Canadians in the name of what he called "the obligations of equality." Before Quebec could fully realize its potential, he said, it would have to match the concessions granted by English Canada with a greater sense of national loyalty.

It was difficult for McClelland to conceal his revulsion for French Canada and what he considered to be its shiftless, whining population. Although he had never articulated the source of his prejudice (like most western Canadians, he had spent his boyhood in complete isolation from French Canadians, believing them to be a jovial, song-singing pack of wood choppers, rollicking somewhere in the eastern forests), it dated from the opening of World War II. Canada had entered the hostilities in 1940, a week after Great Britain, and a full-scale mobilization had been mounted. McClelland—then twenty-one—joined the Army and made his first trip East, to be billeted on the grounds of the famed Canadian National Exhibition on Toronto's lakeshore. There, in a vast temporary camp that had been frantically set up among the old pavilions to process the outpouring of volunteers, McClelland first became aware that this was to be a fight for the English Canadians. Only a few

"Frenchies" had appeared, and as the war progressed, and after he and his artillery unit had been transferred to England, the absence of the Quebeckers became a national scandal. Encouraged by such leaders as Camille Houde, the mayor of Montreal, the French Canadians balked at fighting in what they considered to be an English war. Many consented to join the military forces but refused to sail overseas to aid the King and country of the English Canadians. A similar, even more truculent position had been taken by the French Canadians during the conscription crisis of 1917, but twice during World War II, in 1942 and 1944, the issue of compulsory military service became so heated that it strained national unity. Houde and others went to jail for their intransigence, and English Canadians, especially those in uniform, regarded their refusal to serve as out-and-out treason. Those "zombies," as the French Canadians were called, inspired nearly as much hatred in Alva McClelland as did the "Jerrys" who were goose-stepping across Europe. It was a hatred he had never let die.

EDMUND BALLOT and Régis Saint-Louis stood in rigid silence as the lobby indicator recorded the elevator's steady climb from ground level toward the twenty-fourth floor. Saint-Louis reached inside his bellhop's jacket, seeking for the last time the comforting contours of the two tear-gas bombs stuffed in his belt. Ballot took one final glance down the shadowy corridor, where he could see Claire at the other end, bent over her service cart, rummaging through a pile of sheets and towels. The elevator arrived, a muffled gong preceding the hushed separation of its doors. Suddenly he was there, confronting Ballot and Saint-Louis with his intense stare. A starched public smile was on his face. Ballot's back stiffened in the intimidating presence of the Prime Minister. McClelland nodded affably to the pair as he stepped into the lobby, followed by four other men. Two of them—rather stern, chunky men in dark suits—

Ballot identified as McClelland's personal Royal Canadian Mounted Police bodyguards, while the other pair—both prosperous, well-polished middle-aged men, appeared to be part of the greeting delegation of the Industrial Resources Council.

Briskly leading the way, Alva McClelland angled away from the elevator and headed down the long hallway toward the closed doors of the Kitchener Suite. Stepping in behind to block a retreat out of the corridor, Ballot and Saint-Louis yanked out their gas masks and their tear-gas canisters and watched Claire, perhaps twenty yards distant, who calmly stood her ground, still fussing with her cart. She was directly in their path to the suite, and she waited until McClelland was almost at mid-corridor, a few paces beyond Room 2403. Then she reached into a tray containing a collection of cleaning solutions and lifted out a pair of tear-gas grenades. Triggering them, she turned toward the approaching group and flung them down the hallway. The first one exploded near McClelland's feet while the second unleashed its choking vapors nearer to her, filling the entire space between them with an impenetrable barrier of gas.

McClelland and his party watched this deft, split-second assault unfold like a startled group of antelope. They froze in semi-crouches, wide-eyed, brows stretched, jaws loose, as the bombs blossomed before them. They retreated to escape the gases, only to see Ballot and Saint-Louis heaving another pair of canisters into the corridor. Coughing and gagging, the two bodyguards tried to unleash their weapons, but the agonizing urge to protect their eyes and throats was too great. Their knees buckled and they reeled against the walls in convulsions of discomfort.

Gannet and Ostrand, shrouded in gas masks, leaped out of Room 2403 exactly five seconds after the bombs had burst outside. They stepped into the gray, opaque fumes and shouldered their way into the midst of the four reeling bodies. Ostrand, sighting one of the bodyguards still groping inside his coat, slugged him smartly on the crown with his Browning, but otherwise there was no violence. Gannet found McClelland in the smoke. He was slumped against the wall, his thick frame bent slightly, his knees curling against his midriff. They pounced on him and dragged him like a wounded bear down the hall toward Claire. She appeared out of the smoke, her curly wads of brown hair flaring from behind her gas mask. In her hand was a long-barreled Harrington & Richardson revolver. She was responsible for blocking any aid that might come from the Kitchener Suite, but the big oak doors remained closed during the entire assault. As Gannet and the other men reached her with their helpless burden, she followed them to the service elevator being held by Agnes and Serge Boucher.

Gannet heard a loud, angry shout for help coming from the smoky corridor as the elevator doors shut and Boucher sent the car plummeting downward. They ripped off their masks and took a look at their quarry, still semi-conscious, lying on the floor. He was a larger man than Gannet had expected him to be, heavier through the shoulders and with rougher features than his photographs indicated. "Good God, I can't believe it. The whole thing couldn't have worked better," he said. "We've got him. This is the beginning. The beginning of a new Quebec!" He looked at his watch. It was seven thirty-eight. "The rest of it has started too," he said grimly, looking directly at Agnes. She returned his gaze blankly, registering no emotion whatsoever.

THREE MINUTES EARLIER, a foursome of golfers teeing up for the 160-yard third hole of the Bathurst Hills Golf Club, in the lush residential region north of the city, had watched in silence as a stake-body delivery truck creaked to a stop on nearby Finch Avenue. A tarpaulin was flipped back, revealing what appeared to be a pair of immense bullet tips glinting in the muted light. Within seconds a high-intensity hissing, like that of a giant blow torch, rose out of the truck and the bullet-shaped objects leaped into the sky with their tails trailing long gouts of fire. Letting their five-irons dribble out of their limp hands, the four golfers gaped as the rockets gained speed and burrowed upward into the cloud cover. When only the hollow rumble of the propulsion units remained, they turned toward the truck, which disappeared behind a shaggy stockade of sugar maples lining the fairway. Two of the groups agreed that it was a red Chevrolet. Another maintained that it was an old orange Fargo. The fourth was able to recall nothing but the noise and fire of the rockets.

A few seconds later one of the SAM-10's fell out of the skies and impacted in a wooded corner of Queen's Park, a few hundred feet short of the Ontario Buildings of Parliament. Aside from obliterating a bed of geraniums and knocking over a lonely undergraduate jogger from the adjacent University of Toronto campus, it did no damage.

The other SAM also missed its mark, overshooting the twin crescent skyscrapers of the new City Hall and blasting into the southwest corner of the low, bunker-like outer buildings. Stone fasciae were flung into the air, an expanse of glass was shattered, and a dozen elaborate offices were pulverized, but no one had been near that section of the building. Aside from a retired Royal Canadian Air Force major who was cut on the forehead by a shard of glass while walking his Welsh corgi in nearby Nathan Philips Square, there were no injuries. But the twin explosions had been perfectly timed. Alarms had been registered and all available police and fire units were racing toward the center of Toronto several minutes before any bulletins of trouble concerning the Prime Minister were received.

At precisely the same time that the twin rockets lifted away from the stake-body truck on Finch Avenue, similar units were released from the four bases surrounding Montreal. Three warheads rained down on the Olympic Village, killing twenty-nine athletes, primarily from the Burmese, Greek, and Argentinian teams. Another six rockets exploded against the complex of municipal buildings in the center of the city, with the stock-exchange tower suffering particularly heavy damage. Although they did not understand why Major Salam and Seif were absent, the three men manning the St. Clet installation carried out their mission shorthanded, unleashing an initial volley of two rockets at the Dorval airport main terminal (one of which hit an Eastern Airlines air-freight warehouse, while the other landed harmlessly on a runway perimeter road) and two more random shots in the general direction of the hated Hampstead and Westmount suburbs (one of the missiles landed in a street, shattering a pair of parked cars; the second scored a direct hit on the home of a prominent banker, killing the entire family of five). Within moments after these detonations in Toronto and Montreal, the inhabitants of Canada's two greatest cities were electrified by communal spasms of fear and uncertainty. And at that point they were still unaware that their Prime Minister was locked in a dusty service elevator, being stripped of his clothes.

"A PERFECT FIT!" Gannet exclaimed as Edmund Ballot dived into Alva McClelland's exquisitely tailored blue worsted suit coat. He had already yanked on the Prime Minister's pants, which were slightly large in the waist but fit him nearly as well as they did their original wearer. Ballot had been chosen for the job in part because of his extremely close resemblance in height and build to McClelland. Ballot buttoned the coat at the waist, then pulled a stocking cap over his head, completely obscuring his face. Saint-Louis and Ostrand, still encased in their gas masks, moved to his side and jammed their pistols against his ribs. The elevator stopped on the sixth floor, and Gannet, Serge, and Agnes piled out. Gannet turned to his comrades still in the car and, as the doors slipped shut, shouted, "For Quebec!" Then he and the others rushed for the fire escape and the waiting Econ-O-Line van.

Ballot, Ostrand, and Saint-Louis left the elevator on the main level, which was one floor above the ground. They appeared in the lobby, greeted by the muffled screams of two elderly women in expensive fur coats. Four uniformed Toronto policemen barged up the wide stairs to confront them. Ostrand had his left arm looped around Ballot's throat, while Saint-Louis had his weapon shoved against his supposed victim's temple. The policemen rattled to a stop and stood in a tight formation blocking the masked trio. Ostrand said nothing, but waved his Browning in the policemen's direction, ordering them to stand aside. Outside, through the tinted-glass windows, he saw a wide, grassy courtyard. There, perched like a strange insect, was the Jet Ranger, its monster blades pawing at the air in a slow idle.

One of the main elevators opened and a pair of men appeared. Saint-Louis recognized one as part of the Prime Minister's personal bodyguard. His eyes were a bubbly red and his face was flushed from the tear gas. In his hand was an automatic. The other, a smaller, more pompous man in a dark suit, appeared to be a civil servant. "My God! The Prime Minister!" he shouted when he saw Ballot's clothing. "Stand away! Give them room!" The four policemen stiffened with shock at the identification and within seconds spread away from the stairway, warily moving back to let the trio pass. More lawmen were in their way on the ground floor, but the little civil servant, scuttling along in their wake, sounded repeated alarms about the prisoner's identity and a wide path was opened. Once outside, they saw and heard more police cars, their lights pulsing crazily and their sirens moaning through the mist, converging on the Parkside Inn. All eyes were focused on the three men marching jerkily toward the Jet Ranger, but not a single move was made to impede their progress.

When they reached the helicopter, Saint-Louis roughly boosted Ballot into the rear seat, then leaped aboard himself. Ostrand turned to make one final, menacing gesture at the milling crowd, then pounced into the cockpit as Raymond

LeBarge throttled the Jet Ranger straight upward into the gray soup.

"Not even in my wildest dreams would I have thought this would work so well," Gannet said as he rolled the battered Ford south on the Don Valley Parkway. In the opposite lane, he counted two police cruisers screaming north toward the Parkside Inn. A khaki-colored Jeep was spotted heading in the same direction. "Aha, the Army's out!" he said jauntily. "If the rockets did their work, the Army will have more to do than hunt for their poor lost Prime Minister," Boucher said from the back of the van. Beside him was Claire, still dressed in her chambermaid's outfit. In the forward passenger's seat sat Agnes, stonily watching the road unfold beneath them. Gannet turned toward her repeatedly, but she avoided his eyes. This troubled him slightly but nothing could diminish the triumph of the moment, the knowledge that all of Toronto, all of Ontario, all of Anglo Canada for that matter, was mobilizing to pursue the helicopter in which they believed their precious Prime Minister was now being transported toward a secret prison. How perfectly that ruse had worked, how flawlessly Ostrand, Saint-Louis, and Ballot must have carried out their act as Claire rode the elevator to the basement level and shoved her service cart out a back door and into the open rear doors of the van—a difficult trip, considering that she had been pushing the additional 190-pound bulk of Alva McClelland, who had been wheeled, bound and gagged and inelegantly dressed in his underwear, out of the Parkside Inn in the dirty-laundry receptacle of her cart.

"How is our guest of honor?" Gannet asked after he turned west on Lake Shore Boulevard, headed toward the docks.

Boucher lifted away the pile of soiled towels and sheets and gazed in at McClelland, whose stocky form had been rolled into a wad of arms and legs by the contours of the bag. His lids were half closed, as though the combination of the gas and the trauma of his capture had put him in a mild stupor. "He seems to be resting comfortably, although perhaps he can't breathe very well under all these sheets," Boucher said.

"Leave him under there," Gannet said. "We've been stifled under his dirty laundry long enough. Let him breathe some of ours for a change."

FARNSWORTH propped
himself on the bucking bridge of the *Red Dog* as it pounded
across the angry waves. Spray seared his face and the rain
slashing out of the grimy clouds drenched his body. His leg was
aching horribly, but he was at last engaged in an elemental
brand of competition he understood. For the moment it was the
power of the lake, rolling out the mists at him in legions of
murderous combers, their tops smeared with evil licks of
whitecaps and spume. He smashed his boat against them with
abandon. When they were beaten aside—as they surely would
be, for the seas and the winds were not slowing him very
much—he would seek some kind of resolution to his troubles in
Toronto. He had no idea where he would begin, except that he
was now sure that the *Talon* was berthed somewhere in the
city's relatively small waterfront. It was likely that by the time he
arrived Jarvis Whitby would have obtained some clues as to the
ship's ownership, and that would at least give him some anchor
of fact from which to start. Based on the brief snatches of news
he had received in Cobourg, it sounded as if the operation that
the nigger had made veiled references to was under way, and if

he was able to connect the ship with the FLQ, it might lead him out of the labyrinth of circumstantial guilt in which he was trapped.

In the distance he could see the towers of the Toronto skyline probing above the horizon. Their sheer walls were dappled with lights shining against a smudge of black weather in the western sky. As he pushed the *Red Dog* closer, the great buildings seemed to rise straight out of the water, forming an imposing barrier of concrete and glass along the lakefront. The boldness of the place, with its tallest peaks lost in the soft underbellies of the rain clouds, the endless steps and tiers of its offices alive with illumination, its parkways swarming with automobiles, made Farnsworth feel like a primitive man rafting in from a savage, primeval sea toward the most advanced and civilized metropolis in the universe.

He rounded the four range lights and the red navigation buoy off Gibraltar Point on Centre Island and turned into the slightly calmer waters of Humber Bay. Dead ahead lay the vivid, architectural flourishes of Ontario Place. During their phone conversation at Cobourg, Zach had told him to make for the marina at Ontario Place; he had said that he knew people there and they would make sure that he got a berth. Whitby had added that he should dock the boat and not move—that his situation would doubtlessly clarify itself as the FLQ crisis came into better focus and that independent action on his part would only confuse matters. Farnsworth had given perfunctory assent to this order, but he had known full well he would never carry it out. Too much had happened to trigger his instincts for reaction for him to become a passive witness, hoping that other men's actions might resolve themselves in his favor.

The harbor at Ontario Place was protected by a pair of ancient lake-freighter hulks, their innards filled with cement, which formed a long, curving breakwater. Beyond the marina lay two man-made islands, each meticulously landscaped and dotted with lagoons surrounded by walking paths and a scattering of outdoor cafés, shops, and restaurants. Dominating the complex, and connecting the two islands like a futuristic bridge, was a massive grouping of five steel buildings mounted on giant stanchions rising out of an inner bay. These exhibition halls, with their starkly functional webs of reinforcement cables and girders and open catwalks, had a decidedly industrial look about them, as if they were originally intended as offshore drilling rigs or oil refineries and had been converted to concert halls and display galleries. The severe angularity of these structures was softened by the proximity of the Cinesphere, a massive steel ball—reputed to hold one of the world's largest movie screens—covered with a geometric netting of external tubing for structural rigidity. Below these bold and compelling buildings, which stood in bleached-white contrast to the sullen morning, spread the marina: a network of neat aluminum finger docks crowded with acres of masts and bulky yacht superstructures. As Farnsworth idled the *Red Dog* around the inert bow of one of the old freighters and into the marina bay, he could see little sign of activity. A few people were strolling along the covered catwalks of the exhibition halls, while a man, bundled in chrome-yellow rain gear, forged through the rain, head down, along one of the piers.

Farnsworth tied up along an inner dock, between a darkly varnished yawl and a pudgy, wooden-hulled Pacemaker cabin cruiser. The marina office, its glass walls opaqued by the sluicing rain and condensation, appeared deserted. The whole place was silent, save for the moaning wind and the incessant chatter of sailboat halyards rattling against bare masts. Someone approached, shrouded in an olive-drab parka. The figure was asexual, but its movements were feminine and graceful. Farnsworth limped along the dock and began securing a spring line. He looked up to see the proud, softly featured face of a young girl peering out from under the water-soaked lip of the parka.

"You must be Farnsworth," she said above the wind.

"Huh?" he sputtered. "How did you know . . . ?"

"We got a call that you were coming . . . although with the gale warnings on the lake, we're kind of surprised to see you." She turned to examine the *Red Dog*. "Your poor boat! It must have been pretty bad out there. And your wrists! Good heavens, man, what's happened?"

He stood up from the cleat and rubbed the water from his eyes. "I've had some trouble," he said.

"You ought to see a doctor about those burns," she said.

"Not now." He paused. "What do you know about this place? This harbor?"

"Well, quite a bit, I suppose. I've lived here all my life, sailed around here, worked at this marina, that sort of thing. Why? What do you want to know?"

"I may need some help."

"I can see that," she said, smiling easily.

"No, I mean it. There's some heavy stuff going on."

"You mean . . . the Prime Minister . . . and the rockets?" she asked hesitantly.

"Yeah, maybe. What exactly has happened? I was out on the lake and everything . . ."

"It's pretty bad. Terrorists . . . the FLQ, apparently . . . got McClelland at the Parkside Inn. Somehow they carted him off in a stolen helicopter. But now the news reports some fishermen have found what they think is the helicopter used in the kidnapping . . . up in the Lake of Bays region, about eighty miles from here, in the bush near a little village called Lewisham. They saw it drop out of the clouds and land in a field. Four guys jumped out. A little black truck came out of some nearby woods, they all got in, and off it roared. But there was no sign of McClelland. All very strange. Right now I guess every policeman and soldier in Ontario is rushing up there. There's been no word otherwise. Oh yes, I guess you know they shot two rockets or something at the City Hall and the Houses of Parliament earlier this morning—about the time the kidnapping took place—and the CBC says that Montreal has been hit pretty hard—bridges out, some people killed in the Olympic Village—and the FLQ has made some kind of proclamation claiming to be behind the whole thing. People thought they'd try something around the Olympics, but nothing like this. The French Canadians hate McClelland. I'd be surprised if they haven't killed him already."

"What's your name?" Farnsworth asked abruptly.

"Susan . . . Susan Pritchard," she replied hesitantly.

"Listen, Susan," he said with the rain streaming through his soaked mat of hair and spilling down his wide forehead. "Right now I'm so screwed up I don't really know much of anything, except that I'm trying to sort out a few things that may fit into this FLQ deal."

"Like what?"

"Like where I might find a yacht I'm looking for."

"Look," she said, "it's insane for us to stand here in this downpour. Let me get our first-aid kit while you get out of the rain. I'll be back in a second." She ran toward the marina office. He stood there for a moment, watching her easy, graceful steps, then hobbled back aboard the *Red Dog* and tried to straighten up the rubble of the main cabin before she returned.

"Farnsworth, who are you?" Susan Pritchard asked as she finished dressing his wrists with gobs of antibiotic burn salve and protective bandaging.

"Me? What do you mean?" It had been a long time since he encountered someone who didn't know who he was and what he did.

"I mean, *who* are you? What do you do? Where do you come from?" she asked, her clear, level eyes watching him closely.

He took it for granted that everyone knew about him and his football exploits. This attitude was not a great expression of ego; it was merely a fact that he could not remember his last encounter with someone who did not treat him with the deferential awe accorded an American pro-football star. "I play football. Pro football."

"I thought you might do something like that. Your size and everything. You play for the Argos?"

"The *Argos!*" he said huffily. "Jesus, no. I'm with the Cleveland Browns. Don't you ever read the newspapers?"

"Now don't get all defensive about it, Farnsworth," she said casually. "This is Canada, remember. Another country. Not an American colony. Your Cleveland . . . whatevers . . . and your pro football are hardly household words here. And frankly, if the game is anything like ours, I think it's a hopeless bore. A lot of people bashing their heads against one another. Not for me, Farnsworth." She told him that straight out, in an easy, relaxed way that he liked.

"What can I say? They pay me a lot of money to bash my head and I think it's a gas. So I do it." He shrugged. "What's your thing?"

"I'm in my third year at the University of Toronto. Majoring in international relations. That's the way I bash my head. O.K., now that we've completed all the formalities, exactly what's your problem? Your boat looks as if it's got bullet holes in it, which isn't what we normally expect from our tourist traffic, and you, at the risk of tarnishing your football hero's image, are a mess."

"I've been running on no sleep, spinning my wheels, getting deeper and deeper into a thing I don't really understand."

"And you think it has something to do with the FLQ?"

"Yeah. I'm sure."

"Whose side are you on?"

"Christ, I'm not on any side. That's not the point. Somebody —Frenchmen and Arabs and I don't know who else—killed a buddy of mine and damn near trashed me too."

"Maybe you better call the police."

"That wouldn't be too smart, under the circumstances."

"Farnsworth, you're talking in riddles. Why not start at the beginning and tell me what this whole thing is about."

Inside the *Red Dog*, with the rain pelting against the overhead, he tried to summarize his situation. He told her everything, except for the killing of the two Libyans. "So you see, I'm sure this guy I talked with on that island—that little rat in the glasses—is mixed up in what's going on with the Prime Minister and all that. I can't prove anything, and I sure as hell can't walk into some police station and tell them that story. It just doesn't add up when you say it out loud. But if I can locate that boat, I've at least got a positive identity of *something*. From there I may be able to connect it with the FLQ or the guys who grabbed me. It's a long shot, but I really don't have much choice." He paused. "You think that's all a batch of shit?" he asked.

"No. I believe you," she said flatly.

"If that *Talon* is here in Toronto, how can we find it?"

"I'm not sure. I'll have to ask around. As a last resort, we can try the marinas and yacht clubs. There aren't that many. By the way, have you checked in with customs?"

"I didn't even know I had to," he said.

"Typical American," she gibed gently, "thinks he can come into Canada as if he owned the place. You'll have to get that done, or you'll be in even more trouble. But right now you ought to get some sleep. You doze for a few hours, and I'll try to find out a few things."

"O.K. But first I've got to make one call. C'mon, I'll go back to the office with you."

She slipped ashore in quick, exact motions while he stepped heavily, favoring his bad leg. "Good God, Farnsworth, you *are* a wreck," she said as she watched him clump, in awkward, gate-legged steps, across the dock.

He called Whitby and Landsman from a small office crowded with a dozen young men and women marina attendants dressed in red-and-blue-striped crew shirts. As his collect call was being delayed by an irritatingly persistent busy signal, he watched Susan Pritchard remove her parka and enter into a conversation with two other young women.

She was spare, with sloping, graceful shoulders and straight hair the color of polished walnut. Leaning against a desk with her arms folded and her legs crossed in a mildly boyish posture, she exhibited a breezy lack of primness that excited Farnsworth. Her face was dominated by large, limestone-tinted eyes and a wide, well-proportioned mouth. Her neck and her nose, both of which were too short, disqualified her as a woman of classic beauty, but this was compensated for by a lithe vitality and an open, almost brash self-confidence.

Finally he heard the quick, crisp tones of Jarvis Whitby on the line. After his location and general status had been accounted for, Whitby began speaking in rapid-fire sentences, clicking off banks of data about the situation. "First of all, LaStarza is pissed off. He knows you're gone, and he was raving about all sorts of crazy charges he was going to lay on you. Then this Canadian thing blew open. Now he's beginning to consider the fact that your trawler story may not have been a lie after all. The guy is sore, but if we can make any sort of connection between Roy's death and the FLQ, I think he'll buy it. I'm not particularly worried about that, but trying to sort anything out in this confusion is damn near impossible. According to the news reports, Montreal is in a state of siege. Those crazy bastards have blown out half the bridges, and they're hitting the city with long-range rockets and mortars from close in. That means we'll have to wait for things to settle down before we can even get there to help. Zach was going to drive over this morning but the border's been closed. They turned him back at the bridge. Right now this thing could go anywhere."

"Anybody know exactly what the FLQ is trying to do?"

"Well, you've got to figure it's a move to split Quebec away from Canada, and the news people are speculating they're going to use McClelland as some kind of bargaining pawn. It's been over three hours since they took him and nobody's heard a word. They found the chopper, but no McClelland."

"So that leaves us about where we were."

"Basically, except that I did get hold of Randy Starkweather in Washington—my friend at the Maritime Commission—and he's really thrown himself into the job of finding the *Talon*. Been on the phone all morning, poring through shipping registries, talking to underwriters and brokers all over the damn world. He's dug up a full history of the thing. *Lloyd's Register* and all that. Lemme see here, according to my notes, the *Talon* was built in 1959 in Southampton, England. She served as a commercial North Sea trawler for five years before she was bought by some guy named Bingham—an Englishman—who had her converted into a long-range, seagoing yacht. The job was done by an outfit named Ryder & Lycoming in Yarmouth. He called her the *Lucy Starr*. God, guys give boats stupid names. Anyway, Bingham died in 1968 and the ship was sold through a Miami broker to a guy in Fort Lauderdale. His name I don't have right here, but the ship was renamed *Orion II*. According to Starkweather, it was resold in 1971 to a Canadian named Joseph Regner, who is her present owner, as far as we know. Oh yeah, she's ninety-eight feet long, has accommodations for about eight passengers and six crew, and she's powered by a pair of 525-horsepower Mercedes-Benz diesels, in case you care. Now here's what may be our only usable information. The *Talon's* home port is supposed to be Toronto. The Royal Ontario Boat Club is where she ought to be tied up if she's there. That's very exclusive, says Zach, and you'd have trouble just rolling in and checking out one of their members. But Zach knows a guy who knows a guy—one of those deals—and I think we can get some information about this Regner and then go to the police."

"And in the meantime I sit on my ass here in a goddamn monsoon," Farnsworth said testily.

"What'd you have in mind, Dick Tracy? Your last big investigation damn near had you sucking up sand on the bottom of the lake. Let's let the pros handle this one. After all, we've got too much at stake."

"Like what?"

"Like your career. Like the Ice Man commercials, like a lot of

other deals I've got in mind. You can't just throw that all away
. . . not on some whacky thing like this."

"Roy's death was a whacky thing?"

"No, of course not. But it's too big for you. It's out of your
hands. Just cool it until you hear from me. Don't go running off
half cocked in something that can affect your earning power for
the rest of your life."

"Screw it."

"What?"

"Screw it. I'm going to find that goddamn boat. Then I'm
going to kick some ass."

"Pancho, I'm telling you, stay where you are. You'll just mess
things up again. If you'd used your head with that broad we'd
about have this thing cleared up by now."

"I'll take care of that too."

"You're just pissed off because you bought her full program.
Which didn't make much sense from the start, by the way."

"I don't remember you having much to say about it."

"Oh sure, I figured there was something weird about her,"
Whitby said airily.

"Your ass! You flipped out just as bad as me. Don't give me
that bullshit, Whitby."

"I'm telling you, I figured she was a phony."

"Listen, Whitby, I'm not going to waste any more time. I
don't give a crap one way or the other about how you had the
broad figured. I'm just telling you I've had it with this entire
deal. A lot of stuff has gone down since I saw you. There's
another whole scene out here, Whitby, and it goes a long way
beyond that asshole world of pro football and deodorant
commercials we live in. You sit there. You call the cops. You
pull some strings. You do all the sweet talking. Me, I'm going to
get that boat."

Farnsworth rammed the phone into its cradle and looked
toward Susan Pritchard. "You ready?" he growled.

"For what?" she said uncertainly.

"To find the *Talon*."

"I thought you were going to catch some sleep."

He scowled at her, then moved toward the door, saying, "Think anything you want. I'm finding that boat."

She glanced at her two friends, who stood in stony silence, watching the giant, water-shiny man limp away from them. Susan Pritchard smiled, shrugged her shoulders, and turned to follow him outside.

XII

GANNET LET the wind sweep the cigarette ashes over the rail and across the pasty-gray, rain-spattered water. Beneath him, the *Talon*'s twin diesels transmitted muted thumpings from deep inside the hull and sent faint oscillations riffling through the deck plates. She was headed toward the lake, idling across the inner bay of the harbor toward the Western Gap, which led to Ontario's open waters. He was slouched against the starboard quarter railing, smoking fitfully and watching the concrete mountains of downtown Toronto pass into the mists. The rain was warm, and the storm seemed to be easing, but he gave no thought to the weather. His mind was on other things.

Agnes DePere came out of a door leading from the salon and stopped at his side. She laid her forearms on the railing and loosely clasped her hands. Finally she asked, "Can you tell me what's the matter?"

He paused for a moment, his eyes fixed on a slimy scrap of driftwood that seesawed through the *Talon*'s wake. "I don't really know, but when my fires ought to be burning their brightest, they seem to be going out. It's a weird feeling," he said softly.

"For as long as I've known you, your dreams have centered on a moment like this," she said.

"Dead men are littering my dreams," he answered, snapping the cigarette over the side.

"You knew men would have to die in a war of liberation."

"Sure, the idea was of no consequence to me, but somehow it was purer and cleaner in my mind—a straight and honest fight with our enemies. There's a difference between guerrilla warfare and terrorism, and I'm afraid our fight is rapidly degenerating into raw, blind destruction."

"Are things going badly in Montreal?"

"It's hard to say. The reports are confused, except that we know the Army has overwhelmed the rocket batteries at St. Amable and La Plaine. Papineau—you remember him, the short, bearded welder with the crooked teeth who was in command at La Plaine—made a final radio transmission that they were firing their last four rockets at random toward the center of the city. According to the CBC, a mental-health clinic and a sportswear factory have been hit—perhaps by Papineau's idiot barrage. A lot of harmless men and women have died."

"Still, a few lives for the revolution . . ."

"That only makes sense if you can choose the lives."

"This is a bad time to have second thoughts."

"It's not that I believe any less in the cause of Quebec. I'll never rest until we possess a free, independent state. It's just that now I'm having doubts about my own motivations. Am I in this thing to compensate for my own feelings of inadequacy? I wanted to keep this above the brutality of the Vietcong and Al Fatah. I felt we could isolate our opponents and leave the masses on the sidelines. That's why the taking of McClelland seemed like such a master stroke. With that kind of bargaining power, we might be able to pull the whole thing off with only a few shots being fired. Instant checkmate. Then it began to escalate, and others wanted the rockets and the mortars, and the attacks on the Olympic Village—where every victim was a noncombatant. How can we say that what we bring the people will be any better than what they have? In some ways we've already begun to corrupt what little power we've gained."

"Yet, I've never seen Pierre so exhilarated," she said.

"I told you, there's more than one Pierre Boutette. Revolutionary movements attract strange men, and unless you're careful, the psychotics ascend to power. After all, the National Socialists were a grand coalition of the mentally unbalanced in Germany."

"Yes, but they were fascists."

"The right wing has no monopoly on madmen."

"It's strange, but I thought he was a charming man when I met him. In fact, I saw him a few times in New York," she said.

He turned to look at her for a moment, his face impassive. He said nothing, then returned his gaze to the water. "Don't feel bad. He's charmed a lot of people," he said after a long pause.

"You know, for as long as I've known him, he's protected himself from me. Who is he? Does anyone know who he really is?"

Gannet pulled his glasses from his face and wiped the fogged lenses with a handkerchief. Shorn of the thick rims, his face took on a look of pubescent innocence. He rubbed the glasses clean, then used both hands to position them carefully on his ears. "He's a Frenchman by birth. He claims a noble ancestry from Brittany, although I don't know his real family name. He was deeply involved with the OAS until he was forced to leave France several months before Algeria got its independence. Then he spent some time in Central Africa working with various mercenary units. He sneaked into Canada in 1968 with a forged Portuguese passport and appeared in our ranks a few years later after opening a successful electronics wholesale warehouse in Laval. His politics are garbled; they swing between right-wing nonsense and solid Marxist sentiments. But it was the force of his personality, not his political views, that got him all his support. Until he arrived, we were nothing but a debating society. . . ."

"God, how I remember. Those endless arguments about such trivia," she said.

"Boutette maintained that we were dispersing our energies in pointless rhetoric. He contended that our only common goals were the removal of the Anglo invaders and the preservation of our French heritage. Once that had been accomplished, we could set about creating a new government for Quebec. No amount of theorizing before a revolution can eliminate a state of chaos following its success, he said, and he kept pointing to the American and Russian experiences as examples. Of course, there were counterarguments—more compelling than his, in my opinion—but in the end he won out by sheer charisma and his ability to inflame passions. For the first time, I thought we had a leader with the strength, the courage, and the audacity to galvanize the FLQ into a potent revolutionary force. So I followed him. He negotiated the aid from Libya and he has gathered some powerful financial backing from a shadowy man known only as Regner who lives in Toronto and owns this ship." Gannet stood back from the rail and braced himself with his outstretched arms. He let his head droop between his shoulders. "Boutette also spearheaded the use of rockets on an open city," he added bitterly.

"Are you worried?" she asked gently.

"For myself, no. For what I have tried to stand for, yes," he said. He listened to the rain rattling on the overhead and the squawking of a gull hovering near the fantail. He shielded a match against the wind and lit another cigarette. Taking a long drag, he asked, "Are you still sorry you left New York?"

"Things were good for me in New York. That's all gone now." She shrugged.

"I'd be a liar if I told you I wasn't glad to have you here."

"I care about the revolution as much as you, Bernard. I always have."

"Once I didn't think so. Now I believe it," he said.

"You've got to take me seriously. I need that."

"When this is over, I'd like to think we could sort ourselves out again. When things aren't so screwed up," he said, turning to her.

Agnes said nothing, but cupped his neck with her right hand and began to softly knead the hard braids of muscle. She felt his tense body becoming more pliant under her fingers. Then it suddenly stiffened in alarm.

"That boat! There, in the channel," he said, pointing toward a smudged white shape in the downpour. "It's the American, Farnsworth."

"I don't want him to see me! Not here," said Agnes, bolting for the cabin door. Gannet quickly followed, and positioned himself at a porthole inside the main salon. She moved to an adjacent porthole. "It's him all right," she observed. "With a girl. I never thought I'd see him again alive."

Gannet, his face cracking in a grim, ironic smile, said, "Somehow I felt in my bones we hadn't seen the last of him. When I heard from Serge that he had killed Salam and Seif with his bare hands, I thought perhaps he'd come. Especially after what he was yelling."

"Yelling? What was he yelling?"

"It was hard for Serge to hear him, what with the wind and the general confusion, but he said Farnsworth hollered something like 'Tell the nigger I'm after him,' or words to that effect."

"The nigger?"

"During our little debate we'd made a couple of references to 'nigger.' He doesn't know my name. He knows me as the nigger."

They watched Farnsworth scan the *Talon*'s superstructure.

He had throttled his boat to a stop and lay near the cement walls of the channel as the *Talon* pushed by him. "He'll spot the name on the fantail and then he'll follow us—or notify the police. We've been discovered," Gannet said.

"Why should he recognize this boat?" she asked.

"Because during our interview I got pretty cocky. I said things I shouldn't have . . . including the name of the *Talon* and the fact that it was in Toronto. That's got to be why he's here. I had him completely under my control. Complete control for a few minutes, and I screwed it up."

"What do we do now?"

"Proceed, I suppose. We've come this far. Too far, actually, without a hitch. We'll just have to go on until some sort of a conclusion is reached. But we'd better tell Boutette."

"SO THAT'S FARNSWORTH," said Pierre Boutette as he stood on the *Talon*'s bridge and focused his binoculars sternward. "He doesn't look so big from here."

"Right now his size doesn't matter so much as his mobility. He gave us unexpected trouble before. I think he can do it again," said Gannet.

"Women fret, men fight, Gannet," snapped Boutette. "We are being followed by one man and a girl in a small boat. It is not a NATO armada, or even the Canadian Navy. It is one man and a girl in a small boat, Gannet, and I'd appreciate your explaining exactly what sort of a threat they pose to us."

It was Boutette's way of repeating a position with which he did not agree, then rephrasing it into a question and disdainfully flinging it back at its source. Gannet viewed it as a simplistic, sledgehammer debating tactic, designed to blunt, rather than answer, opposing opinion. Boutette had used the technique with startling effectiveness in the faction-ridden councils of the FLQ. Gannet stood for a moment, watching Boutette, the frustration building inside him. He was tall, and slight, with a pipe-straight spine. His hair was combed back in low, shiny black waves. When he talked his thick eyebrows tended to dance in coordination with the rise and fall of his wide, curving upper lip. Dressed in a pair of flawlessly pressed khaki pants, an expensive black turtleneck, and a pastel-blue windbreaker, he seemed drenched in self-confidence. Everything from his voice, which crackled with the authority and the lucid tones of a professional broadcaster, to his posture, to his hair, which refused to be ruffled by the wind, exuded a regal sense of command. Gannet felt this, and try as he might to resist it, could not help but falter in the presence of the primary energizer of the most critical phase of the revolution.

"That man and his small boat have been the only trouble in an otherwise perfect operation," Gannet said. "For four days now, he has blundered in and out of my life, very nearly messing up our final offloading operation at Yellow Squaw—and worrying the hell out of us that we'd been discovered. Then he killed two of your Libyan friends. Now he's here. He's trouble."

"Not *my* friends, Gannet, friends of the revolution," snapped Boutette. "We'll avenge them. Farnsworth will pay for that. But what can he do to us? Even if he scuttles off to the police and they come after us, what difference does it make? Below us, neatly tied in ribbons, is Alva McClelland, the Prime Minister of Canada. As long as we have him as hostage, we are invulnerable. There is no reason to alter our operation to the slightest degree. If Farnsworth chooses to trail along, it will only hasten his death."

Gannet knew the plan. At precisely three o'clock that afternoon, about four hours hence, with the *Talon* steaming in the middle of Lake Ontario, its powerful transmitters would be fired up. It would be about fifty miles east-southeast of Toronto and about twenty-five miles due south of the nearest point on the Canadian shoreline, near Bowmanville. In this position, the *Talon* would be in mid-lake straddling the United States–Canada international border. Broadcasting on three military and public frequencies that would surely be monitored, the clear, authoritative voice of Pierre Boutette would, after a lengthy preamble outlining the well-known FLQ grievances against the Canadian government and the Anglo-American power structure in Quebec and its French-Canadian quislings, make a formal declaration announcing the formation of the independent state of Quebec. Its borders would conform to those containing the present Canadian provincial territories of Quebec. Boutette's demands included the immediate removal of all Canadian military personnel from Quebec territory, the release of all political prisoners being held by the government, and Canadian recognition of the provisional government of the Free State of Quebec. In return, the FLQ promised a cease-fire and the opening of a seven-day truce period during which free movement across the new frontiers would permit citizens of both nations to relocate at their own free will. This would include, according to the text, "the representatives of Anglo-Canadian and foreign financial interests—primarily from Wall Street— who have exploited and raped French-Canadian resources for centuries. These men should be tried and punished for their repeated larcenies against the Québecois, but in the interests of reconciliation, they will be permitted to leave the new state in complete freedom, although all financial assets are irredeemably frozen by the provisional government." The truce period would also bring the opening of formal talks between the Canadian government and the new state of Quebec. Free and open navigation of the St. Lawrence Seaway would be perpetually guaranteed to Canada and the United States. Negotiations would hopefully lead to the beginning of normal diplomatic and trade relations. It would also be understood that Canada would exert the most energetic restraints possible "to prevent the United States from playing its traditional role as the most brutal and ruthless force for repression of personal liberty and self-determination in human history.

"If the Canadian government chooses to observe these simple

conditions, it can look forward to the immediate cessation of fighting by the ever-increasing ranks of the Army of Free Quebec and the creation of a constant, yet proudly independent ally devoted to friendly coexistence within the great northern half of the hemisphere. If Canada chooses not to observe the sovereignty of the Free State of Quebec, it will assure itself of a long and bloody war of liberation that will most surely resolve itself in favor of the oppressed peoples of Quebec. In addition, the provisional government will have no choice but to institute criminal proceedings against Prime Minister Alva McClelland, whom it now holds as a political prisoner. The charges would involve repeated high crimes of political repression and economic exploitation against the people of Quebec. The punishment for such a conviction would be death.

"In the event the Canadian government misjudges our intentions or our claims, the provisional government provides this opportunity to Prime Minister Alva McClelland, who is being held safely in our custody, to explain the magnitude of the situation."

Boutette would then broadcast the voice of McClelland—recorded at gun point if necessary—reading the following prepared statement: "This is Alva McClelland, Prime Minister of Canada. We are at a turning point in the history of the North American continent, and I urge my associates in government and my fellow countrymen to regard it with maximum seriousness. It is imperative that you carefully consider the demands of my captors. In this way, not only will my survival be assured, but more important, the growth and prosperity of Canada and Quebec will be guaranteed."

Gannet had to give Boutette credit for the awesome bombast of the message and the bluff it contained. But he doubted that it would work. Too much depended on the reaction of the Quebec working classes, and he believed that the rocket attacks on Montreal would inhibit the people as well as the government, thereby stunting the spontaneous street action that was necessary to support the bargaining that centered on McClelland. Gannet had counseled that the rockets be used as a second line of attack—as a desperate backstop if all else failed—but he had been defeated in the face of Boutette's bold arguments for a single, all-out deathblow to the establishment.

The *Talon* rounded the buoy guarding Gibraltar Point and set an eastward course into the lake. Boutette stepped smartly off the bridge, heading for the main cabin to recheck his speech and to confer with the radioman, a fellow Frenchman and former OAS comrade named Mercier. The winds were sagging, although the *Talon* was wallowing through a nasty following sea that caused her round-bottomed hull to dip and yaw in reaction to the waves that rose up against her old lady's stern. She was crankily answering her helm, and Serge Boucher was spinning the varnished wheel—first in frantic revolutions to starboard, then back to port—in order to maintain her heading. "Goddamn, I can't imagine this old bitch in the North Sea," complained Boucher.

"She might be happier where the waves are higher but come at longer intervals," observed Gannet as he entered the pilothouse and balanced himself beside Boucher. He said nothing else for a while. The only sounds in the cabin were the low grunts and occasional curses of Boucher and the polyglot rumblings and sloshings caused by the interaction of the ship and the water.

"What do you make of the crazy American back there?" asked Serge.

Gannet turned toward the aft windows of the pilothouse. Beyond the stubby stack and the cradled lifeboat, out across a quarter mile of water, he could see the bow of Farnsworth's Bertram pushing through the *Talon*'s wake. "I wish he wasn't there," he said evenly.

"Twice we've failed to kill him. I'd like another chance at that bastard. So would Delisle. That was a bad scene on the lake."

"You were fools to follow Salam's orders."

"He said you authorized them. What were we to do?"

"It's too late to argue about that. But the fact remains that Farnsworth could be quietly locked in the cellar at Yellow Squaw Island instead of stalking us like a mad shark," said Gannet sharply.

"Boutette says he can't hurt us. I agree with him. What can he do? Ram us with his goddamn little yacht?"

"If I were a superstitious man, I'd call him an omen. A bad omen."

"How can you worry? Christ, man, the operation is perfect. Mercier just brought a message that says that things are going beautifully in Montreal. The mobile mortar units are raising holy hell, and we seem to have neutralized the police. The blown bridges are keeping the Army practically at bay, just as we expected. What more do you want?"

"I want popular support. Until we get that, the killing and the destruction will mean nothing," said Gannet.

"That will come. When the Anglos realize that their beloved Prime Minister is in our hands the whole scene will change. As they falter and our people understand that we have a serious claim to power, they'll pour into the streets. Right now they're sitting on the fence. As Boutette says, it's a victory for us if they simply remain neutral."

"Are you sure they are neutral?"

"Oh, a few of them—the same old cowards and crooks and ass kissers—are staying with the government, but the masses seem to be waiting to see how strong we really are. The key is that fascist we've got below. He's the greatest bargaining token imaginable."

"The next few hours will tell," mumbled Gannet.

"You always did worry too much, Gannet. Come on, forget that fool slogging along behind us. Up ahead. There's the future. Keep your eyes forward. We'll clean up the debris in our wake later."

THE FIRST HOUR had
passed quickly, as their animated conversation about the sighting of the *Talon* propelled time forward at an accelerated rate.
Farnsworth and Susan Pritchard had been heading up the
harbor channel, on their way to the Royal Ontario Boat Club,
when the *Talon* appeared in front of them. Farnsworth had
throttled back the *Red Dog* and let the larger ship glide past.
"That's it . . . that's the son of a bitch that got Roy," he had
said ominously as the stern swung into view and the block letters
spelling out TALON, ROBC appeared against its black hull. He had
turned into her wake and followed as she stood out toward the
lake. The *Red Dog* had loafed behind the *Talon*, pointing away
from the great city until its last shining spire had disappeared.

"Have you any idea what we're doing out here, Farnsworth?"
Susan Pritchard asked coolly.

"What the hell do you mean by that?" he challenged.

"Well, we've been following that evil-looking ship up there
for quite a while now, and I was just wondering if you had any
plan, or are we just going to trail it until it sinks or something?"

"You nervous?"

"No, not particularly. It's just that it doesn't seem to make much sense to bounce around in this rotten weather without some notion of what you're going to do. After all, if you really believe the people on that ship are involved, let's radio the police and let them handle it."

"The radio's busted."

"O.K., then let's go back and report it in person."

"Like I said, they'd think I was nuts. Plus the fact that they're going crazy trying to find McClelland and everything. And I'm not letting those bastards up there get out of my sight. I owe them something."

"C'mon Farnsworth, what are you going to do, board them like Errol Flynn?"

He turned to her, meeting her unswerving gaze. He nodded his head in resignation and smiled. "Just my luck, to find the only wise-ass chick in Canada," he said.

"I don't know about you, Farnsworth. I guess you're just like all the other big, dumb Americans who come to Ontario Place. They all roll in on their yachts—older and fatter than you, and generally louder and drunker, but full of that same kind of incredible arrogance. Do you have any idea what that does to other people—all of your self-confidence?"

"Never thought about it."

"Well, you ought to think about it. Here we are, a pack of poor little Canadians huddled next to America like a pack of puppies at their mother's breast."

"You sound like that weirdo on the island."

"A lot of Canadians feel that their lives are too closely entwined with the Americans. For years we were nothing but a barren outpost of the British Empire. Then we turned into an American satellite. You can't imagine how dull life used to be in Canada, mainly because we didn't have any sense of self. Half the time we were trying to be Victorian Englishmen and the other half trying to act out middle-class American fantasies we saw on television. The result was a kind of frumpy routine. If you ever read any old Canadian novels you'd find that they all had somebody freezing to death. Honest, that was the most dramatic death imaginable—for some poor fool to lie down in the snow and freeze!"

"You aren't going to freeze today . . . that much I'll guarantee."

"Don't be so sure. Two years ago I was crewing on a friend's Cal 27 in the Freeman Cup. I went overboard out here, and I looked like a snow cone by the time they fished me out."

"Serves you right for hanging around those blow boats," he said.

"Careful how you talk. Sailing is a way of life for me."

"Have you got anything going? I mean, are you hooked up with some guy?" he asked abruptly.

"No, not really. Not right now. Why do you ask?"

"I don't know. I'm so wasted, nothing in my head comes out straight. I was just thinking I'd feel worse about getting you involved if you were somebody else's chick. But that's crap."

"You know, Farnsworth, this morning I decided I wasn't very happy. For years I've convinced myself that I wanted a career in teaching. I would get my degree and find myself a quiet little university, maybe in western Canada. Then suddenly this McClelland business and the FLQ did a funny thing to me. I thought, God, all this time I've made a commitment to order and reason, a belief in the latent rationalism of mankind, and suddenly it's all messed up. Turned upside down by a few madmen. All that certainty has been destroyed. First by the FLQ and then by you."

"Me?"

"You, Farnsworth. A few hours ago my life was as predictable as the full moon. Now I have this weird feeling that it's building up to some kind of cataclysmic change . . . and that feeling started in me when I spotted you stumbling off your boat like a wounded gorilla. Now it's getting stronger and I don't really like it."

"Don't feel bad. Six months ago I thought I was so tough and clever that I could tell you exactly what I'd be doing five years from now. Now I'm not sure what the hell is going to happen even in the next five minutes," he said.

"It does funny things to your head, suddenly realizing that you have very little control over what is going on around you," she added pensively.

"I was beginning to think there was nothing I couldn't control—or at least influence favorably—until all of a sudden Roy got shot. I still can't really believe that happened. All that smug, structured shit, blown away in the night," he said.

She silently tugged at a strand of wet hair, then pushed it over her shoulder. Brushing another lock away from her face, she tucked it behind her right ear and turned to Farnsworth. "I didn't mean to mock you with that crack about Errol Flynn. It's just that . . . we don't seem to know what to do," she said.

"I know it's stupid. I just haven't any idea what else to try. I can't let that ship float away. It's my only contact. I've got to stick it out as long as I can."

"I understand."

"You want to go back?" he asked.

"Why should I want to go back? I think you're right; the police would probably figure you were crazy. No, we don't have much choice."

"You've got no stake in this."

"Keep going, Farnsworth. It's long past the time for turning around," she said brusquely.

He idled ahead, keeping a constant range behind the bobbing stern of the *Talon*. He made no attempt to peel off and head toward Toronto. "Listen, those guys up there don't kid around. They could have anything on that goddamn ship . . . rockets, machine guns, you name it. This isn't just a question of injecting a little inconvenience into your life. In the next few minutes both you and I could be just so much raw meat for the sea gulls. Does that sink in?"

"Just keep going and let's not think about it," she snapped.

"O.K., but if something happens, get below and lay down between the forward vee berths. No, better yet, the hatch between the engines. Get in there. That'll give you better protection."

"What about you, Farnsworth?"

"I'll probably be down there with you," he said, forcing a weak smile.

"I'll stay. Up here," she said.

"Can you run a boat like this?" he asked.

"Of course."

"Can you fire an automatic rifle?"

"You know, I've never shot a gun in my life," she said, her voice straining for levity. "And up until about two seconds ago, I was very proud of that."

XIV

ALVA McCLELLAND, Prime Minister of the Commonwealth of Canada, sat on the edge of the bunk and rubbed his eyes. The dull light from the porthole, coupled with the residual irritation of the tear gas, made him want to close his lids and fall back on the mattress where he had been bound since being secreted aboard. A burly, silent man had left the small cabin moments earlier after untying his legs and wrists and removing the blindfold that had been wrapped around his head, and McClelland forced himself to remain upright in order to determine his situation. He had known from a variety of tactile and auditory messages—the movements of the hull, the cloying dampness, and the faraway, tympanic beat of the engines—that he was on a ship. The magnitude of the noises and the slow, mannerly rolls and pitches suggested that the vessel was of substantial size, on a substantial body of water, which had to be Lake Ontario. He stood up and suddenly felt dizzy. He slipped back onto the bunk, then tried again. Bracing himself against the outer bulkhead, he peered through the porthole. Armies of dark rollers, some dappled with whitecaps, appeared to be escorting the ship. Unless the wind had changed radically in the hours since his capture, McClelland guessed from the direction of the seaway that the ship was on an easterly course. He was in a cabin in the fo'c'sle, on the port side. The space around him was constricted, only large enough to house the bunk, a small stainless-steel washbasin, and an empty clothes locker.

The mahogany-paneled door snapped open with authority and McClelland watched a tall, dark-haired man in a turtleneck step into the cabin. He turned to confront him, rising to his most formidable and dignified posture in order to unleash a tirade of indignation upon his jailer. And then came the clammy realization that he was clad only in a pair of rose-tinted skivvies and a white undershirt. He stood in silence as the man tossed him a clump of clothing, which thudded against his chest and fell into his tardily outstretched arms.

"Our conversation might gain more dignity if you were dressed, Mr. Prime Minister," said the man with disdainful precision. McClelland fingered a pair of rough-twill pants, then quickly pulled them over his thin, parchment-white legs. As he buttoned a denim shirt around himself, the man resumed speaking. "I am Pierre Boutette, Mr. McClelland, provisional leader of the Front de Libération du Québec, an organization with which I am sure you are familiar. You are, quite obviously, our prisoner. Regrettably, your presence within our ranks is no more pleasant for us than it is for you, and in view of your penchant for solid Tory good sense, I am sure that we can expedite our business as quickly as possible, and to our mutual satisfaction."

"I have no business with you barbarians. Do you understand the magnitude of what you've done? You'll pay for this insult to the Canadian people with your lives!" McClelland yelled.

Boutette glared at McClelland, a tolerant smile slicing his face. "You are as fatuous in private as you are in public. At least you get points for consistency. No, McClelland, the Canadian people—at least those with the greed and stupidity to support your policies—will have to live with the insult. You are quite effectively cut out of the herd and there is very little your cronies or your hoodlum police or your army and navy can do about it. In fact, before we waste a lot of time with more of your asinine posturing, it might be of service to us both—and to the causes we serve—to bring you up to date on what has happened in Canada since you became our prisoner this morning.

"Your seizure was but a small part of a massive and long overdue uprising by the citizens of Quebec. In a series of perfectly coordinated operations, the FLQ has militarily neutralized Montreal. Most bridges leading to the city have been interdicted and neither the city government nor the Canadian Army has real influence in the area. Heavy fighting is under way in certain sectors, and the rich suburbs of your compatriots, especially those of Hampstead and Westmount, have received deadly mortar fire. It would be overstating our case to imply that we have control of Montreal. The salient point is that the Canadian government does *not* have control. Therefore, much blood will be shed before any sort of resolution is reached, unless you, McClelland, exhibit perfect judgment. You are the key to peace on this continent." Boutette finished speaking and watched the Prime Minister. He had rehearsed this confrontation many times, imagining a multitude of responses McClelland might provide. His wildest fantasies had the Prime Minister staggering under the weight of the news and, flabby and tear-stained, scurrying to carry out the FLQ's bidding. But that was too much to hope for. Boutette was too hardened and cynical a man not to know that everyone invests his enemies with nonsensical combinations of strengths and weaknesses. They are on the one hand clever, ruthless, crafty, analytical, perfectly organized zealots. Then again they are narrow-minded, arrogant, decadent, dull-witted, barbaric cowards. Actually one's enemies tended to be quite like oneself and Boutette understood this. In the end Alva McClelland reacted much as he would have himself—as he had expected.

The Prime Minister's face blossomed with color. He was trying to maintain his composure by folding his arms across his chest, but the wide stance, the arched back, and the slightly protruding pelvis revealed that his body and his mind were bristling for a fight. "Listen, Boutette, or whatever your name is, you aren't goddamned fools enough to think that Canada is going to be blackmailed out of Quebec simply because of me? Are you actually so ignorant that you thought we'd never considered such a possibility? We have hundreds of contingency plans that provide for the orderly function of government in the event of my accidental death, assassination, or even kidnapping. Whether I am there or not, whether I am dead or alive, you and your pack of maniacs will be crushed. Do you understand what I am saying? Quebec is part of Canada and it will remain so, regardless of what happens to me."

"They said you were a gritty bastard," smiled Boutette. "Unfortunately, guts often nullify wisdom."

"Time is passing. Men are dying. Surely, you must have something in mind," challenged McClelland.

Stiffening at this outburst, Boutette subdued an urge to lay a hard, sweeping blow on the stolid face confronting him and snapped, "First, you'll find out the scope of this mission. You are aboard the *Talon*, a specially fitted trawler-yacht with oceangoing capabilities. For the past year and a half it has been engaged in special missions for the FLQ, primarily in the movement of men and military matériel into Quebec. She is an extremely ingenious ship, laid out like a luxury yacht, but actually designed to operate as a mobile communications center. Behind the bulkheads of the main hold—which has been converted into a pair of guest staterooms—are concealed a number of high-powered transmitters. Within the two masts are retractable antennas which permit us to transmit over vast distances."

"Get on with it, man, you're wasting Canada's time!"

"You bastard! Shut your mouth when I'm speaking!"

screeched Boutette as he took a pair of quick steps toward McClelland and laced him across the head twice with his open right hand, stiff-elbowed, as a man might swat at a gyrating housefly. The force of the blows sent McClelland staggering back against the bulkhead, where he leaned with his bleached-blue eyes malevolently welded on his captor. Breathing quickly, Boutette stepped back and continued, his voice louder and his words quicker than before. "Your voice, McClelland, your crazy fascist voice, will soon be released from those antennas! Your words will trigger the birth of a new Quebec. The statement has been prepared. And you will read it. Yes, you will read it, you Anglo son of a bitch, or you will face a tribunal of the provisional government right here on this ship to answer for your repeated offenses against the people of Quebec. And, McClelland, if you believe nothing else I've said, believe that the penalty for conviction is death. See how much good your contingency plans do when your body is rotting at the bottom of Lake Ontario!"

Vibrating with anger, Boutette burst out of the cabin, cursing wildly as he inelegantly stubbed his foot against the bulkhead coaming. Saying nothing more, he swept by Marcel Delisle, who stood somberly in the passageway, ready to lock McClelland's door behind him. Rushing past the radio room, where Mercier was reaching to adjust a dial, Boutette trundled up a companionway and into the main cabin. Agnes DePere was sitting, stiff and unsmiling, in a lounge chair, her head cupped in her right hand. "Where's Gannet?" he demanded.

"Up there. With Boucher," she said, gesturing loosely in the direction of the bridge.

Boutette walked quickly to the port-side door and stepped onto the deck. He was about to spring up the ladder leading to the pilothouse when he heard the clatter of feet above him. He looked up to see the slight frame of Gannet half sliding, half stepping down the ladder toward him.

"McClelland, is he O.K.?" asked Gannet in alarm.

"He's all right, the crazy old bastard. We may have more trouble with him than we expected," said Boutette.

"That may not be all. I was just coming to tell you. Farnsworth's trying something," Gannet said, looking over Boutette's shoulder and off the port quarter of the *Talon*.

Boutette twisted in place and his eyes immediately zeroed in on the low, wide, white shape of the *Red Dog* surging closer. It was perhaps two hundred yards astern, but the size of its foaming bow wave indicated it was cutting the distance at full throttle. He could see that a girl, her hair streaming in the wind, was at the helm, while Farnsworth seemed to be climbing back onto the flying bridge with a long, dark object in his hand. "Well, well, see what your man has in his hand," mused Boutette.

"Er, my glasses," apologized Gannet.

"A gun, Gannet, some kind of rifle or automatic weapon," said Boutette. "Whatever that idiot has in mind, we'll at least be able to get him out of our hair earlier than expected. Keep your eye on him while I get Delisle. I know Marcel wants the honor of killing him."

XV

CROUCHED LOW, his bad leg braced against the bridge superstructure, Farnsworth had Seif's AK-47 wrapped in his hands, where it appeared to be no larger or more lethal than a concert flute. Susan Pritchard was beside him, pointing the *Red Dog* toward the port quarter of the *Talon*, her lean body canted forward, rising and falling on the suspension of her calves and knees, as if she were in the saddle of a giant horse. He knew this might be a futile gesture, a childish attempt to extract revenge, much as a kid might fling a stone through a tormentor's window. But he had to leave his mark. The *Red Dog* had run perhaps a hundred and forty miles since its last refueling and its tanks held barely enough gasoline to get it back to Toronto. The chase would have to be broken off, but not before he left a clot of 7.62mm Russian bullets plastered against the bulkheads of the *Talon*.

He waited as the trawler loomed up, then caught sight of two men watching him from its deck. The smaller of the pair, dark and owlish, prickled in him a signal of recognition. He jerked the chunky hardwood stock of the AK-47 into the crotch of his shoulder and watched the outlines of the man sweep through the ramp sight on the end of the barrel. "The nigger! It's the nigger!" he yelled in angry triumph. At that moment the nigger's companion—dressed in a black turtleneck and blue wind-breaker—slipped through the nearby cabin door. Farnsworth yanked at the trigger and the AK-47 turned into a midget jackhammer squirming in his arms. The longer he kept the trigger pressed, the faster it seemed to fire, until the detonations condensed into a single ugly racket. Smoke spewed into his face, and from the corner of his eye he could see the gleaming brass shell casings spilling out of the madly oscillating receiver like broken teeth. His initial volley had been aimed at the nigger, who had flung himself to the deck like a rag doll. Unable to exercise precise aim with the weapon, Farnsworth had merely hosed the side of the vessel with bullets, letting them spray in random clusters against the steel and wood. For a moment he had tried to direct fire at the pilothouse, but finding he could not steady on a target even that bulky, he went back to scatter shooting until the AK-47 gobbled its last round and went inert in his hands.

Susan Pritchard wheeled the *Red Dog* into a long, gentle left turn away from the *Talon* while Farnsworth dropped the automatic rifle to his side and tried to assess the damage. "That guy . . . that guy I told you about who had me on the island—the nigger—that was him. That little bastard is on there. Which means something, goddamnit. I only wish I knew what. Susan, swing around and we'll make another pass." He dropped down the ladder to the main deck and scurried into the cabin to rummage through the mess in search of the extra thirty-round banana clip. Finding it between the galley seats, he snatched it off the deck and rose up to see the boxy contours of the *Talon* slogging along a quarter mile distant. He watched it for a moment, recalling that it was from a similar angle and range that he had first seen it—four days earlier.

GANNET SKATED, face down, into the shelter of the main cabin. He sighted Agnes, kneeling behind a rattan chair on the starboard side. The rug was strewn with shattered porthole glass and a brass table lamp had spilled on the floor. He had no chance to speak before Boutette and Delisle stomped into the cabin from the forward passageway. Delisle led the way, lugging what Gannet recognized as a Mauser MG42 machine gun dating from the World War II Wehrmacht, one of the finest lightweight combat weapons ever built. Behind him, following in a frantic, stumbling lockstep, was Boutette, carrying an armload of fifty-round 7.92mm ammunition belts. They were crunching across the broken glass, headed for the port-side door, when Boutette suddenly stopped. His eyes widened and his head arched upward and swiveled slowly in an animal perception of alarm. "The ship! It's off course! We're swinging well off to starboard. Gannet, get up to the bridge and find out what's wrong. We'll take care of Farnsworth." Gannet leaped off the deck and sprinted toward the starboard door while Delisle and Boutette disappeared with their machine gun.

The *Talon* was heeled over in a steady turn, and by the time Gannet reached the bridge he could see that her wake was scarring the lake surface in a wide, foaming crescent. The pilothouse appeared to be empty. Serge Boucher was lying on the floor, his limbs stretching away from his body at odd angles. On the left side of his neck, at the base of his skull, was a deep, juicy wound. A glazed smear of vermilion spread from beneath him and it filled the pilothouse with the meaty aroma of raw, ripped flesh. Gannet turned, seeking the source of destruction. He found it in a port-side window glass, where a single hole, surrounded by a frosted penumbra and fracture lines, pocked the lower right corner. A random shot from Farnsworth's volley had struck Serge Boucher, and he was dead. Gannet began to rise, then stopped once again and lifted Serge's Llama automatic from his belt and jammed it into his rear pocket. Then he grabbed the wheel and swung the *Talon* back on course.

FARNSWORTH could see a pair of men running along the *Talon*'s port side. Reaching a position where the deck ran athwartships in front of the main-cabin superstructure, they threw themselves down with what appeared to be a long black pipe. On one end of the pipe was a V-shaped brace of smaller pipes—a bipod mount for the Mauser. The *Red Dog* was charging toward the *Talon*, this time swooping in from almost directly abeam. Straight ahead, Farnsworth could see the pair fiddling with the weapon, trying to engage one of the glinting snakes of ammunition in the feed tray. "Those guys have got a machine gun up there," he shouted to Susan Pritchard. "When I tell you, whip that goddamn wheel over to full port and hit the deck." Then he knelt against the flying bridge, wedging himself between the seat and the bulkhead and propping the AK-47 in his arms. He slammed the new magazine into place and yanked the bolt to transport the first cartridge into the breech. He saw one of the men with the Mauser reach for the cocking slide. Farnsworth fired, flinching slightly. He aimed low, assuming that the jerking recoil would raise his line of fire. BRRRRRRRRRaaaammmmm! The AK-47 belched a tentative six-round volley, which was answered by a dreadful, deafening report and a blossom of fire that enveloped the entire cabin of the *Talon*. Susan Pritchard screamed as the shock waves powered against her and an oven-like balloon of heat whooshed past. A second detonation shook them and flung smoking fragments of wreckage high into the air. Farnsworth cowered in dazed amazement, watching like someone who had just dislodged a pebble that had triggered an avalanche.

Susan managed to turn the *Red Dog* from the heat and fire

and, after making a broad loop, she slowed in order to witness the fiery convulsions of the stricken trawler. "Good Christ, what have I done?" Farnsworth whispered, dropping the AK-47 on the seat behind him.

GANNET found himself lying on the starboard wing of the bridge, being swallowed in the smoke that billowed up from the explosion. He did not know how he got there. His survival mechanisms operating at full intensity, he pulled himself to his feet and groped toward the ladder. Finding it, he tumbled to the shelter of the lower deck. The core of the fire was on the other side of the ship, and he could hear its ominous moaning, like a berserk oil furnace, and see the heavy smudges of smoke pouring over the water. He was in a pocket of fresh air, and he took a moment to assess his damage. Aside from seared eyebrows and a deep ache that ran the length of his left arm, he seemed to have survived the explosion unharmed. Agnes! Agnes! Where is she? His mind labored with the problem, trying to orient itself in relation to her last remembered location. Gannet pushed his way into the main cabin, which was misted with an evil-smelling fog of smoke. Glass and broken furniture were spilled across the room. He found the lounge chair he had last seen her kneeling behind. Agnes was next to it, groggily perched on her hands and knees with her head drooped forward and her long hair dragging through the litter on the deck. A splotch of red, like a small hibiscus, glowed in her hair near her left temple. Saying nothing, he hauled her to her feet and pulled her outside. She sagged against the railing, but from the firmness of her muscles and her relatively stable bearing, Gannet suspected that she was merely dazed and bore no serious injury. "C'mon, the fire is spreading. We've got to get forward. Let's move it!" he said as he wrapped his arm around her and pointed her toward the bow.

They moved away from the fire, down a short ladder and onto the main deck. The *Talon* was chugging in a vast, blind circle and the wind was blowing the fire and heat off the stern. It was cool where they stood, trying to regain their equilibrium and to understand what had happened. Bright fissures were rupturing the thick clouds and the sun was beginning to probe through. The storm was dead. "Your head . . . let me look at your head," Gannet said, reaching for her. He looked at the bloody spot in her matted hair, gently touching its perimeters with his fingers. "It doesn't seem too bad," he said.

She watched the fire pouring across the cabin. Flames slithered out of the portholes and the white bulkhead paint was bubbling and scorching like burnt meringue. "What in God's name happened? That blast . . . the fire. How . . . ?"

"I don't know. One minute I was at the wheel. There were a few shots. Then bam! It blew me right out of the pilothouse. After that, I found you." He looked at the flaming ruin. There was a white-hot core at the corner of the cabin where Boutette and Delisle had tried to position the Mauser. "I think I know what happened," he said slowly. "The fire is worse where the tanks of liquid propane gas for the galley cooking and refrigeration were located. Farnsworth must have accidentally hit them."

"What about Pierre and Marcel? Are they O.K.?"

"There's no way. No way at all. The explosion was only a few feet away from them," he said.

"Oh no!" she protested, as a convulsion of shock vibrated her body. She put her hands over her eyes and appeared to shrink in grief and despair. "And Serge? Where's Serge?" she asked.

"I'm afraid . . ."

"Goddamnit, goddamnit, goddamnit!" she screamed. "The glorious revolution. Nothing but dead men!" He reached for her, but she twisted away from him and bent over, sobbing.

He stood beside her, idly rubbing her back in a feeble attempt to relieve her sorrow. The fire was building toward a celebration that would consume the entire ship. Lying to, a white dot on the sun-spangled waves, he saw Farnsworth's boat, intensifying his leaden sensation of defeat. "C'mon," he said quietly, "we've got to get off this damn thing. There's a life-jacket locker on the fo'c'sle." He gripped her arm and pulled her toward the bow.

Agnes DePere sat down on the anchor winch, stiff and silent, while Gannet rummaged through the locker, finally emerging with a pair of orange kapok life jackets. He walked to her and held out one of the jackets. She took it. Then, her voice tight and husky with emotion, she asked, "What about Mercier? And the Prime Minister? What about them?"

"Fuck the Prime Minister."

Her face took on a gray, granite dullness. "Will the murder of a helpless man make it better? It's over, Bernard. Done. Finished. Blood is washing around your feet. Keep it off your hands."

He stared at her for a moment, his body rocking in rhythm with the motion of the ship, then he let the life jacket drop out of his hands. Gannet walked to the nearby hatch and slipped down the ladder into the crew's quarters. He went to the portside cabin where McClelland was imprisoned and tried the latch. It was locked. He slammed his small body against the stout mahogany twice and was repelled. The passageway was filling with smoke. He heard coughing. It was Mercier who appeared out of the darkness. He was a chunky man with wheat-colored hair, which was now smudged and singed. Spotting Gannet, Mercier dropped the fire extinguisher he had been carrying and staggered toward him. "Hopeless," he said. "The fire will get to the fuel tanks soon. She'll burn to the waterline in an hour."

"There are life jackets on deck. Help me get McClelland, and we'll move out of here."

Mercier started past him. "*We're* going. Boutette's orders were that if anything went wrong, I was to kill the bastard. Success or failure, he wasn't going to leave this ship alive. You know that, Gannet."

"No, I didn't know that."

"Now you know. Let him fry."

"He's going with us, Mercier."

"Take your choice, you little bastard. Either you go out with me or you stay here and get broiled with him. That's your choice," he said, spreading his clenched fists away from his body.

Gannet yanked the Llama 9mm out of his pocket, but Mercier detected the movement and lunged at him with a wild, looping right hand that arched down like a mallet head. Gannet sidestepped the fist and swung the automatic at Mercier's head, missing. A second swipe caught Mercier on the back of the neck, staggering him. Gannet cracked him again, and he toppled onto the deck. Emitting low growling noises, Gannet stood above the downed man and cocked the pistol. He bent over, pointing the barrel at the bridge of Mercier's nose. Then the gun wavered and his thumb released the hammer. He dropped the weapon and reached for a ring of keys on Mercier's belt loop. The fourth key unlocked McClelland's stateroom.

McClelland said nothing as Gannet swung open the door. He was standing in the middle of the cabin, his expression tense and uncertain. "We're leaving the ship," said Gannet blankly.

"Kill me now. I won't play any of your games," said McClelland regally.

"I'm not here to kill you. I'm offering you a chance to escape from this ship, which is going to explode and sink. If you want to stay, that's your choice." Gannet spoke in a clinical monotone as he tried to suppress his revulsion for the man he confronted.

"I demand . . ."

"You demand nothing!" Gannet shouted. "This bloody ship is finished. It's a funeral pyre already. I don't give a goddamn whether you live or die, I'm just here to tell you if you want to leave, *leave*. If you want to stay, *stay*. You silly, bullheaded idiot!" Gannet turned and left the cabin. He stepped on the ladder that led upward to the sunny rectangle in the deck as the smoke eddied around his feet. Halfway up, he felt the rungs jiggle with the addition of extra weight. Another man was climbing out. He did not look back. He knew it was Alva McClelland.

XVI

THE WAVES, less harassed by the wind, shimmered with scattered sunlight like crinkled cellophane. Farnsworth was heading south. The American shore was closer and, because of following winds and seas, offered quicker refuge for the *Red Dog* with its rapidly draining fuel tanks. Behind him, over the horizon, he could still see the stain of black smoke that marked the grave of the *Talon*.

Bernard Gannet was sitting on the afterdeck of the *Red Dog*, leaning against the starboard bulkhead, his knees drawn up against his body. Agnes sat beside him, her legs extended straight in front of her. She was leaning her head on Gannet's shoulder. Her eyes were closed. Near them, three orange life jackets lay on the deck, draining water into the scuppers. In the cabin below, Susan Pritchard was tending to the few scratches received by her Prime Minister during his recent ordeal.

Lying near the flaming trawler, Farnsworth had seen Gannet, Agnes, and McClelland tie on the life jackets and tumble into the water. He had maneuvered closer and hauled them into the boat. Farnsworth had evidenced no reaction on seeing Agnes, except to bare his teeth in disgust as he elevated her above the water, much as he might have exhibited an undersized bass on a stringer. Gannet had come next, and Farnsworth had muttered, "You lose, nigger," and yanked him so hard that he nearly looped him over his head on the way aboard. "My God, that's McClelland!" Susan Pritchard had blurted as he was pulled out of the water.

It had been a strange moment for Farnsworth, seeing Gannet and Agnes again. The intensity of their last encounters had seemed to compensate for their brevity, and he had felt that he knew them better than he did—much as if they were long-lost, much-despised relatives who had suddenly appeared. It was as if repeated family rumors had invested them with too much guile and nastiness and, as they huddled, soaked and beaten, like a pair of half-drowned puppies, his fevers for revenge were cooling. Agnes, her face shining amid the smeared tangle of her hair, looked angelic in repose. Gannet, tiny by Farnsworth's standards to begin with, looked no more worthy of fear or hatred than a harshly punished child. The holocaust on the lake had purged him of his urge for retribution and he felt that the whole ugly affair was winding down. It meant little to him that the lost Prime Minister of Canada was on his boat, and that the world would have to wait perhaps another hour before he would reappear, healthy and whole, in an obscure Lake Ontario harbor. Farnsworth was going to Oak Orchard Creek. According to his charts, it was the closest port, and his plan was to steer south until he picked up a landfall, then to head eastward until he reached Oak Orchard. There he would call the New York State Police and wash his hands of the entire affair. He wanted that. There were many pieces to be mended with LaStarza, but that would come easily, once he had produced his three passengers for the authorities. He pondered the arrival of the yapping press, pawing at him with their felt-tip pens and their Sony tape recorder microphones and scanning him with their Arriflexes and their wind-up Bell and Howells. His story was long and confused, punctuated by death, and he wondered how much he would tell, and what it would mean for his career. A numbness was coming over him, partly from the outright exhaustion of his mind and body, and partly from the trip-hammer power and proximity of the violent incidents. Roy's death, once central to his thoughts, had been nudged aside by a chain reaction of his own kidnapping, the killing of the Arabs, the destruction of the *Talon*—and he tried to sift through them in search of some meaning or justification for his involvement.

Alva McClelland bounded onto the flying bridge and sat down. "Pancho Farnsworth, you deserve a medal," he said jauntily. He was still covered with the damp, wrinkled clothes Boutette had given him, but aside from a small welt above his right eye, to which Susan had applied a light fog of antiseptic, he had that intangible, inner luminescence of authority. Perhaps it was his perfectly groomed hair, or his ruddy, tanned complexion, but Alva McClelland carried himself like a man familiar with riches and power. "These are insane circumstances in which to meet, but I can't imagine a more opportune moment for you to have arrived on the scene. Quite frankly, I thought the final countdown had begun. Even when that scum set me free and handed me the life jacket, I thought they were going to kill me."

Farnsworth said nothing. He eyed the Prime Minister and produced a faint smile and nodded an acknowledgment.

"You know, Farnsworth, I'm quite a fan of your American professional football. You may have heard of Wolcott Jenner, who owns a fleet of ore carriers in Cleveland. A fine man, and a great Browns booster, by the way. I've heard him mention your name, and it's a pleasure to meet you."

"Thanks. You seem to have survived without a lot of damage," Farnsworth said unenthusiastically.

"I'm fine," McClelland said. "But I'm extremely concerned about the situation in Montreal. That maniac on the boat—I can't recall his name—told me that the city was under a state of siege, and I'm very anxious to reestablish contact. My reappearance may be enough to break the back of this wretched insurrection. Your, er, Miss Pritchard told me that your transmitter is broken, so I assume you're making for the nearest port. It may be that the Montreal story is a complete fabrication, but I've got to find out as quickly as possible. These Frenchies have a way of exaggerating things, but you can't be too careful. This is the boldest, most insane thing they've tried yet, so you can't tell how much else they've attempted."

"He was telling you straight. Montreal's a mess," said Farnsworth.

"Those bastards," snarled McClelland.

"When men get strung out far enough, they'll try anything."

"Are you suggesting you think they have a reason for such criminal acts?" asked McClelland.

"I'm not suggesting anything, except that nobody takes risks without some motive. It's not what I think; it's what they think. They must think they're getting ripped off or else they wouldn't have tried such a far-out thing in the first place."

"You disappoint me, sir. You may be a fine athlete but your political senses are badly dulled. If you have ever been to Montreal, you know it is one of the most prosperous cities in the world. A showpiece of civilization."

"I've heard people say that Montreal's slums are the worst in North America—and they're full of French Canadians who are either unemployed or underpaid," Farnsworth said, showing his irritation at the smugness of the man beside him.

McClelland shrugged and smiled thinly. He began to nod his head in a patronizing display of patience. He paused for a moment, gathering his thoughts. "You know, Farnsworth, I can talk to you more easily than some other men. We do after all understand the uses of applied power, and I'm sure that you are not naïve enough to think that what you read in the press is gospel. My private contention is that these Frenchies who infest Quebec have been a millstone around Canada's neck for two centuries. A backward, bead-clutching pack of primitives who have steadfastly refused to join the rest of Canada in any meaningful sense. They have tried to remain a nation apart, spurning our language, dragging their feet on the development of the province's abundant resources, clinging to the Roman Church, and, worst of all, repeatedly refusing to fight in their homeland's wars. No, Farnsworth, please don't waste your sympathies on them."

"If they're so worthless, why don't you let 'em go?"

"Separatism? God, how that word sickens and infuriates me. The idea of giving that lazy tribe Quebec's riches in ore, oil, and timber is as idiotic as turning America back to the shiftless Indians."

"So what are you going to do?"

"What do you mean?"

"Well, you've got a goddamn revolution on your hands."

"I like your simple approach to things, Farnsworth. It's refreshing. This is the last spasm of the FLQ and of separatism. Trudeau could have done it in the October crisis of 1970, but he lacked the stomach. He invoked the War Measures Act, then failed to use it as a scalpel to carve out every last malignant cell of separatism. This time it will be different."

"What about those two down there?" asked Farnsworth, motioning toward Agnes and Gannet.

"They'd better enjoy the fresh air, because they're breathing their last of it," said McClelland, his voice edged with triumph.

"Doesn't it matter that they helped you off that ship? They saved your life."

"I thought I'd give you credit for that, Farnsworth. It would make a great deal more sense to the press, and would considerably simplify the job of prosecution. Surely you understand that." McClelland's face lit up with a satisfied leer.

Farnsworth turned and looked at McClelland head on, slowly scanning his face—the arched eyebrows, the steady, cocksure blue eyes, the straight, high-ridged nose, the ample mouth, and the haughty, jutting chin. He was silent for a while. Then, in hard, deliberate tones that prickled with disgust, he said,

"McClelland, you are as bad as the rest of them." He turned toward the *Red Dog*'s controls and yanked the throttles back to idle and pulled the clutches into neutral. The boat nosedived to a stop, sending Agnes and Gannet skidding across the deck. They watched in alarm as Farnsworth shoved his way past the Prime Minister and gimped down the ladder from the flying bridge. "Pancho, is everything all right?" asked Susan, appearing out of the main cabin.

"It's perfect," he snapped as he brushed past her, headed toward the forward vee berths. A fat green-canvas bag was stuffed between the bunks. Farnsworth swung it into his arms and, taking two quick steps to the cabin door, flung it out on deck at Bernard Gannet's feet. "Pump that up!" he snarled at Gannet, and climbed back to the bridge.

"Get below, McClelland, I'm tired of your shit," Farnsworth said. Alva McClelland stared at him for a moment, searching for a retort. Finding none, he squinted his eyes in a subtle signal of defiance and disappeared. Farnsworth restarted the boat and turned to check Gannet's progress. He had already extracted the Avon Redstart dinghy from its carrying bag and was connecting the bellows pump. Farnsworth stood up. His leg pulsed with pain. Ahead he could see a flat ridge of trees on the horizon, punctuated by an occasional silo. It was the New York State shoreline: lonely acres of peach and apple orchards, interrupted by colonies of summer cottages. Susan Pritchard appeared beside him. "Pancho . . . what are you doing? The Prime Minister is extremely upset. You must have really insulted him."

"He insulted me. The racist bastard."

"What are they doing with the life raft?" she asked, motioning toward Gannet and Agnes.

"Susan, are you with me?" he asked abruptly.

"I'm with you."

"You're the only good thing that's come out of this whole rotten mess. I just want you to know that," he said. He paused, lowering his eyes, rubbing the stubble of beard on his chin.

"We've been hurting a lot of people lately. Too damn many. It's time to quit."

Gannet had the raft bulging with air. He assembled a pair of short varnished-wood oars and stood up, an uncertain look on his face. Farnsworth stopped the *Red Dog* once more. Leaving the bridge, he dropped to the deck and pitched the raft into the water with a single movement. Holding the painter, he hauled the little craft against the hull and turned to Gannet and Agnes. His face was severe and unsmiling, but the rage had drained away. "Get in," he said bluntly.

Gannet stood there, his jaw hanging loose, groping to comprehend.

"I said, get in the goddamn raft!" barked Farnsworth.

"I don't understand," said Gannet.

"See that land? That's the United States. Maybe, with a little luck, you can get a break. The shore is deserted farmland. You stand a better chance than if you go back to Canada with your Prime Minister."

Gannet looked at Agnes, who was avoiding Farnsworth's eyes. They started toward the raft. McClelland reappeared at the cabin door. "Farnsworth, I demand an explanation! Those people are my political prisoners. They are wanted for high crimes against the Commonwealth of Canada. If you aid in their escape you are an accessory, and I will see that you are punished severely!" he shouted.

"Shut your mouth," said Farnsworth ominously. "This is my boat, in my own country's waters, and I'll do as I damn please."

"I will not tolerate this! This is an international offense!"

"Don't you realize those two saved your life?" Farnsworth shouted. "Doesn't that mean anything?" He took a menacing step toward McClelland.

Falling back, McClelland screeched, "It means nothing in the face of the crimes they have committed. Let them go and you'll pay. I swear!"

"Who do you think will believe your story? Like you said, it was us—Susan and I—who picked you up from that burning ship. We just found you floating in the water. You were deliriously talking about a man and a woman, but we figured it had something to do with your state of shock." Farnsworth's face spread into a stiff, ironic grin as he spoke.

McClelland spun around, looking up at Susan Pritchard on the flying bridge. "You're a Canadian citizen, young lady. You must support your Prime Minister. Otherwise, it's treason!"

Susan Pritchard regarded McClelland, her eyes filled with disdain. "Pancho and I saw the same thing," she said, and turned away.

"Farnsworth, you have one last chance," McClelland threatened.

"Wrong again!" snarled Farnsworth as he lunged toward McClelland. Peering down, his wide, deep eyes prickling with anger, he pressed his face close to the Prime Minister's until the tips of their noses nearly touched. "Listen, you dumb son of a bitch, my patience is starting to run out. In one way or another, you owe your life to everyone else on this boat. You are at the bottom of the heap. Right here, in this time and this place, you don't mean shit. And if I hear any more out of you—any more of your goddamn orders—I'll heave your ass over the side."

He stepped back from McClelland, heavily canting his weight on his good leg. He sucked in several deep breaths while keeping his eyes locked on the most powerful man in Canada. "Now I'm going to show a little mercy. *Mercy*, McClelland, do you know what that means?" he asked, ominously feinting a move forward. McClelland's eyes widened in a flicker of alarm, and his head vibrated in eager, helpless assent.

Farnsworth turned away from the Prime Minister. "Now we're beginning to understand each other," he said. Lifting the oars off the deck, he handed them to Gannet. With shaky, uncertain movements, Agnes climbed into the bobbing life raft.

It was Gannet's turn to get aboard. He stepped to the rail of the *Red Dog*, then looked at Farnsworth. His body was wobbling with fatigue. His eyes seemed drained of life. "I only want you to understand one thing," said Gannet. "That night on the river, with the Libyans. That was not what I wanted. That you've got to know."

"Whatever was, was," said Farnsworth grimly. "All I know is that it's time we stopped trying to kill each other. Now get off my boat."

"Pancho, you can never know—but I'm sorry," said Agnes softly.

"We're all sorry. The whole goddamned world ought to be sorry," answered Farnsworth.

Gannet climbed into the dinghy and fixed the oars into the molded-rubber oarlocks. He stared at Farnsworth, his face clouded with emotion. He began to say something, then grasped the oars and took the first stroke. Farnsworth tossed the painter onto the bow and let the tiny boat have its way. Susan came to his side, and they watched the raft bobbing toward shore, its two passengers bent low against its gunwales. It was silent, save for the soft wind, the sloshing of the lake against the hull, and the muted murmur of the *Red Dog*'s idling engines. The clouds were gone.

Tomorrow would be warm and clear.